NEW YEAR, NEW PLANET

My Holiday Tails

Marina Simcoe

To my Captain

New Year, New Planet
Copyright © 2021, 2023, 2024 Marina Simcoe

Marina Simcoe
Marina.Simcoe@Yahoo.com
Facebook/Marina Simcoe Author

New Cover Edition
Cover image source: Depositphotos
Spelling: English (American)
Editing by Cissell Ink

New Year, New Planet is a Science-Fiction Romance. It contains graphic scenes of intimacy. Intended for mature readers.

No part of this book was produced by generative AI. Written by the author.

Chapter 1

Tessa

"Everyone needs an adventure in their lives, Tessa!" Bree yelled from the common area of our apartment.

"I have lots of it. My entire life is an adventure," I yelled back from behind the partially closed doors of my bedroom. I closed the tiny hooks on the side of my black-and-white, polka-dot skirt and zipped up the zipper, getting ready for the new-year's party.

I've been traveling for a living most of my adult life. We were in the city of Voran on Neron, a planet only a handful of people from Earth had visited.

Wasn't that an adventure already?

And before taking the job that had brought me to Neron, I'd worked on luxury yachts back on Earth, traveling all over the Caribbean and the Mediterranean.

"Your life is not an adventure, Tessa," Bree argued. "Because you don't actually *live* it. You work. And when you have time off, you read in your cabin. You have every chance for an adventure, but you never take it. It makes no difference that you're on a spaceship or on another planet. You don't go out. You see nothing. You may as well be back on Earth in some shitty small town, working in a hole-in-the-wall diner. You don't *live* the adventure, you skirt right by it."

Her words scraped unpleasantly inside me. It hurt. Probably because Bree was right. I preferred to stay safe.

My very first job actually was in a diner. My biological parents hadn't been in the picture since my birth. My foster family had made sure I'd been fed and clothed while growing up, but once I turned eighteen, they gave me a suitcase and wished me a happy life.

I wasn't angry with them. They'd helped me get my driver's license, my first job, and my first apartment. They still sent me a Christmas card every year. But once I'd left their house, I'd always known I had no one but myself to count on.

As a waitress in a diner, I'd worked hard, taking as many shifts as was physically possible. One night, a customer had witnessed me resolving a nasty situation at three in the morning—a drunk was harassing another waitress. The witness had been impressed with the way I handled it. He'd turned out to be the owner of several luxury yachts he rented to wealthy clients, and he'd offered me a job on the service crew.

Since then, my life had become a string of trips, ports, and endless travels.

Bree was right, however. I'd been to many countries but had hardly experienced their culture. I rarely met new people, and preferred to stay in my cabin, reading.

"Come on, Tessa," Bree exclaimed. "We're on a freaking alien planet, girl! You need to live a little."

I smoothed my hands over my dark hair, then closed the tiny silver buckles of my black Mary Jane shoes and grabbed my purse.

"I'm trying." I stepped out of my bedroom into our living room that burst with vines and flowers in the typical Voranian fashion. "I've agreed to come with you on this double-date, haven't I?"

My lifestyle wasn't conducive to building and maintaining relationships, but sometimes loneliness got the best of me. Tonight, the prospect of going out and meeting new people made me feel more excited than apprehensive.

New Year's Eve was my favorite holiday, and I was looking forward to the party.

Bree gave me a measuring look, taking in my outfit of a cup-sleeved blouse, flared polka-dot skirt, and black heels.

"What?" I ran my hands down my skirt, feeling self-conscious under her scrutiny.

Bree was dressed in a scarlet mid-thigh-length dress with an open back that complemented her golden-red hair in a most stunning way.

Unlike me, Bree never missed an adventure. She also never failed to tell Lucy and me about her escapades.

Lucy was another woman from Earth, who came to Neron with our ship and was sharing the apartment with Bree and me. She was sitting on a white couch in front of the large white-screen TV. A Voranian movie was playing, but Lucy had it on mute, quietly listening to our conversation instead.

Bree yanked my sleeves down to expose my shoulders.

"Not too bad, but something is missing..." she muttered, staring at me like I was a picture in a museum and she was trying to appraise me. "I see you're going for a kind of sexy librarian look. Sweet and smart. That's good. Guys like it."

Was *that* what I was going for? I just put on the only skirt I owned that wasn't a part of my uniform.

"The red lipstick is great. But this purse needs to go." Bree tugged at the hard-shell bag I had in the crook of my elbow. "Get rid of it."

I clutched the handles tighter. "My purse? No way. My entire life is in it."

Bree wouldn't let go, though.

"You don't need to bring your entire life on a date. Leave it here. It makes you look like a librarian."

"But you just said guys liked that look!" I protested.

She blew out a breath, clearly exasperated. "Men want a 'librarian on vacation.' A demure, quiet girl ready to let loose. This purse says a 'librarian at work'—the one who's more likely to hiss at them to be quiet than let them ravage her."

Did I want to be "ravaged" by someone?

Living a proper life had kept me safe and mostly out of trouble. Sometimes it got excruciatingly lonely, though.

I had no family. The only friends I had were my co-workers. Like most people in this world, I often longed for a connection. In my case, however, that could only be a very short-lived connection before I was off to another port, country, or planet. Even that happened rarely. It'd been over a year since a man had last held me in his arms.

"Fine..." I set the purse on the side table by the couch. "But I need these two things from it." I took out my glasses and my wallet.

"You don't need the wallet. I have the invites." Bree flashed two glossy, hologram-enhanced cards to me. "These will pay for food and drinks."

"But my glasses..." I held on to my red cat-eye frames.

My farsightedness wasn't bad. I needed glasses to drive, to read the street signs and such, but I went around without them otherwise. I liked having them with me, though. It made me feel more confident and secure.

Bree squinted at the glasses in my hands, tapping her chin with her finger.

"Let me see." She took them from me, then perched them on my nose.

I immediately slid my finger up the bridge of my nose, adjusting the position of the glasses.

"You know? I don't hate it," she announced, giving me a critical once-over again. "They look rather trendy, go well with that sexy librarian thing, and add a splash of much needed color."

I caught my reflection in the floor-to-ceiling window. The sun had long set. The dark sky outside turned the glass of the window into a navy-blue mirror.

At almost five feet ten inches, I was taller than most women I knew. There was nothing dainty or delicate about my body, either.

I had strong shoulders that looked even more prominent now that Bree had exposed them. My hips pushed the soft folds of the skirt out quite a bit. I had a waist but nowhere thin enough for a man to circle it with his hands—no hour-glass figure here.

"It's cute, Tessa." Lucy said softly, tucking a strand of her blond hair behind her ear. "You look beautiful."

"Thank you."

Unlike Bree and me, Lucy wasn't a flight attendant. She worked for the human branch of the Earth-Voran Liaison Committee, the organization that was in charge of any joint projects between humans and Voranians. That included the marriage program that started several years ago and the transportation operations that had begun with it. As part of the crew operating a spaceship from Earth, Bree and I fell under their jurisdiction, too.

Lucy's assignment on this trip was to travel to the planet Aldrai. The Aldraians had recently expressed an interest in a marriage program with humans, and Lucy's task was to evaluate their planet as a suitable environment for our men and women.

Unlike Voranians, who had a severe shortage of females due to their birth rate being heavily skewed in favor of males, Aldraians had a healthy balance between males and females born.

Their interest in humans as spouses had other reasons. Aldraian pregnancies were few but resulted in many babies born to one woman. By mixing the genes, they hoped to achieve more frequent pregnancies but with fewer babies. It would significantly improve Aldraian female health, without a drop in population growth, and give a chance to more people to have a family.

Unlike Voranians, whose marriage agreement with us involved only women, Aldraians were looking at opening their program to both women and men.

"You need more color..." Bree muttered under her breath.

She plucked a red flower from the nearest vine and stuck it be-hind my ear.

"Here." She leaned back, admiring the results of her work. "That's better. Guys around here adore flowers."

Winter lasted almost six months in Voran, but Voranians loved summer and decorated their living spaces with an abundance of living plants.

The apartment where the three of us stayed was in the building of the Liaison Committee. The inside looked like an actual garden, with garlands of flowers dripping from the walls and ceilings. Pots with tall lattices of vines served as partitions throughout the living areas. And a sophisticated Artificial Intelligence system oversaw the maintenance of this indoor paradise.

People of Voran had adapted the methods of Aldraians of growing and tending to plants. The Voranians adored greenery. Aldraians must love it even more. From the little I knew about Aldrai, it was a garden planet. People literally lived in their gardens there. They didn't even bother with building houses.

The two men that Bree had arranged for a double date with us tonight had come from Aldrai.

I touched the flower above my ear.

"He'll love it," she assured me.

She'd only met one of the men. Once.

The two Aldraians had come to Voran for business and were staying in a hotel nearby. Bree ran into one of them in a café in a glass covered walkway that connected the hotel with our building. They'd chatted. As it'd turned out, both men had received the invitations to the New Year Celebration event organized by the Liaison Committee, too.

Lucy had adamantly declined both the double date and the invitation to the party. In a moment of weakness, I'd promised Bree I'd come to keep the second guy company.

The whole aspect of a blind date was nerve-racking on its own. Add to that the fact that the man was an alien from a planet where no human had even been to yet... Well, my hands turned sweaty every time I thought about it and my heart thundered so loudly, I feared a heart attack.

Unlike me, Bree looked rather bouncy. Her green eyes shone with excitement.

"Are you sure you don't want to come with us, Lucy?" she asked.

"No. Thank you." Lucy shook her head, adjusting the elastic waistband of her sweatpants. "I need to get some rest. My flight is tomorrow morning."

Bree laughed. "Mine too!"

Our spaceship was leaving for Aldrai at nine in the morning. Because we only had one passenger on this flight—Lucy—only one flight attendant was required. Bree was scheduled to work tomorrow. But it hadn't stopped her from accepting the invitation to the event tonight.

"Sleep is overrated." Bree headed for the door. "Are you ready to have some fun, Tessa?"

"Sure." With a wave at Lucy and a longing glance at her comfy position on the couch, I followed Bree out of the apartment.

"So, you've never seen an Aldraian before?" Bree asked as we walked down a long hallway to the glass-tube elevator.

"No." Aldraians never came to Earth. And there weren't many of them here, on Neron. "I mean I've seen pictures of them, once or twice."

The images were blurry in my memory. I recalled the males of that species had horns, and women had three pairs of breasts—due to the births of multiples, I assumed.

"Well." Bree chewed on her bottom lip. "Their men are not what people would call 'pretty boys.' You know?"

"What do you mean?"

Bree made a face, tilting her head. "Well, no one on Earth would call Voranians beautiful, either, come to think of it."

Voranians were very much scary looking, with their horns, hooves, and charcoal fur. Yet I found many of them agreeable. Alcus Hecear, the Voranian representative to the Liaison Committee with whom we'd interacted the most, was charming. I liked him a lot.

We stopped in front of the elevator, and I pressed the button. "There's nothing wrong with Voranians. They're nice people."

"So, you're okay with horns?" Bree asked.

"Sure. Why not?"

She squinted at me as we stepped into the elevator. "I mean like a *lot* of horns?"

"What are you talking about?"

She bit her lip. "Aldraians look...different. I just don't want you to be disappointed."

I shrugged. "I honestly don't care about their looks."

Going on a blind date with an alien, one had to expect something different, right?

"Listen," I said. "It's not like I'm going to marry the guy. I'm just there to keep him company while you're...doing whatever it is you're going to do with the other one. And anyway, looks don't matter as long as they're decent people."

The elevator stopped, and its doors opened.

"Right." A mischievous spark flashed in Bree's eyes. "Though, I rather hope Prug isn't going to be *decent* with me tonight."

Chapter 2

Tessa

"There they are." Bree tossed her long, wavy locks over her bare shoulder and adjusted her dress around her chest—preening like a beautiful, exotic bird.

The two of us had already taken our seats at one of the round tables scattered around under the enormous glass dome on the rooftop of the building.

Arches of brightly colored flowers marked each of the entrances, and people poured in from all directions.

Most of the guests were Voranian males. A handful of them had a human woman on their arm. The marriage program between humans and Voranians had been active for a few years now. However, human women were still a rare sight in Voran. Marrying one was considered a great honor in Voran, one that few men earned.

The two males who headed in our direction weren't Voranians, and they certainly stood out from the crowd.

Bree rose in her seat, waving at them.

"They may look rather ugly," she reminded me apologetically. "But please give them a chance. It'll be worth it, I promise."

On the first glance, the Aldraians appeared even more "scary-looking" than Voranians. There was something extremely intimidating in the way they plowed through the crowd toward us.

A race that lived in gardens and dedicated a huge chunk of their history to perfecting plant-growing techniques looked nothing like the flower faeries one might expect them to resemble.

The best comparison I could come up with when watching them stomp our way was a pair of rhinos moving on hind legs.

A row of thick, curved horns graced the middle of their heads, like a mohawk. Two more horns, one on each side of their skulls, slightly curved inward, making it look as if the men wore tall, massive crowns on their heads.

Short, wider horns also grew from their shoulders in thick clusters. It appeared as if their brawny bodies were encased in armor under their white clothes—tight, sleeveless shirts and loose pants.

The entire place shook from the footfalls of their brown boots. The delicate glasses and silverware on the table clinked as the two came closer. I gripped the edge of my chair, bracing for an earthquake or a building collapse that seemed eminent with their approach.

With my nerves strung tight, I was ready to bolt before saying a word to either of them. Only their bright, friendly grins helped me remain in place.

"Hi, Prug, sweetie," Bree cooed, flying up from her chair to greet the one with the skin the color of wet sand.

The other one was slightly darker, his coloring a bit warmer—deep caramel or light umber. He nodded to Bree, then turned to me, his smile spreading wider.

"Tessa?" He stretched his hand, palm up, to me.

Shit. Why had I never asked Bree for his name? I'd been so overwhelmed by the very idea of a blind date with an alien that I'd forgotten about the most basic things.

I got up, awkwardly shoving back my chair.

"Um..." I lifted my hand, too, unsure what he was expecting me to do with it.

"I'm Greyx." His smile grew warmer, radiating through his features and lighting up his bright orange eyes from within. He took my hand, turned it palm down, then placed it on top of his, palm to palm.

"Gray...ex," I repeated, taking extra care at pronouncing the foreign sounds of his name. "It's nice to meet you." I pressed lightly on his palm. It was warm and surprisingly soft. In contrast, the top of his hand appeared plated, just like his shoulders, with hard ridges over his knuckles.

Prug elbowed Greyx. "We'll go get us some drinks. What would you like, ladies?"

"Champagne would be lovely," Bree murmured, hanging on Prug's arm.

"I don't think they have Champagne here," I pointed out, not sure where to look. Greyx's smile urged me to grin back, and the loss of control was unnerving.

"True. It isn't Earth. So, no Champagne." Bree pouted. "Well, just get us something light and bubbly, then. Sweet, if they have it. But not bitter, please. I can't stand Voranian wine. It's too strong."

Prug frowned in a visible concentration, trying to memorize her instructions.

Bree peeled herself from his side, and the men headed over to one of the robot-powered carts with drinks that whirred between the tables on the other side of the room.

The space was filling in quickly. I spotted Alcus Hecear from the Liaison Committee. He entered, holding hands with another Voranian male. Dressed in a lime-green suit with pink embroidery, the representative had his horns painted with tiny multicolored dots, like confetti. His partner was wearing a similarly bright outfit. Most Voranians—male and female—loved bright colors and didn't shy from expressing it through their clothing.

"So." Bree leaned to me across the table, her eyes following the backs of the two Aldraians walking away. "What do you think?" She plucked a baby-blue berry from one of the several square trays of food on our table.

"They're nice." I had very little to go by. The brief encounter didn't give me much to judge the character of either of the men. But they both seemed friendly.

"Not too ugly, are they?" She winced, shoving another piece of food, something that looked like a small ball of cheese, in her mouth.

"Ugly? No." Chewing on a stick of curried meat, I followed her gaze to the Aldraians. They might be visitors from another planet, but they behaved in a sure manner here, comfortable in their own skin. Their confidence was attractive. And the physical strength that radiated from their massive figures made me intrigued. "They're unusual looking. But they are from another planet, so it's to be expected."

"They sure make up for the lack of good looks with their *skills*." Bree wiggled her eyebrows.

I rolled my eyes, hiding a smile behind my hand. "When did you have a chance to find out about their skills? You just met Prug yesterday."

She grinned. "I got a *preview* on the way from the café when he walked me to our apartment. Oh, and earlier, with his hands under the table in the café..." She let her voice trail off, her expression turning dreamy.

I laughed. "It didn't take him long at all."

"Why wait?" She shrugged. "They're leaving Neron tomorrow. Tonight may be my only chance to fuck an Aldraian."

I snorted a laugh, then grabbed a piece of fruit from a tray and shoved it into my mouth.

Some people collected post stamps and rare coins. Bree had been assembling her own collection of alien dicks. Since we'd landed on Neron, she'd slept with a couple of Voranians and even scored a night with a Ravil somehow. She told Lucy and me all about her conquests. I didn't mind Bree's stories. Listening to them was entertaining and even exciting, like living an adventure through her.

It didn't surprise me that Bree would jump on the chance to add a new specimen to her collection.

"You didn't make any promises to Greyx on my behalf, though, right?" I felt the need to clarify.

"Of course not! I mean, fuck him if you want, but I gave him no reasons to expect sex with you tonight."

I fidgeted with a narrow utensil on the table. "Good."

One-night stands never worked for me. I had to spend some time with the person to feel comfortable enough around them to relax and enjoy myself. Sadly, I rarely had much time to spend in any one place.

Of course, that didn't mean I couldn't have a great time and enjoy the party tonight. The slow music pleasantly floated under the glass dome. The food tasted nice. And the company of the Aldraians was welcome. My first impression of them wasn't bad. I hoped they found me agreeable, too.

A New Year's celebration always held hope and excitement for me. I was glad to discover that Voranians celebrated the start of a new year, too.

The Voranian head of the state, Governor Drustan, was a social man who loved to party. He insisted on celebrating every holiday in existence. Every year since he came into power, he'd been throwing a lavish ball on New Year's Eve at his palace.

Tonight's event was an echo of the Governor's ball. Bree and I weren't important enough to attend the Governor's palace. But the Liaison Committee organized an event on their own, inviting all their employees and members from both sides, humans and Voranians.

The Aldraians must've gotten the invitations as representatives of the planet also considering joining the alliance.

"You know they have tails?" Bree whispered in my ear, unexpectedly.

I stared at her in surprise. "No, they don't."

I might've slid my gaze a bit lower than their backs as Greyx and Prug had walked away to get us drinks. I'd noted they had nice backsides, but I hadn't seen any tails.

"They hide them," Bree explained excitedly. "It's not polite in their culture to display one's tail in public. Prug said they even have a special kind of porn—a tail porn." She giggled. "Normally, they tuck their tails in their pants. A secret appendage, hidden from view. Kind of like a second dick."

All other species in this part of the galaxy displayed their tails openly. Voranians had arrow-tipped ones. Ravils' tails ended with a tuft of fur. And Ivodians, I'd heard, were especially proud of their nine long, flexible tails that they often displayed fanned out behind them.

"What's wrong with having a tail? Why hide them?" I wondered out loud. "What do their tails look like?"

Bree flashed me a wicked grin. "Maybe Greyx will show you his?"

"Show her what?" a voice said at our side.

Absorbed by the naughty tail tales, I hadn't noticed that our Aldraians had returned. They must've moved more softly this time, since each carried two drink glasses in their hands.

Greyx was the one who'd asked the question, taking his seat to my left. And he was now staring at me expectantly, waiting for an answer.

"Oh... Nothing—" I blanched, my face heating up.

"Your tail," Bree murmured in a seductive voice, leaning to him over the table.

"My tail?" he asked. Incredibly, the skin over his cheeks tinted with a warm glow. The man was blushing!

Prug guffawed loudly, making the dishes on the table clink as he plopped in the seat next to Bree.

She nudged me with an elbow. "Tessa has never seen an Aldraian tail."

"Well, I…" Afraid to meet his eyes, I sank my gaze into the golden-orange liquid in the glass that Greyx had deposited in front of me.

I felt his mortification with my skin, wishing I had stuffed a bunch of cheese balls into Bree's mouth before she'd said anything about his tail.

Thankfully, Greyx recovered quickly. His easy grin returned.

"I bet not many people here have," he said in a light tone of voice.

The Aldraian phrase he used was longer than what my translator implant conveyed to me. The sound of his language—smooth and strong, with a rolling ramble to it—was pleasant to the ear.

Prug took a drink from his glass. "No Aldraian has seen everything human women have to offer, either," he murmured, nuzzling Bree's ear. "I'll show you mine if you show me yours."

"We don't have tails, silly." She giggled, sliding her hand up his arm.

"I'd still like to take a look."

The forearms of both Prug and Greyx were enclosed in gray bracers with soft ridges on the back. Made from a soft, rubber-like material, it wasn't clear whether the bracers had any practical application or were simply worn for fashion.

"I hope you'll like it," Greyx said softly at my side.

"Like *what?*" Flustered, I fisted my hands in my skirt.

Was he talking about his tail? His "second dick" as Bree had put it?

"The drink." He pointed at the glass in front of me. "It's a mix of fruit juice and alcohol distilled from flowers."

"Oh. The drink… Yes. Thank you." I released a breath and lifted the glass shaped like a large sphere to my lips, then took a sip.

The cool liquid had a fresh, crisp taste with a hint of sweetness. It reminded me of a watermelon, with just a hint of fizzy bubbles. The fuzzy effervescence from the drink bubbled through me, relaxing my muscles and easing the awkward tension inside me.

"It's really good." I raised my brows in surprise at how much I liked it.

Greyx leaned back in his chair. Satisfaction spread on his face, softening the hard angles of his features.

"It's the favorite drink of my sister. I figured you may like it, too." He popped a berry into his mouth, looking as comfortable as could be now that his tail was no longer the topic of conversation.

I watched him over the frame of my glasses that had slid down my nose. "How many sisters do you have?"

His grin unexpectedly slipped away. "One."

"And brothers?"

"None." His voice sounded clipped.

Having just one sibling was highly unusual for an Aldraian. Their pregnancies often delivered a dozen babies or more each.

I had questions, but Greyx's expression told me he wasn't in the mood to discuss his family. We had just met. I had no right to pry. So, I changed the subject by pointing at the drink in his hand—a thick, green-brown liquid, poured into a wide, stocky glass. "What are you drinking?"

The deep crease on his forehead below his front horn smoothed out.

"*Kartig.*" He raised his glass. "Brewed with bread and seaweed."

"Sounds...yummy." I made a face, not hiding my skepticism.

He laughed.

"Want to try?" He offered me his drink.

I shook my head, smiling. "I don't think I should."

"You may not get another chance."

His simple words resonated with me on many levels.

Bree was right when she said I'd been skirting an adventure. How many chances to experience something new had I missed in my twenty-seven years? This might be the grossest drink I'd ever drink. But it very well might be the one and only chance for me to taste it.

At least, I could say I'd tried.

"Okay." I set down my glass and reached for his.

"No." He raised an eyebrow ridge, jerking the glass out of my reach. "I don't trust you to hold it. One sip, and you'll fall in love with it. You'll drink it all, and I'll get nothing."

He was clearly teasing. Humor bounced bright in his eyes.

"I hardly doubt I'll fall in love with *this*." I grimaced. "No offence, but it doesn't look that appetizing."

"Oh, you have no idea what you're missing here. Looks can be deceiving." He raised the glass to my mouth. "Try it."

I leaned closer, parting my lips. "Just make sure you don't spill it on me. I don't think I'd ever get this color out of my clothes."

His mouth curled into a soft smile.

"I'll be gentle," he promised.

The purr in his voice rolled over me, prickling the skin on my bare arms.

Carefully, he touched the rim of his glass to my lips, then tipped it a little, letting me take a sip.

The liquid was thick and textured like tomato juice. The savory taste reminded me of seasoned green vegetables with a hint of anchovies. Not what I expected, but pleasant and satisfying.

"It's more like a meal than a drink," I said, leaning back.

He hummed in agreement.

"It helps to drink some water with it." He waved at a nearby drone that flew around with a pitcher of water and a stack of glasses.

Before the drone reached us, Greyx stretched his hand to my lips and slid the pad of his thumb over the corner of my mouth. Startled, I had no chance to react.

"A drop got away," he explained, licking the drop of his *kartig* off his thumb.

I watched his very human-looking pink tongue in amazement. He flicked it out, catching the drop on it, then hid it behind his firm lips. Unlike the tongue, his lips weren't pink at all. They were just a shade warmer than his skin, very much the same color of burned caramel as the rest of him.

His coloring darkened a bit on the clusters on his shoulders and on the plating on the back of his hands and arms. It lightened to golden-brown on the very tip of his horns that looked polished as if from a good use. I wondered if the Aldraians really used their horns for something or if that resulted from cosmetic polishing.

He cleared his throat. And I realized I'd been staring at him for way too long.

Judging by his easy-going smile, though, he wasn't affected by my way-too-close attention. He appeared to study me back, with a glint of amusement in his orange eyes.

"Care to dance?" I heard Prug asking Bree.

Slow music drifted under the glass dome. A Voranian band was playing from a low, round stage to the left, decorated with garlands of flowers.

There wasn't a designated dance floor here. But with the widely spaced tables, couples had more than enough room to float and twirl between them.

Prug dragged Bree to a free spot between the tables. The two made no particular dance moves. Both just shuffled from foot to foot with her arms linked around his middle and his hands roaming all over her.

I turned my attention back to Greyx. Fascinated, I kept catching myself staring at him, no matter what part of his body my gaze landed on.

At that very moment, it landed on his arm, just above the elbow, as he rested it on the table. Since he was sitting next to me, I could see most of his arm. The plating on the back of it was flat, slowly growing

into the raised bumps and peaks over his shoulder, like a rock forma-
tion.

"Would you like to touch?" he asked, catching me ogling him
again.

I blinked. "Touch what?"

"Me," he said simply, stretching his arm on the table for me.

"Oh, no..." I pressed my hands together, as if they would jump
out on their own and start pawing all over him. "I'm..."

Touching him seemed like asking for trouble.

"Go ahead." He rolled his arm from side to side, displaying the
hard nob over the elbow on the outside and the thick bulge of his bicep on the inside. "Aren't you curious how it'd feel?"

"Well..."

What was I supposed to say to that? That I really, really wanted
to rub the hard parts of him, to see if the plating was external like a
turtle shell, or if it was a thick layer of skin like on a rhinoceros?

It could come with the desire to explore further. And I had no
idea where exploring his softer parts would lead.

He kept his arm in front of me like an offering. "I, for one, am
dying to know what your skin feels like."

"Oh. It's...just skin." I glanced at my own—to me, very ordinary
looking—hand.

"It seems so tender, unprotected, and soft," he murmured, leaning closer.

Way too close.

I should've moved away, even if that meant taking my chair with
me. But a tendril of his scent reached me—warm and earthy, with
a hint of spice from his drink on his breath. And instead of moving
back, I leaned forward. "You know how it feels. You've touched my
hand."

"True." He nodded. "It'd be only fair, then, if you touched mine,
right?"

That wasn't how it worked, I wanted to argue. We'd both touched hands. But he lifted his arm off the table, turning his hand palm up and... I couldn't resist.

"I suppose..." I mumbled, trying to focus entirely on the hand and not think about the mountain of a man attached to it.

"There you go. You have five minutes to do with it as you please." There was a smile in his voice.

I knew he must be looking at me with that sunny twinkle of amusement in his eyes, but I didn't move my attention from his hand, afraid to meet his eyes. Instead, I slid the tip of my finger along his palm.

He exhaled a short laugh, closing his hand into a fist so fast he nearly trapped my finger in it.

I glanced up at him in question.

"It tickles," he explained innocently, making me burst into laughter, too.

Who knew this build-like-a-rock, hard-plated male would be ticklish?

"Where else are you ticklish?"

"I don't know." He grinned. "That'd require some testing."

I arched an eyebrow at the challenge in his voice, suddenly wishing I could explore much more than would be appropriate in a public place.

"I'm not done with your hand yet. My five minutes aren't up," I reminded.

"Right." He unclenched his fist, but turned his hand palm down now.

I touched the wide, pointed bumps over his knuckles. The tips of them were glossy and hard, like bone or shell polished to a shine. The base of the bumps gradually gained some subtlety. His skin drew over the bone between the ridges.

I slid my fingers over the rubber bracer, then felt the inside of his elbow and higher up his arm. Here, his skin was soft and warm, stretched over the hard curve of his bicep underneath, with no plating at all. I let my fingers explore more freely, splaying my hand over his skin and squeezing his arm.

After a few more seconds, he audibly sucked in a breath.

"Ticklish again?" I teased, raising my eyes to his.

There was no amusement in his expression now. Trimmed with thick, dark-brown lashes, his eyelids dropped, shading his eyes. His irises grew darker and redder somehow, turning the color of terracotta. The intensity in them sent a flock of warm tingles through my chest.

"Not ticklish. Something else..." His voice sounded rougher than before. The rumble in it resonated through me, making me squirm in my seat.

I jerked my hand away.

He kept his gaze on me. "You've strayed way past my hand, Tessa. Now, I'll need to touch something of yours to make it even."

The look in his eyes promised so much more than handholding. A thrill of anticipation buzzed through me. His stormy eyes didn't scare me. On the contrary, the dark expression in them excited me.

He'd managed to put me at ease, and now he was making me want more.

I rested my chin on the back of my fingers, my elbow propped on the table. "What would you like to touch?"

"Your hair." Taking a strand that had made it out of my up-do, he slid the curl between his fingers.

"My hair?" I mumbled, utterly confused. I would consider giving him permission to touch anything that wouldn't get us kicked out of the party, but he went for a hair strand he could've snagged any time.

"It's so dark, as if colored with coal," he murmured, making the lock slide between his fingers. "Even darker than Voranian fur. And so smooth."

"Don't Aldraian women have hair?" I asked, amazed by his fascination.

"They do. But their hair is always straight and the same color as their skin—shades of brown. I've never seen black hair before."

"Well," I said as he continued to play with that one strand hanging off the side of my face, the back of his fingers grazing my cheek. "That's my natural hair color. It's hard to change it since it's so dark. And no, I certainly don't paint it with coal."

He looked at me, his gaze scattering from my eyes to my lips, then back to my hair. Letting go of the strand, he slid a caress above my ear, then moved his hand to the back of my head.

Technically, this was still only my hair he was touching, but the nature of his touch had changed. He gripped my bun above my nape, bringing my face closer to his.

His lips parted, the tip of the tongue darting out to wet his bottom lip. I swallowed hard, halting my breath. My heart raced. I knew we were a heartbeat away from a kiss, and everything inside me wished for his lips on mine.

The music changed. Its languid flow that had been easy to ignore suddenly leaped to a fast, upbeat tempo. The first loud cords sounded like an explosion in my mind. I jerked back and out of Greyx's grip, losing the moment with him.

He didn't appear as if he'd lost anything, though, seizing the opportunity instead.

"Finally!" He shot me a smile. "My type of music."

He shoved his chair back, energetically rising to his feet, and grabbed my hand. "Let's dance, Tessa!"

"What? No!" I protested, clinging to the table with my other hand. "I don't dance. Definitely not to...this."

The music skidded and rushed with the ferocity of white water over rapids. Most couples returned to their seats. Those who remained hopped and jumped as if suddenly possessed by demons.

"I can't do *that*." I shook my head.

"Of course you can." He dragged me out of my chair. "That's the best kind of dancing—no dancing skills required."

He drew me to him, and I had to let go of the table lest I drag the tablecloth off with me.

"Come." He led me to an open space. "And don't worry. You don't need to do much. All this dance requires is a little jumping and a lot of enthusiasm."

Well, he most definitely didn't lack in the enthusiasm department. Excitement burst in his bright eyes. His wide grin drew me in more powerfully than even his strong arms.

"Put your hands on my shoulders," he ordered.

I hovered one of my palms over the hard clusters on his shoulders. The only smooth place was a couple of inches next to his neck. Here, two gold-embossed leather straps held the front and back panels of his shirt together. Several more short belts like that buckled along the side seams, too.

Putting a regular shirt on would be impossible for Aldraians, I imagined, with all the horns and bumps on their head and shoulders. Their shirts were constructed from two separate panels held together by leather straps with decorated buckles. They must put them on like two pieces of armor from the human medieval times, buckling the two parts together afterwards.

I stared at his shoulders with trepidation, unsure where to put my hands.

He took my hand in his.

"Like this." He carefully placed my right hand between the hard bumps on his left shoulder, then wrapped my fingers around a short, thick horn growing in the middle. "That's the only one that's sharp enough to hurt you," he explained. "Hold on to it and stay away from the pointy tip."

I nodded, mimicking the position with my left hand on his right shoulder.

"Ready?" he said, smiling, his voice low and warm.

"No—"

He grabbed me by the waist and swung me around.

I wasn't a petite girl, never had been. But his massive size made me feel tiny in comparison. The strength with which he lifted and twirled me in his arms made me feel weightless.

"Jump, Tessa!" he shouted over the music, leaping in the air.

I had no choice but to jump with him. My heels hit the polished wood floor when I landed.

He glanced down at my feet.

"You're wearing the perfect shoes for this." He nodded approvingly. "Strapped to your feet, so you don't lose them."

This dance sure could blow one's shoes off their feet.

After a few more of uncoordinated jumps and leaps, I started figuring out the pattern of the dance. Greyx leaped to one side, taking me with him, then he jumped on the same spot a few times, quickly alternating his feet. After that, he leaped to the other side, all the while progressing forward in circles.

I made an effort to follow his lead as well as the crazy rise and fall in the music. The steps weren't difficult. The hardest part was to maintain the neck-breaking tempo. I was quickly running out of breath, trying to keep up.

I panted, but couldn't help laughing. "This is actually fun!"

It was impossible not to laugh when leaping into the air like a madwoman.

"I told you!" He exhaled a burst of laughter, too, his expression a pure glee.

We made another circle of leaps. My heels beating staccato on the floor. My skirt swishing through the air with each twirl.

My face heated, my glasses sliding down my nose. My breathing rushed out of me in rugged panting. My lungs burned, as if I was running a marathon. And I didn't want this to stop.

Greyx's bright eyes watched me with delight. My face hurt from smiling so wide, but I couldn't stop smiling.

A crackling of microphone cut over the music, but we kept dancing. Neither of us was ready to quit yet. The music kept playing, and Greyx was taking me for another loop between the tables.

"Ladies and gentlemen," a male voice sounded. Alcus Hecear was speaking into the microphone. "In honor of the tradition of our human guests, we're going to sound a bell for each of the twelve last seconds of the passing year."

A bell rang, followed by another one shortly. It wasn't quite the same sound as beating of the clock back home, but it was close enough. Gratitude tugged at my heart with emotion. It was very thoughtful of the Committee to bring something from Earth's traditions into their celebration.

"It's also customary in some parts of the Earth to kiss your partner after the last bell," Alcus Hecear announced. "I quite like that part myself." He grinned at the Voranian male standing at his side, the same man he'd come with.

"Four!" Alcus yelled into the microphone, counting the bell rings.

"Five!" Everyone under the dome shouted at once.

Alcus put down the microphone, letting the crowd count the rings. The music quieted for a few seconds.

Greyx spun me one more time, then stopped abruptly, holding me in front of him.

"Ten," he said softly, counting the next ringing of the bell.

His eyes on me, he drew me closer.

"Eleven," I said along with the shouting crowd.

I opened my mouth to count the very last ring of the bell, but the word never left my lips.

"Twelve!" the crowd yelled.

And Greyx's mouth was on mine, swallowing the last count. His firm lips were surprisingly gentle at first. The tip of his tongue stroked my tongue tentatively, as if tasting the waters before taking a plunge.

I gripped the horns on his shoulders tighter. He pressed me to him, my feet lifting off the ground.

In his arms, I felt like I was flying. My mind was spinning out of control in a dance wilder than the one he'd just taken me on. It was a freefall, and Greyx was falling with me.

He deepened his kiss, his tongue invading my mouth as if it'd always belonged there. He moved his hands higher up my back.

My fingers weakened, letting go of his shoulders. I slid my palms down his chest. The muscles under the thin material of his shirt were firm and chiseled, but there was no hard plating here. Through the layer of his shirt, I felt the warmth and subtle give of his body.

I slid my hand up, cupping his jaw as he devoured my mouth. I wished for this moment to last forever. I didn't want this kiss to end. I never wanted to leave his arms...

Greyx was not one-night stand material. He was what heartbreaks were made of. And with him, my heart wasn't safe.

Pressing both hands into his chest, I leaned back, breaking the kiss.

"Happy New Year!" the crowd cheered.

"Happy New Year," Greyx echoed.

His lips, the color of black cherry after our kiss, stretched in a smile. The glint in his hooded eyes held a promise. It was so easy to get lost in their depth.

"Happy New Year," I said softly, my words lost in the noise of the cheering crowd.

"Tessa!" Bree shouted next to us, swinging in Prug's arms. "Happy New Year, girl!"

Her lipstick was gone, as mine must be, too. Her hair was mussed. A strap of her dress was hanging loose off her shoulder.

"We're leaving," she happily announced. "It's Prug's last night on Neron." She ran a finger along Prug's jawline. "He wants to spend it with me."

Last night.

True. She'd mentioned before they were leaving the planet tomorrow.

Greyx's jaw ticked, but he said nothing.

Bree ran her hands over Prug's wide chest. "I have to make sure he has a night to remember. He's so curious..." She rose on her tiptoes, placing a kiss on Prug's lips.

"Can't wait to find out what you hide under that dress," Prug growled. Leaning his head, he sucked Bree's bottom lip into his mouth.

I stepped out of Greyx's arms and straightened my blouse. "Bree, are you going to his hotel?" There was something predatory in the way Prug was staring at her, and not in a good way. Besides, as a team lead, I had to remain sensible even on the first day of the new year. "You have to work in the morning, remember?"

Bree released a dramatic sigh, adding an eye roll for a good measure. "Work is not going anywhere."

I took her by the arm and leaned closer to gain a modicum of privacy, which wasn't easy with Prug hovering over us. She wouldn't let go of his shirt.

"You have a flight tomorrow morning, Bree," I said sternly, willing her to take it seriously. "You need to get some sleep tonight, and you can't drink anymore. Okay?"

"I know, I know." She waved me off. "We won't take long. Right, baby?" She gave Prug a smoldering look.

"We'll see." He smirked, with a glint of a canine from under his curled lip.

I darted my gaze between the two.

"Bree, I'll leave, too, if you come to the apartment with me, now," I made a last attempt, already knowing I was fighting a losing battle.

Greyx shifted at my side. "Do you have to leave, Tessa?"

I glanced at him.

Heat simmered deep in his bright eyes. Like Prug, he was certainly "curious," too, but Greyx's smile seemed kinder and so much more appealing to me than Prug's predatory smirk.

Unlike them, I wasn't simply *curious* about sex with an alien. Neither was I interested in assembling a collection of extra-terrestrial conquests like Bree.

I liked Greyx. He deserved more than becoming "a dick" in any collection. And I, too, wanted more than simply a one-night stand. I wished we had a chance for a second date and more time to get to know each other. But in my current life, relationships weren't possible.

Greyx brushed my fingers with his, but I shrank away from him, thwarting his attempt to hold my hand.

"I should go," I said, not meeting his eyes. "Are you coming with me, Bree?"

"Oh no, I'm not letting her go anywhere," Prug said, tightening his arms around Bree, as if she were his rightful prize.

"I'm not going to the apartment yet." She laughed, tipping her head back.

Bree was a grown woman. This wasn't her first night out on her own, nor her first alien man. I couldn't drag her to the apartment against her will.

"Okay, well…" I gave up. "Just make sure you're back on time." I glared at Prug in warning. "I know where you're staying. If Bree is not home safely in the morning, I'll come searching for her myself."

He just smirked again.

Greyx studied me carefully, his orange eyes focused on me intently from under his dark, prominent brow ridges. I couldn't escape his stare. I felt it on me, tangible, like a touch.

"I'll walk you back," he said firmly.

I wanted to say that it wouldn't be necessary. It was just a long elevator ride and a brief walk through a hallway. I didn't even have to go outside. But he already placed a hand on the small of my back. My thoughts scattered at the contact. My knees grew weak, and I leaned into his side, stealing a few moments of his closeness.

"Okay…" was all I muttered.

"Have fun, you two," Bree cooed in a sing-song voice, wiggling her fingers at us.

I shook my head to let her know she was mistaken about my intentions, but she had already turned her attention back to Prug, who slid his hand down the deep plunge of the cut-out on the back of her dress.

With a slight press on the small of my back, Greyx directed me to the nearest exit.

"I'm on the thirty-sixth floor," I warned him.

The thirty-sixth floor was a long way down from the rooftop, way past the floor with the walkway to his hotel. Voranians' skyscrapers were freakishly tall. So tall, in fact, that people in Voran used personal aircraft instead of cars for transportation, flying from roof to roof.

"I know," he said, matter-of-fact.

I glanced at him above my glasses. "You know where I live?"

"Prug told me. I think he learned it from Bree."

"And you don't mind leaving a party just to walk with me?"

"The party was only fun because you were there," he replied earnestly.

I adjusted my glasses awkwardly, feeling a warm blush flooding my face at his compliment. I wished I had my purse with me to occupy my hands. Without it, I feared Greyx would get hold of my hand, or worse, that I might grab his.

"Did you have fun?" he asked me when we reached the rounded glass doors of the elevator.

"I did," I blurted out. "It was probably the best New Year's celebration of my life."

"Then why leave so early? Do you also have to work tomorrow?"

"No. I'm off."

The elevator came, and we got on. The glass elevator shaft was located on the outside of the building. We plunged into the dark winter night, surrounded by flowers inside and the intense heat radiating between our bodies.

He took a step closer, skimming his hands up my arms.

"Spend the night with me, Tessa." His voice was low, but the words came out with force. Half-plea, half-order. "I'll make sure it'll be a night you'll never forget."

I believed him. But that was a problem, too, wasn't it? An amazing night with Greyx would still only be one night. He'd leave in the morning. And then, I'd spend the rest of my life trying to find someone who'd be half as good at making my body sing by just rubbing my arms the way Greyx was doing right now.

Wouldn't it be better not knowing what I was missing?

It felt safer that way. And safe was what I did best.

The elevator stopped and the doors opened.

I practically ran out, not giving him a chance to either stop or follow me.

"Thank you for everything." I hit the button of the floor with the walkway to his hotel on my way out. "It was a fun party."

The doors closed.

The elevator soared up, taking with it my last chance to change my mind.

I was glad it did.

I really was.

I had to be.

Nothing happened. There was nothing to miss or regret.

Nothing.

Except that now it felt like yet another experience had passed me by.

Chapter 3

Tessa

One day, I would stop traveling. Eventually, I would find a stable job that would allow me to stay in one place for a while. Hopefully, it'd pay at least half as well as working on the spaceships did.

One day, I might run into a man whose kisses would make my toes curl and my heart flutter the way Greyx's did. And I'd be in the position to hold on to that man and give our relationship a chance.

One day...

For now, I quickly washed off my makeup, changed into my nightshirt, and climbed into the comfy, round bed that was all mine for the next two weeks.

I closed my eyes and prayed that the one glass of liquor I'd drank at the party would perform a miracle and let me fall asleep without being taunted by the sweet memories of muscular arms twirling me in a dance or of smiling, sun-colored eyes.

I must've gotten lucky, falling asleep fairly quickly—and deeply. Because when the loud pounding on my door came sometime later, waking up was hard. It felt like breaking through the surface of a dark, muddy ocean.

"Tessa! Tessa!" Lucy's voice shouted on the other side of the door. "Wake up!"

I peeled my eyes open and sat up. It was morning already. The large, floor-to-ceiling window of my bedroom displayed the pale blue and faint yellow of the washed-out winter sunrise.

"Tessa!" Lucy demanded. "Get up!"

Lucy never *demanded* anything. Shy and quiet, she'd never raised her voice before for as long as I'd known her, which was almost six months now.

Something must've happened.

Swiping the covers aside, I climbed out of bed.

"What's going on?" I slid my door open, coming face to face with Lucy.

Her fist raised, she was about to pummel at my door again. She was fully dressed in jeans and a white crochet sweater with pearly buttons in the front. Strands of blond, wavy hair that had strayed out of her ponytail stuck out wildly. Her big blue eyes appeared larger than ever, open wide.

"It's Bree..." She gestured over to the couch.

Bree curled in a corner on it. Still wearing her red dress and sparkly heels, she sobbed loudly.

With a jolt of shock, any remnants of sleep vanished.

"Bree!" I rushed to her. "What did he do to you?" I immediately assumed Prug was the one to blame here. I'd left Bree with him, after all.

I sat on the couch next to her and touched her shoulder. "Should I call the police or whatever they have on Voran instead?"

Lucy hovered nearby, her face pale like the snow clouds outside the window. "I think it translates as 'the police' here, too," she said through the hand placed over her mouth.

Bree shook her head. "No... No police."

"At the very least, I'll have to let the Liaison Committee know," I insisted. "I'll call Alcus Hecear—"

I made a move to get up, but she grabbed the hem of my night-shirt, pulling me back to the couch. "Don't... It's stupid."

"What do you mean 'stupid?'" I bristled. "If the asshole abused you in any way—"

"He didn't." She sniffled. "Well, not like that..."

I took her shoulder again and leaned sideways to better see her tear-stained face. Last night's makeup streaked her face. Her long hair was tangled and matted, her dress stained.

"God, Bree, you look like shit."

"Thanks," she scoffed, wiping her nose with her arm. "I feel like shit, too." She winced, resentfully squinting at the pale light from the window.

"I'll get you some water." Lucy trotted over to the kitchen area.

I brushed Bree's hair away from her face. "Are you going to tell me what happened? Or do I have to track Prug down and interrogate him?"

She huffed a humorless laugh. "You would, wouldn't you?"

"Damn right, I would! And I wouldn't be too picky about my interrogation methods. Did he hurt you? Did he make you do anything you didn't want to do?"

She shook her head again, with a hiccup this time.

"We fucked. But I wanted to fuck him. And it was...fun." She glanced up at me from under the tangled mess of her copper-red hair. "I got to see his tail. Apparently, it's super sensitive." She snorted another laugh.

My worry eased somewhat.

Lucy padded back with a glass of water. Bree emptied it in a few long, greedy gulps.

"Why are you crying, then?" I asked and immediately regretted it as her eyes welled with tears again.

"You know what that asshole said to me?" she sobbed with a sniffle.

"Who?" I blinked. Was she still talking about Prug? Was he the asshole, after all?

Lucy grabbed the empty glass out of Bree's shaking fingers.

"We had great sex, right?" Bree bawled. "I came like a gazillion times. He did, too. All freaking night. Then, he watched me getting dressed, and I asked, 'Do you like what you see?' And... and he said, 'Sure.' But he sounded funny, so I asked him what he meant. Then he told me that human women looked weird..."

She burst into another bout of tears, wailing loudly. Lucy ran back to the kitchen to get more water. I patted Bree's shoulder.

"Well, he's from another planet," I said. "*Weird* is to be expected. Aldraians don't exactly look like someone we're used to seeing, either, right? You called them ugly, remember?"

"Yeah, but I didn't tell him that to his face!" she yelled through tears. "He was so mean about it, too. He said that us having only two breasts makes it look like something is missing, like we're not whole, you know? Lacking. He told me he was curious what it'd be like to fuck a human, but it turned out 'underwhelming.' He'd rather stick with Aldraian chicks from now on. Because they have *six* breasts, like every woman is *supposed* to have."

Anger stirred in me. I felt offended for every human woman out there. I forced my voice to remain calm, even as I seethed inside.

"He was drunk," I offered, in an attempt to console Bree.

"He's an asshole!" she screeched.

"Well, that, too," I agreed.

Lucy rushed in and shoved another glass of water into Bree's hands.

"It's eight o'clock," Lucy said softly, nervously glancing at the white screen of the TV displaying the time of all known planets.

Eight o'clock?

Was it that late already?

"Shit! The flight!" I jumped to my feet. "Bree, you need to be at the terminal, like right now!"

"Awww..." she released a loud wail. "You're such a freaking goody two-shoes. Always so on time and so very proper." She tossed her head back, then crashed face down onto the couch cushion.

Goody two-shoes? Because I show up for work on time?

"Bree, you knew you had to work. You promised!"

She just mumbled something incomprehensible into the cush-ion.

"I don't think she can do it," Lucy stated the obvious.

If Bree didn't come to work this morning, I believed she'd be fired. And all because of some alien idiot saying stupid things to her? Or was there more than that?

I shook her shoulder. "How much did you drink last night?"

To my knowledge, there was that one glass of flower liquor, the same one I had, which was fine and long ago to be perfectly legal.

Without lifting her face from the cushion, she raised her right hand up, with all five fingers outstretched.

"Five?" I asked to make sure. "You had *five* drinks?"

She lifted her left hand, too, holding out five more fingers.

"Holly shhh... Bree! What were you thinking? They'll fire you if you don't show up. And if you do show up in this state, they'll most definitely fire you, anyway."

She cried loudly. And I plopped back on the couch next to her.

This wouldn't be the first violation on Bree's part, but it'd be the most serious one to date. Even if I could somehow shake some sense into her, wash her up, and send her to the spaceport, she was not in the position to work this flight.

There was only one solution.

"I'll have to take your shift," I said.

A loud snoring came from the cushion—Bree's only answer.

"Could you?" Lucy pleaded, both hands pressed to her chest. "If they cancel the flight today, it may screw up the rest of our schedule, including the return trip to Earth."

That was entirely possible. We had just over two weeks left in Vo-ran. A round trip to Aldrai was five days. Plus, Lucy had a week's worth of visits scheduled on Aldrai to assess the living conditions on the planet.

We were running tight as it was. Delaying a return trip to Earth wouldn't be easy, considering the amount of work and the number of people involved in interplanetary travel. And all because of a flight attendant who partied a little too hard the night before.

Bree could be in so much trouble.

I glanced at her. Curled into a ball in the corner of the couch, she looked younger than her twenty-five years. Combined with the pitiful state of her outfit, it tugged at my compassion, making it hard to be mad at her.

"Well, I did get a few solid hours of sleep, and I'm legal as far as alcohol goes." I glanced at the clock again. "Just give me fifteen minutes to get ready," I said to Lucy, who exhaled in relief. "Call the taxiplane, or whatever they have here to take us to the spaceport. If we hurry, we should make it."

I took a quick shower, then dried my hair and got dressed in record time. Any trace of lingering tiredness was gone. I quickly messaged our crew scheduling and the captain of the flight, letting them all know about the switch.

After packing my things in my carry-on, I grabbed my "librarian" purse and put my glasses on.

Meanwhile, Lucy had taken Bree's shoes off, covered her with a blanket, and put a fresh glass of ice water on a side table next to the couch.

"I left a message on her tablet, explaining what happened," Lucy told me as we were leaving the apartment. "She may not remember it otherwise."

I sighed in answer, shaking my head. I'd never missed a shift in my life without a very good excuse, even when I was working in a hole-in-the-wall diner for shitty pay. And maybe that made me "a goody two-shoes," but it was hard for me to imagine someone being this careless with a good, well-paying job. I'd worked much harder for far less money before not to appreciate what I had now.

That said, Bree was sweet and personable when she was sober. She'd always been there for me, ready to help when needed. And I would hate to see her fired.

Hopefully, things would work out well in the end. For all of us.

Chapter 4

Tessa

With passenger space travel still being very new, there weren't that many spaceship flight attendants on Earth. I hadn't known jobs like this existed until a client who had rented the luxury yacht I'd been working on told me about it.

He worked in executive management of the human branch of the Earth-Neron Liaison Committee. My service skills on the yacht had impressed enough to encourage me to apply for this position. The money was amazing, and the prospect of visiting other planets sounded exciting, so I had applied and then happily accepted the job when they'd offered it to me.

The travel time to Neron from Earth was five months one way. With the necessary rest and layover time, a round trip took an entire year.

I didn't mind. No one was waiting for me back on Earth, anyway. I had no family to miss me. And by the time I took the job, I'd been well used to the nomadic lifestyle. When working on the yacht, I'd often celebrated each new year in a different country. This year, I'd rung it in on a new planet, instead. It wasn't that much different.

Despite the long, rigorous training I'd been put through before starting this job, working on the spaceship was similar to working on a yacht or even in a diner. All of it was customer service, first and foremost.

Common sense, pleasant manners, patience, and thick skin were valuable attributes in any job I'd done.

Punctuality was crucial.

Lucy and I arrived at the Voranian spaceport with only a minute to spare. The anxiety that had gripped my chest since that morning only let go when I spotted the massive gray shape of our interplanetary shuttle docked on the glass-covered platform. Our ship was at least ten times as big. However, since this was a much shorter trip, with only one passenger on board, it'd been decided to use the shuttle instead.

Alcus Hecear met us on a pathway between the trimmed hedges on our way to the shuttle. Despite the snow and freezing temperatures outside, here under the glass dome, flowers bloomed and shrubs remained as green as ever.

"Flight Attendant Lucas," he addressed me in the Voranian way, using the work position as part of my name. "Representative Kowalski." He tipped his horns at Lucy in greeting. "I've come to bid you goodbye and a safe trip."

"It's very nice of you, Representative Hecear." Lucy offered him her hand, and he took it between his two.

Alcus had changed from his bright party outfit of last night into the white-and-gold uniform of the Liaison Committee. However, his long, slightly curved horns remained painted with the multi-colored confetti-dots, as were his hooves, I noticed when I bowed my head in greeting.

"I saw the change in your crew this morning." He turned to me, enclosing my hand in both of his in the Voranian handshake. "And I wanted to make sure you're aware of the two new passengers joining you on this flight."

I straightened. "More passengers?"

"Yes. General Wrun and First Lieutenant Mazex. I sent their names to everyone on your flight yesterday."

I didn't doubt he'd sent them. Bree most likely had it in her communication folder somewhere. Obviously, she'd been in no position to forward the information to me this morning.

"The general and the first lieutenant were supposed to take an Aldraian Army ship a week from now, but their plans had changed. The Army petitioned for the seats for them on the first available spaceship traveling to Aldrai, citing urgency of their departure. Yours was the soonest flight we could arrange for them. Their tickets have been approved by your authorities and paid for by the Aldraian Government. But I thought I would let you know in person, since the increased passenger load means triple the amount of work for you, Flight Attendant Lucas."

Legally, I was allowed to serve up to twenty passengers on my own. The two extra ones didn't add that much workload. However, it was very thoughtful of Alcus to make it all the way here this morning to tell me in person.

"It's very sweet of you, thank you," I said sincerely. Alcus had proven to be one of the nicest people I knew. I wished he would accept addressing me by my first name. *Flight Attendant Lucas* was a mouthful. "I promise to look after them."

Alcus boarded the shuttle with Lucy and me. The extra passengers weren't here yet. Alcus went to speak with the flight crew in the front while I showed Lucy to her cabin, then put my bag into the crew cabin with bunk beds.

After making sure everything was in order and ready for the two-day trip, I stood by the ramp at the door, waiting for the new passengers.

It didn't take them long to arrive.

I heard their heavy stomping way before the two emerged from between the rows of green hedges.

Standing straighter, I smoothed down my uniform—a teal dress and a gray cardigan—and plastered my best professional smile on, ready to greet them.

My polite smile wavered, then disappeared completely as the two men came closer. They were wearing black and gold clothes today instead of the white outfits they had on last night. But there was no mistaking them; they were the same men I'd met at the party last night.

I recognized the happy grin and the bright orange eyes of the one in the front.

"Morning, Tessa," Greyx greeted me, the ramp vibrating under his heavy footfalls.

Prug leered at me, falling half a step behind Greyx. "Hi there."

I froze, words and thoughts deserting me.

"Welcome aboard!" Alcus Hecear rushed from behind me to greet them. "General Wrun." He tilted his head in greeting, and Greyx placed his right hand on the left side of his chest with a slight bow of his head in return. "First Lieutenant Mazex." Alcus repeated the ritual with Prug.

Holy cupcake with sprinkles on top! These were my two extra passengers. And by the sound of it, they were high-ranking officials in the Aldraian Army.

I clutched my hands together, struggling to breathe.

How was I supposed to know that the man I danced with and *kissed* last night was a freaking general? And that he would end up on my freaking shuttle this morning?

Should I have known?

There weren't that many Aldraians in Voran. Other than these two, I hadn't seen any at all. Both Greyx and Bree had said they were on Neron for business. With so few Aldraians on this planet, it would've been logical to assume that it was some kind of important interplanetary business. They wouldn't come to Neron to sell vacuums or encyclopedias door-to-door, for goodness' sake.

I'd never asked Greyx about his job because at no point had it been important. I never thought I'd see him again. And anyway, my mind had been entirely occupied with other things. Like how amazing Greyx's hands had felt on my waist and how wonderful his kiss had tasted.

In any case, not spending a night with him now seemed an even wiser decision. Him being a general only widened the distance between us.

Just like Prug, Greyx might've ended up disappointed with my inadequate number of breasts anyway, had I mustered the courage to get naked with him.

The memory of crying Bree stirred the anger against Prug inside me again.

Alcus chatted with the two Aldraians for another minute or so. He wished them a pleasant journey home before departing, while I stood nearby, still solidly frozen in shock, my face burning hot like a heating lamp.

"Tessa. Can I talk with you for a moment?" Greyx turned to me.

I cleared my throat, willing my voice not to shake, even as my violent blush couldn't be helped.

"Welcome aboard," I said brightly, stepping back from him and into the main passenger cabin.

"Tessa, please..." Greyx followed me in.

"It's *Flight Attendant Lucas*." I jerked my chin up. The sunny spark dulled in his eyes, and I softened my voice a bit. "You can call me 'Miss' if it's more convenient."

Hell, I'd go by "Ma'am" or even "Excuse Me" if that helped keep some distance between us.

This was *my* world now. The shuttle was my place of work. Here, I had a clearly defined role, and Greyx was no longer my blind date. He was my passenger.

Dating was complicated and unsettling. Working was something I knew and did well.

"Gentlemen, allow me to show you to your cabins." I kept my tone and expression neutral, snapping back into the working mode.

"You can leave your luggage there." I gestured at the suitcases in their hands.

Prug brushed by Greyx, stomping down the wide aisle between the seats toward the area with the passenger cabins.

"It's a long flight," he smirked, measuring me with a glance as he passed by. "She'll come around."

Greyx ignored him, keeping his attention on me and not moving a step away.

"I'm at work," I explained, turning toward the aisle to the cabins, too. "I need to do my job."

Greyx followed Prug and me to the sleeping area at the back. I made sure to put these two as far from Lucy as possible. I wouldn't put it past Prug to try sneaking into her cabin sometime during the flight. The way he'd looked at me, I didn't trust him to stick with his "Aldraian chicks only" resolution. In fact, I didn't trust that guy at all.

The moment Greyx took his attention from me to poke his head inside his cabin, I slipped away, heading to the front of the spacecraft. There, I briefly talked to the pilots, then got ready for take-off.

Both Greyx and Prug were in the main cabin already when I made my way back. Lucy was also seated in one of the wide leather seats, reading something on her tablet.

I started the passenger briefing. "Please remain seated and wear your seatbelts during the take-off until the captain makes the announcement that it's safe to remove them."

"And when will that be?" Prug grimaced. He looked displeased to stay put even for a little while, but fastened his five-point seatbelt, anyway.

Lucy clicked hers on, too.

"Usually, it happens shortly after we leave the atmosphere," I replied to Prug, maintaining a professional manner, though his whiny tone made me cringe inside. "Then, all of you are welcome to join me in the lounge in the front of the spacecraft for refreshments."

I carefully avoided looking at Greyx, fixing my eyes on Prug's horns instead.

When I turned to go to my seat behind a partition in the front, I caught a movement from the corner of my eye. Greyx was rising from his seat—with the obvious intention of following me.

Spinning to face him, I hissed, "Please remain in your seat, sir."

Of course, he didn't listen.

Getting hold of the short horns on his shoulders, I shoved him back into his seat.

He plopped down on his butt, too stunned to fight me.

"Seat," I ordered, my heart pounding, my composure torn to shreds like fog in the wind.

He was just another passenger, for goodness' sake. I'd dealt with lots of unruly ones before. I could put this one back in his place, too.

I reached around him, yanking the seat belts from the back and the side of his chair, then snapped all five ends together by the buckle in his lap, one by one.

"For. Your. Safety," I punctuated each word with another click of the buckle, strapping him in his seat securely.

So, he couldn't follow me.

So, I would get some time to catch my breath, to gather my thoughts, to figure out what the hell I was supposed to do with my blind date suddenly turning up at my workplace.

"Stay," I gritted through my teeth, like he was a dog—a far from obedient one, too.

With the last click of the buckle, I propped my hands onto his thighs and took a second to catch my breath.

His warm, spicy scent drifted around me. There was a streak of fragrance—something like an expensive wood and citrus—a cologne or hotel soap, maybe? But the warm, male scent of his skin was the most alluring. It rushed my senses. Memories of us dancing together flooded my mind—me, wrapped in his arms and this scent of his, made stronger by the clean sweat he'd worked up while dancing.

I glanced up. Blood rushed from my face, then back to it again. My heart seemed to send it all over my body, with no rhyme or reason. A few strands of my hair were hanging in front of my eyes. My neat bun must be falling apart from my efforts to restrain this massive alien.

He met my eyes, a smile playing on his lips. The familiar spark of amusement lit his eyes. Something else danced within their depth—dark and heated. Lifting his hand, he brushed the hair away from my face, moving the strands behind my ear.

All thoughts flew out of my head. All emotions slipped into the background. The only thing that remained was an overwhelming desire to kiss him.

My elbows buckled, nearly sending me into his lap. With shaking hands, I used the horns on his shoulders for support and straightened out.

"Please remain in your seat at all times until the captain's announcement," I mumbled breathlessly.

Spinning on my heel, I stumbled behind the partition. There, my knees gave in, and I plopped into my seat, finally able to breathe again.

What was I going to do for the next two and a half days of the flight?

If he kept looking at me like that, with that smile on his lips and fire in his eyes, I simply didn't stand a chance.

Chapter 5

Tessa

The take-off seemed much shorter than usual. I was still racking my brain, trying to figure out what I was going to do about Greyx...

General Wrun.

He was a fucking general!

I might not know much about Aldraian Army, but a rank of general carried weight in any army, human or alien. Greyx was someone important.

And I...

Well, girls like me didn't end up with generals, did they?

He hadn't told me who he was because it didn't matter whether or not I knew it. He was leaving the planet this morning. Had Bree been just a tiny bit more responsible, I wouldn't be here today. Even if Greyx knew he'd be traveling by our shuttle, he didn't know I'd be here. In fact, I'd explicitly told him I wouldn't, I had a day off.

When he'd asked me to spend the night with him, he had every reason to believe he'd never see me again afterwards.

With a long sigh, I clutched my hands together in my lap.

Maybe we should talk. He seemed to want that very much. It might be best to clear things up. Then, I could continue doing my job in peace and treating him as just another passenger. Maybe that was what he wanted, too.

If only his proximity didn't have the most devastating effect on my composure.

A bell clinked pleasantly, jolting me out of my thoughts.

The captain made his announcement, and I heard the belts clicking open in the passenger cabin.

Despite my best intentions to talk with Greyx and clear things up, the urge to flee propelled me out of my seat.

I rushed to the lounge in the front of the spacecraft and made it behind the counter the moment the first passenger showed up—Greyx.

He looked around the room furnished with comfy armchairs and tiny round tables, then spotted me behind the slick bar counter lit with white and blue lights and beelined my way.

I inhaled slowly.

I could do this.

I could face the unstoppable force moving toward me like a tornado, threatening to sweep me off my feet.

"How can I help you?" I blurted out before he had a chance to even open his mouth.

"Tessa, listen..." He didn't stop at the counter, walking around it, as if to join me behind it.

I quickly raised both hands, waving him back. "Please keep out of this area, sir. For...um, hygienic reasons."

He stopped abruptly, giving me a puzzled look.

I spotted Lucy lingering hesitantly behind his back, and I grabbed onto that chance of interruption like a drowning woman onto a straw.

"What can I get you?" I asked Lucy brightly.

Greyx turned to see whom I was talking to.

"Um." Lucy glanced at him, hesitantly. "A chamomile tea, please? But I can wait. The gentleman was here first."

"The *gentleman* hasn't made up his mind yet," I said with force, hitting the button on the electric teakettle.

I grabbed a mug from under the counter and a coaster from a box nearby, then slammed them both onto the counter.

Prug sauntered in. He threw a lazy look around the room, then headed over to the bar, too.

"Hey, do you have anything for a headache?" He winced, rubbing his forehead.

Must be a hangover. Serves him well for saying nasty things to Bree.

"I'm afraid I have nothing that would work for an Aldraian," I lied. To my knowledge, our biology had been found similar enough for human painkillers to be effective on Aldraians.

Prug was lucky I didn't give him a whole bottle of laxative. The prospect of him hogging one of the lavatories for the rest of the day and possibly making a mess I would then have to clean up was the only thing that held me back from doing that.

"Give me some human painkillers," he groaned, squinting against the light. "At this point, I don't give a fuck."

I straightened, rolling my shoulders back and pushing out my *two* breasts.

"Oops, sorry, I'm out of those, too," I bit out.

A bone-chilling flash of rage rushed through Prug's dark-orange eyes. I wondered with horror if Bree had been lucky to suffer only the wounds from his words last night.

"You need to get some sleep, Prug," Greyx said with a low growl of warning in his voice. "Just give him some water, Tessa, please."

I filled a glass with drinking water, then slid it along the counter toward Prug.

The water in the kettle boiled, and I made Lucy's tea, concentrating on not burning my hand with Greyx watching my every move and Prug still hovering nearby.

"Lucy!" I called to where she had gone to sit in an armchair by the far wall.

"I'll take it to her." Greyx grabbed the mug off the counter. The thick ceramic mug looked like a tiny teacup in his large hand.

"You don't have to. I can—" I tried to protest, but he swiped the coaster off the counter, too, and headed in Lucy's direction.

"Hey." Prug leaned my way the moment Greyx had left. "Where's your cabin, sweetie?"

"Mine?" I stared at him in shock.

Was this jerk hitting on me?

The nerve of this guy!

He rubbed his forehead again, tightly shutting, then opening his eyes. Prug was clearly in pain, and he was trying to score a tryst on my bunk instead of going the heck to sleep?

"You have some spunk," he drawled. "I like a challenge."

I splayed my hand on my breast-less stomach. "I don't have what you want in a woman, buddy. And you certainly don't have what I'm looking for in a man. I suggest you stick to dating your own kind from now on—or better yet—your own hand."

A violent spark crossed his expression. He reached over the counter, as if to strike or grab me.

I shrank back, tripping in my flats.

Greyx

THE PALE HUMAN WOMAN with the light-colored hair that almost matched her skin blinked at him with her large blue eyes as he approached.

"Here is your tea." He set the mug on the small table in front of her and gave her a big smile, hoping to ease the terrified expression on her face.

The smile didn't help. The woman—Lucy, Tessa had called her—shrank deeper into her seat, watching him cautiously.

She had been casting timid glances at Prug and him ever since they had boarded. Her apprehension wasn't surprising. Each of them was at least twice her size, and everything in this human-made shuttle looked so small and dainty to him, including both women.

Maybe Lucy found his long canines intimidating, it occurred to him. He toned down his smile, hiding them behind his lips.

"Thank you for the tea," Lucy half-whispered, dropping her gaze to the mug.

Tessa had also been shy around him, especially at the beginning. But she never seemed to be terrified of him. On the contrary, he got the impression she quite enjoyed looking at him, even as she'd been avoiding eye contact this morning.

He wasn't entirely clear on her reasons for that, but he fully intended to clarify them soon.

Turning back to go to her, he saw Prug lurch at the bar counter. Tessa paled, recoiling from him. Prug reached for her, and Greyx's blood boiled.

In two leaps, he was back at the bar.

He struck, hitting Prug square in the jaw.

The male staggered backward from the blow but managed to remain upright.

Greyx raised his fist, ready to strike again. Blood pulsed hot through his muscles, urging him to fight, but he held back. Beating up an inferior was unbecoming of a leader. However, just the thought of Prug's hard knuckles anywhere near Tessa's soft, delicate skin drove him mad with rage.

"Care to explain what you were going to do to Tessa, Prug?" he demanded through his clenched teeth.

Prug's sandy-beige face took on a sickly yellowish tint.

"Nothing..." he said quickly. "I'm..." His shifty eyes stopped at the drinking glass on the counter. "I just reached for my water."

Greyx swung his glare to the glass, then back to Prug again.

"Take it," he growled. "And leave."

With a furtive glance at Tessa, Prug snatched the glass, then stomped to the exit, muttering under his breath.

Tessa watched the male depart, pale but visibly composed. He wished he could grab her in a hug or at the very least touch her hand, but the invisible wall she'd put around herself by acting professional and reserved kept him at bay more effectively than the bar counter between them. She obviously tried to convey she didn't need to be comforted, no matter how much he wished to comfort her.

"Are you okay?" he asked.

Her chest rose and fell with a long breath—the only sign of any distress. Color returned to her cheeks.

"I'm fine." She blinked, adjusting her sweater. "I've dealt with worse."

Rage burned inside him, urging him to find Prug and punch him again. Once hadn't been nearly enough. Twice wouldn't be either, he feared.

She lifted her clear gray eyes at him.

"Nothing happened," she said firmly, looking perfectly in control. As soft and delicate as she appeared on the outside, there was strength inside her that amazed and impressed him.

"*She'd do well in the Army,*" flashed through his mind, even as any threat of danger to Tessa made his stomach churn.

"Everything is fine," she repeated. "Nothing happened. He was reaching for his water." She narrowed her eyes. "And he *got* it."

He studied her face, trying to read her true feelings. It wasn't easy; her features were pleasant but foreign. Humans' expressions, he'd learned, overlapped with those of Aldraians. The strong feelings and emotion, such as fun, pain, or anger, seemed to be expressed in a similar way. However, some subtleties still escaped him.

Was she trying to cover up Prug's actions? Would she rather put the incident behind her and move on? Or was she telling the truth, and he'd misread Prug's intentions in the first place?

Despite her claims, she seemed pleased with his punching Prug. A corner of her mouth lifted slightly in a satisfied smile.

She turned around to the medicine cabinet on the wall and took out a clear pack with two small round tablets in it.

"Here." She placed it on the counter. "Give these to Prug with water before he goes to bed."

He squinted at the pills. "It's not a laxative, is it?"

That would be a subtle but effective way to get even with Prug if the male had truly tried to attack her.

She snorted softly, her features relaxing. "No. It's painkillers. But I did entertain the laxative idea briefly."

It amused him that she did.

"You don't like Prug, do you?"

"No," she confessed. "I know his type. I've seen a lot of men like him during my years of working in the service industry."

He flicked his gaze to the pills on the counter. "Why give him the medicine, then?"

She shrugged, grabbing a rag to wipe the counter that didn't need to be wiped.

"He's in pain," she said softly. "I don't want anyone to suffer, even if they deserve it."

She had a kind heart.

He cared little about her dislike of Prug. He wasn't fond of the male, either. Prug wasn't his first choice as a partner on this trip.

Much more important were her feelings for *him*.

"Do you dislike me, too?" he asked cautiously.

Last night, he'd believed she liked him, but he wasn't so sure about it this morning. Worry tightened around his heart as he waited for her answer.

It mattered how she felt about him. Because his own feelings for her had been growing.

When he'd returned to his hotel room after the party last night, he searched the Liaison Committee's directory for Tessa's name and read everything they had publicly available about her. But it was so little. He wanted to know more about the strange human woman who had somehow made him feel as if he'd known her all his life.

As much as he regretted her declining to spend the night with him, he wished for more than just one night. He knew she was leaving this part of galaxy soon, way too soon. And regret filled him, bitter and strong.

He couldn't let her go without seeing her again, without making sure she wasn't going to disappear from his life for good.

The timing was wrong. He had obligations on Aldrai that involved an important off-planet assignment his team had been working on for months.

Finding her on the shuttle this morning was an amazing surprise. Now, he had the time to get to know her a little better, to hopefully figure out how to keep her in his life. Except she was acting as if she wanted to have nothing to do with him at all.

She raised her gaze to his face.

"No. I don't dislike you, Greyx." She shook her head with conviction that allowed him a breath of relief. Her dark eyebrows moved close together. "Do you think I do?"

She worried about what he thought. That was a good sign—indifference would have been much worse.

He perched on a barstool and leaned on an elbow. He had to choose his words carefully, and he needed to be completely honest. He sensed Tessa wouldn't accept half-truths. Neither did she strike him as a woman who could be bought with cheap compliments.

This might be the only chance he got.

"Tessa..." He loved the sound of her name, savoring it on his tongue. "I had an amazing time last night. I like parties. Being around people relaxes me." For the past seven years especially, he had preferred being with people either at work or elsewhere—anywhere other than back at his family home, where loneliness reigned with tormenting silence. "I love to dance. But I didn't expect to enjoy it as much as I did last night. And it only happened because of you."

"Me?"

"Yes. I thought you had fun, too."

"I did." She sounded sincere, which made his hope grow.

"Then why are you avoiding me today? You won't even look at me."

This was one of the little subtleties of her body language he couldn't figure out. It was no longer shyness on her part, but something else.

She lifted her eyes again, briefly focusing on his abdomen, then slid her gaze up his arm, across to his chest, darted up to his lips, then to his eyes. Her blush deepened before she snapped her attention back to the rag as she vigorously rubbed the same perfectly clean part of the counter.

"There's just no safe place on you for me to look, is there?" She muttered as if to herself.

"Safe?" What did she mean by that?

She blew out a breath, finally tossing the rag away. She met his eyes, but her expression was somber.

"What is it you want with me, General Wrun?"

General.

It sounded cold and distant, no doubt how she'd intended.

He winced. "Please, call me Greyx."

"No matter what I call you, it won't change who you are." She searched his eyes with hers. "Why didn't you tell me you were a general?"

Was that what it was about? His rank?

Unlike in Voran where a rank became a part of a person's name, titles and positions meant little on Aldrai, especially outside of one's professional life.

"It didn't come up." He shrugged. "We're not as formal on Aldrai. Ranks aren't used outside of work."

She tucked a stray strand of hair behind her ear. "I wish I'd known."

He peered at her closely. "Why? Is my position more important to you than my name?"

She flinched. "It's not like that."

"I didn't hide it," he protested. "My rank is right here in plain sight."

He pointed at the leather straps that held the two panels of his shirt together at his neck. The straps also served as epaulets.

He was wearing his black every-day uniform. The white one was reserved for special occasions. For combat, there was a range of colors and patterns, each matching the climate and landscape of the location where a battle was taking place or where an assignment took him.

The buckles and the embossed characters on his epaulets were in gold, not silver like on the dress uniform he'd worn last night. But the insignia on them was exactly the same.

She studied the writings carefully. "I—I've never seen a uniform of the Aldraian Army before."

He nodded.

"Understandable. I'm not familiar with the military insignia of every army on Earth, either. This here..." He circled the character in the center of the epaulet. "Means 'general.'"

She leaned over the counter, examining his shoulder. His attention whizzed away from their conversation and to how close she was to him. He could take her face in his hands and lean down just a little to kiss her again.

The phantom memory of their last and only kiss tingled on his lips. She remained serious, and he longed to see her smile again. He missed the glow of excitement she had in her eyes last night when they danced.

Dammit, he'd sweep her into a dance right here, right now, if it helped shake off that cool, reserved expression of hers.

A ray of genuine interest broke through as she examined his epaulettes.

"It looks like an ink spot," she muttered under her breath. "With short drips, like legs of an octopus. This picture means 'general?' Is this your written language?"

He swallowed thickly, stuffing his hands into his pockets lest they reach for her on their own accord and spoil everything. He needed to tread carefully. One wrong move, and he sensed she'd withdraw and hide behind her walls again.

"Yes," he said calmly. "Unlike Voranian language, on Aldrai we don't use letters to form words. We have images for each individual word."

"Are all images in the shape of blobs like that?"

Blobs?

Her choice of words made him laugh. The deep sound didn't scare her. On the contrary, a tiny smile tugged at her lips in response.

"Voranians love to joke," he said, "That when Aldraians were developing their written language thousands of years ago, they must've just dripped paint on a piece of parchment and assigned meaning to every splash."

She giggled softly. The skin on his arms pebbled with pleasure in response to that sound. Warm tingles rushed down his body, tickling along his tail and pooling hot in his groin.

This woman would be the end of him. And he didn't mind it one bit.

"I can see how that would happen!" She exclaimed excitedly. Humor sparkled in her gray eyes behind her glasses. "An ancient Aldraian was padding along a scroll of parchment with a brush dripping paint."

He couldn't tear his eyes away from her smiling mouth, remembering the taste of her kiss.

Her smile faltered under his close attention. "So…" She twisted a button on her sweater, risking ripping it off. "Do you have a blob that means Tessa?"

"Tessa…" Her name slipped from his lips like a sigh. "We need to use two 'blobs,' one for each syllable." He paused, imagining both characters side by side. "They'll look beautiful together."

She blinked, that gentle warm blush appearing on her cheeks again. A dreamy smile was playing on her lips. He felt like he had finally blasted through her walls and this was again the woman he'd held in his arms last night. Refraining from kissing her became even harder.

"What are you planning to do once you get back home?" she asked.

Obligations weighted heavily on his shoulders. He had important things to do. Though nothing seemed as important as keeping her in his life.

"I won't stay on Aldrai for long," he explained grimly. "I'll have to leave again."

"When?" Was it a disappointment in her eyes?

"The day after our arrival."

"Not long at all." She sighed. "Where will you be going?"

He flexed his jaw, gritting his teeth. "I can't tell."

"Is it for work?"

"It's classified."

Light dimmed from her expression. With the tip of a finger, she drew circles on the shiny countertop and kept silent.

He couldn't stand this any longer. This trip wasn't the end. They might have to part after two days, but it would never be for long. Fuck, he'd go all the way to Earth if that was what it took for him to have a second date with her.

"Tessa." He grabbed her hand.

She snapped her gaze to his. "Greyx, I—"

Alarm blasted out of somewhere.

Tessa jumped, startled, and gripped his hand tightly.

Her fear zapped through him with shock.

"Warning!" a male voice shouted through the intercom. "This is the captain speaking. All passengers return to your cabins and lock the doors. The flight attendant..." The man hesitated. The uncertainty in his voice was unnerving. "Take cover, Tessa. We have a breach."

Chapter 6

Tessa

What happened?

Greyx glanced my way, a question in his eyes. Wide-eyed, Lucy stared at us from her seat, both hands clutching the mug with her tea.

This was *my* ship. I was in charge of their safety. And I had no clue what to do. Because I didn't know what was going on.

"A breach," the captain had said.

But I had no procedure for that, no checklist. A breach had never been covered during my training. It simply wasn't considered as something that could happen.

Thoughts and questions flashed through my mind at lightning speed. I focused on just one—the captain had given us instructions. He'd told me what to do.

"Return to your cabins..."

"Lock the doors..."

"Take cover..."

"To the cabins. Quickly," I said to Greyx, surprised at how calm I sounded.

Stepping from behind the counter, I gestured to Lucy to join us. Leaving her mug on the table, she ran to me.

The three of us were halfway across the lounge when the intercom sounded again.

"Unauthorized docking. Intruders. From the luggage port," the captain informed us.

"Intruders?" I echoed, stupefied.

How was that even possible? Had someone docked with us mid-flight?

The captain's words confused me, but they appeared to have a very different effect on Greyx. Understanding flashed through his eyes. He jumped into action, taking charge. "Where is the luggage port on this vessel?"

"Underneath." I gestured at the floor. "But the access to it is at the back. In the tail."

"That's where the sleeping cabins are, too." His brow ridges shifted together. "Don't go to the cabins, Tessa." He placed a hand on my shoulder, holding me in place. "How many flight crew do you have?"

"Three. The captain, the first officer, and the on-board engineer."

"Do they have weapons?"

"No." I shook my head. "No weapons are allowed on board." There was no need for them. The war in this part of the galaxy was long over. These were peaceful times.

"Go hide in the cockpit," Greyx instructed. "I'll deal with whoever the intruders are."

"You? How?" I fought the urge to grip his arm, to beg him to stay with me.

He cupped my cheek briefly, stroking my face with his thumb. The tenderness in his eyes was heartbreaking. I didn't want him to go running headfirst into danger.

"What if you get hurt?" I asked, unable to keep the worry out of my voice.

The familiar, playful smile broke out on his face—so out of place for the situation, but so comforting.

"I'm not easy to hurt, Tessa, even unarmed."

He grabbed the edge of one of his arm bracers. With a soft suction sound, the bracer separated from his arm, revealing a row of short horns on the back of his forearm. Curved like harpoons, they were flattened from the sides and looked sharp like a saw.

Aldraians had built-in weapons, it seemed.

Peeling off the second bracer, Greyx headed for the exit from the lounge.

He glanced over his shoulder at me one last time before rushing out of the room. "Stay safe."

"You, too. Please..."

Lucy gripped my arm. "Tessa... What's happening?" She sounded frightened out of her wits.

A part of me wanted to run after Greyx, to see the danger we were facing. A more practical part wished to heed his order, find a safe place, and wait it over. Greyx didn't become an army general for nothing. He and Prug were much better equipped to deal with whatever was happening out there.

"We need to hide," I said to Lucy and patted her hand reassuringly.

"Hide where?" She darted a look around the lounge.

Greyx said to go to the cockpit. By the protocol, the cockpit locked automatically in case of any trouble, and I wasn't sure if the pilots would be able to open it for us. The captain had said for me to "take cover," not to come to them.

Still, it was worth a try.

"Come." I tagged Lucy across the lounge.

A crashing noise came from the direction Greyx had left.

Lucy jerked and stiffened.

Sounds of punching, grunts, and groans approached, getting closer.

The fight broke out. Too close. Way too close.

Dread seized me, chilling me from the inside.

"Get behind the bar." I shoved Lucy behind the counter. "Stay down."

Frantically, I rummaged inside the bar for anything that could be used as a weapon. I hoped for a knife, but my fingers landed on a corkscrew bottle opener.

A figure appeared at the entrance. He looked nothing like any species I'd ever seen. With vividly green skin and four legs. His eyeballs were suspended on antennae above a bald head.

They rotated as he took in the room.

I ducked under the counter, hoping he hadn't seen me.

Lucy's entire body was shaking, and I brought my finger to my lips, urging her to be quiet.

The shuffling of his feet moved across the lounge.

Freezing terror creeped down my spine. My teeth chattered.

The footfalls of the green alien sounded right on the other side of the bar. Crouching low and halting my breath, I gripped the handle of the corkscrew tighter in my hand.

"Huh!" A sharp inhalation of air above our heads had the effect of a gunshot on me.

Shaking, I glanced up, meeting the bulbous yellow eyes of the alien. They swayed on the antennae as he was sitting on top of the bar, peering at us behind it.

He reached for me, and I jumped up. Panic surged through me.

"Stay back, Lucy!" I yelled.

Whipping around, I dashed from behind the counter.

"Hey!" The green alien leaped on top of me, knocking me off my feet.

I slashed my corkscrew at him.

The sharp end scratched his side, making him yelp.

Shaking him off, I scrambled to my feet and ran to the exit, his footfalls right behind me.

"Got you!" A hand slammed into my shoulder. "Stupid female."

I spun around, slamming my knee between his legs. It happened to be the wrong pair of legs, with nothing vital between them. He barely grunted from my blow, unfazed.

Grabbing me by my neck, he nearly twisted my head off my shoulders.

I cried out in pain.

"Stupid, stupid female," he hissed in a language that had an awful amount of clicking sounds.

He shoved something long and shiny into my neck. It pressed cold and hard to my skin. A sharp stabbing pain made me scream. His green face swam in front of my eyes, then distorted into a swirl of color. Black took over the green.

Then everything went dark.

Chapter 7

Tessa

Darkness receded like a suffocating, muddy tide. Bright light filtered through my eyelids. Cool air brushed against my bare thighs.

Bare?

Was I naked?

I drew in a breath. The tightness of my bra appeared to still be there. If I was naked, then only from the waist down.

Something touched me. The sensation was still muddled. I couldn't tell whether those were hands, or tools, or something else entirely.

Prodding.

Poking.

No!

I wanted to scream but couldn't. I wished to run, except my limbs wouldn't move.

"Do you hear me?" a voice asked, with the dreadful clicking sound.

"Yes." The word sounded in my ear. It took me a moment to realize it had come out of my mouth. "Who are you?"

The memories of the green, four-legged alien attacking me floated into my mind. Then the anger flared.

"Who the fuck are you?" I yelled. "Let me go!"

Something poked at my head, just behind my ear. A clunking sound reverberated through my skull.

"Ouch!" I whimpered.

Another series of clicking sounds came from the green guy, only this time I didn't get their meaning.

I tried to move but couldn't. At least, I still had my voice.

"What do you want?" I pried my eyelids open.

Dirty yellow light shone somewhere high above me as I lay on my back.

Green faces floated in the light puddle. Their eyes dangled on skinny antennae.

Behind them was a dark metal ceiling, and below it a circle of windows, like in a medical theater back on Earth.

Dark shapes moved on the other side, like shadow puppets. All had antennae on their heads. Except for one.

One dark silhouette was larger than the others. His arms folded across his wide chest, he wasn't moving, staring down at me. A tall crown graced his head.

Somehow, I knew this wasn't a crown but horns—a row of them in the middle and one on each side.

Greyx.

I wanted to call to him. But something thick and heavy flooded my veins again. It made me sleepy, depriving me of the ability to speak.

Greyx...

A tear trickled down my cheek before the muddy ocean closed over me again, cutting me off from the rest of the world.

NEXT TIME I WOKE UP, I was lying on my side, on a hard surface. I opened my eyes quickly and without difficulty. My awareness seemed to be sharp, my brain functioning.

Patting my sides, I was relieved to find all my clothes on me—the teal dress of my uniform and the gray cardigan. My bra, my underwear. Even my shoes were on my feet.

My glasses were gone, though.

Unsettling feelings vibrated inside me. I didn't need my glasses to see my surroundings right now, but not having them made me feel like something important was missing. It made me feel even more vulnerable in this place.

Getting up, I took in the small, dark room with the metal, riveted walls. The thick door with a barred window made it look like a holding cell. Even before I shook the door, I knew it'd be locked.

This *was* a holding cell.

Where was I?

I was exploring the wall opposite to the door when the lock clinked open. I whipped around as a green alien shoved a bowl inside my cell.

"Wait!" I rushed to him, but he shut the door in my face. "What do you want with me?" I yelled through the barred window.

A series of clicking sounds came in reply. He appeared irritated, but I had no idea what he said. I understood the green alien back on our spaceship perfectly well. Which meant their language was one of those programmed into my translator.

Why didn't I understand this one?

Then, I remembered the pain behind my ear as I'd laid on the table.

I stiffened. Did they cut my translator out?

I'd gotten my implant during my job training. The translators were widely used by all alien races. Many had them implanted at birth. On Earth, they were mandatory for those involved in interplanetary travel.

A small disk, not much bigger than a watch battery, would be implanted in the area behind one's ear. It connected to the person's brain and conveyed the meaning of a spoken word directly to it. The sophisticated program seamlessly translated the meaning of each word or phrase into the equivalent or most appropriate expressions for the other person to understand, which made for a smooth, fluent conversation with any alien being.

It required a sophisticated surgery to implant the translator. Attempting to take it out without having adequate medical skills could result in a serious injury, brain damage, or even death.

Nothing I'd seen so far about this place spoke "sophisticated" or "adequate medical skills."

Fighting a rising panic, I brought my hand over the spot on my head where the translator should be. I expected a scar, shaved hair, blood, maybe. But there was nothing. Just smooth skin and my hair. Like usual.

No pain, either.

I believed I could even feel the little flat disk of the translator under my skin.

Maybe the green ones just tampered with it from the outside, rendering it useless?

I released a breath. At least no one had cut my head open.

The rest of my body felt okay, too. There was no pain or even soreness, just the phantom memory of the cold, clinical touch. Lifting my skirt, I didn't find any scars or bruises, either.

They might have done some tests, but it didn't appear there'd been any surgeries. Not yet, at least.

Somewhat calmer, I eyed the bowl the green alien had left behind. It was food, I assumed. Though it did not look very appetizing—roughly cut pieces of a fruit or vegetable with white flesh that had a sickly violet tint.

I brought the bowl to my nose, taking a tentative sniff. It smelled like cabbage or turnip, with a hint of mint, like toothpaste. The skin of the vegetable was black and thick. I was hungry, but was it safe to eat?

Would the nasty green people try to poison me? They'd had plenty of opportunities to kill me when I lay unconscious on their examination table.

With a sigh, I sat on the floor and placed the bowl in my lap. Lifting a piece of fruit in my fingers, I took a tentative bite. It was hard and crunchy, like a raw turnip, but it tasted slightly better than it smelled.

Hungry, I ate the entire piece, then took another one.

The fact that I was here alone felt comforting in a way. It meant they might not have found Lucy. If so, she would be safe, back on our shuttle.

This place wasn't for a delicate girl like Lucy. Everything frightened her—thunderstorms, loud noises, darkness. When we'd moved into our apartment in Voran, she'd made me inspect every pot and vine of the flowers growing there, to make sure there weren't any bugs inside.

Bree was often annoyed with her. But Lucy's timidness tugged at my protective instincts. She needed to be looked after.

I understood why the Liaison Committee had chosen Lucy to travel to Aldrai to report on the living conditions. If Lucy found life on Aldrai tolerable, chances were any other human would do fine there, too.

I finished the food. My stomach was full, but not happy. It rumbled and churned.

A yellow eye poked through the bars of the window. The lock clicked open again.

"Listen!" I hurried to the green dude.

There were two this time. Like the one back on my shuttle, neither of them wore any real clothes. Instead, they had belts with pouches strapped all over their slim, agile bodies. One had a piece of cloth tied around his middle. The smooth crotch of the other one remained exposed. Several coils of thick rusty chain were wrapped around his waist.

The second one stood behind the first, holding a long, spear-like stick with two sharp prongs on the tip pointed my way. He gave me two warning clicks with his tongue, shoving the stick in my direction. Would he really poke me with those pointy ends if I disobeyed? I didn't feel like provoking him just to find out.

Since they had disabled my translation device, it was safe to assume they had no desire to communicate with me. Still, I tried.

Lifting both hands up in a placating gesture, I took a step back.

"I just want to speak to someone about...um, my situation," I said, keeping my voice neutral.

Neither of them responded or even acknowledged if they heard or understood me.

With the second guy threatening me with prongs, the first one produced a long metal strip from the hook on the chain around his middle. Coming closer, he clipped the strip around my waist.

"What's this?" I gripped the strip, trying to pry it off me. But there was no give in the metal and the lock held firmly.

The one with the chain clipped the end of it to the ring on my metal belt. Opening the door to my cell wider, he tugged on the chain, obviously urging me to get out.

Had they understood me after all? My heart beat faster with hope. Were they taking me to someone who could explain to me what I was doing in this place?

I remembered seeing Greyx's shadow behind the window of the room where they had examined me.

What if they were taking me to see him?

Behind my cell was a long, wide corridor constructed of dark, roughly hewn rock.

Rock was not a suitable material to build spaceships, which could only mean we must be landside, on a planet. The question remained, which one?

My captors stopped in front of tall double doors. Thick and heavy, with wooden beams across them, the doors looked like the gate of a medieval castle.

Noise filtered through them—growling, crashing, and slamming.

My skin prickled with trepidation.

"What's there?" I half-whispered.

Not dignifying me with an answer, one of the green guys yanked down a large, rusty level on the wall while the other one unclipped the chain off my metal belt.

One side of the door cracked open. A wide stripe of red light hit the stone floor like a splash of blood. The noise burst through the opening—deafening and crashing.

One of the green aliens shoved me forward roughly.

"Nope, not going there!" I dug my heels into the floor.

The brutal noises and the ominous, blood-red light gave me no desire to find out what was happening on the other side. I wanted no part of it.

The green, four-legged assholes weren't putting up with my resistance. The one with the stick poked me in my backside with it.

The prongs pierced through the material of my dress. Shock shot up my body, crippling my muscles and sending me to the floor.

I screamed in agony.

The aliens rolled me across the floor, shoving and pushing with their feet, until I found myself no longer on the floor but on a fine sand, awash in the red light.

The door behind me slammed shut.

Chapter 8

Tessa

I winced and blinked in the red light.

Something hard suddenly crashed on top of me. It was heavy, with sharp edges.

With my muscles still twitching from the shock of the pronged stick, I gathered my limbs under me and crawled out from under the heavy weight.

Scrambling to my feet, I looked at the thing that had crashed into me.

It was a giant bug!

Its head had been ripped off. Six legs spasmed. The purple segmented body contracted, then stilled. Two long, fleshy tubes tipped with sharp spikes on each side of the bug drooped lifelessly.

Horror engulfed me at the sight of the monstrous abomination. Even dead, it looked terrifying.

I staggered backward on my shaking legs until my back hit the door.

Something leaped my way. Another creature I'd never seen before. It was round and spotted like a piece of granite, but I got no chance to notice any details.

Something jumped from the side. Lashing with a pale, yellowish tentacle through the air, the new creature sliced off the head of the granite-spotted one.

With a choked scream, I scurried out of the way as its massive, headless body crashed to the ground at my feet.

A scaly tail with a barb on its end came out of nowhere, whizzing by my ear with a loud hiss.

"Shit!" I jumped away, just in time.

What was this place?

Hell. No doubt.

Panting, I frantically tried to get my bearings.

Fine white sand sprawled far and wide. Piles of rocks and patches of sparse vegetation interspersed it.

A tall, metal wall ran around the space that must be larger than a football field. And there was no roof. The eerie, red-streaked sky hung low over the arena. The light came from a huge, crimson sun that took up at least a quarter of the open space above.

The most fantastic creatures, large and small, had been hoarded in here. None seemed to have any desire to coexist peacefully. They tore, stabbed, and bit at each other. No one stopped until their opponent was dead. Then, they moved on to another one. They fought like wild beasts, and none of them looked sentient.

Shaken to the core, I inched along the wall. A jolt of pain shot up my hand when I touched the metal. I yanked my hand away.

The walls passed a charge, similar to electricity. Its purpose must be to force the creatures closer to the center of the arena. Whoever was in charge here wanted us to fight, not to cower by the walls.

I wasn't much of a fighter. Without any weapons whatsoever, I stood no chance against the monsters armed with spikes, claws, and teeth.

Frantically, I scanned the arena for a place to hide.

A tall, waif-like creature, with gauzy wings or fins on its back, stood on its hind legs. It swung its front legs, tipped with long curved claws, at a giant insect with a scorpion tail.

I crept out of their way, trying not to attract their attention.

With a loud hiss, the scorpion-like thing lashed its long, barbed tail over its shoulder. The barb sliced off three claws of the tall creature, then embedded into its slim neck. Bright red blood sprayed its silvery-white wings. Then, the poor thing collapsed to the ground.

The scorpion monster pivoted my way.

With a squeak of horror, I scrambled away from the lash of its tail. I tripped and fell, rolling in the white sand.

A gush of green liquid splashed next to me—the scorpion's blood. Its smashed head was squished between two massive forearms armed with harpoon-like horns.

The arms opened, letting the dead scorpion creature drop to the ground.

Greyx stood behind it.

My heart fluttered and skipped at the sight of him.

"Greyx!" I jumped to my feet and...froze.

The scowl on his face was unrecognizable. His eyes darkened—the pupils dilated so wide, the irises turned into slim bands of dark gold.

His cinnamon skin was splashed with blood of all colors. It dripped from his horns. Rivulets of dried blood streaked his face and shoulders. And his forearms appeared washed in blood.

He didn't look like a savior, but a murderous monster in the heat of a rampage.

"Greyx?" I stumbled a step back.

He sucked in air through his nostrils, his chest expanding. His scowl deepened. Violence pulsed in his eerie eyes. His upper lip curled, baring his sharp canines. He lowered his head, as if aiming his horns at me.

Fear seized my heart. I'd never been afraid of him before. But I felt terrified now. Shaking head to toe.

With a loud screech, a long, slimy creature threw itself on Greyx. Glistening purple and red, it had an elongated body and two heads on snake-like necks. They undulated like tentacles, aiming to wrap themselves around his neck.

He roared, grabbing each neck in one hand. Tossing his head back, he roared. The sound reverberated through the arena, momentarily drowning out the noise of the battle. By rotating his wrists, he wound the snake-like neck around his arms, then yanked them apart, ripping the purple-red creature in half.

Blood gushed, splashing Greyx's chest.

Another creature attacked him. Then another.

He tore and ripped, spearing some on his horns and crushing others with his forearms. The moment one opponent fell dead, he searched for another, unstoppable in his murderous spree.

The fight took his attention from me. He circled the arena, moving farther and farther away.

Greyx was the only one I knew here. Someone who could possibly help me. But the image of his murderous scowl froze in my mind, stopping me from following him. Going after him through the crowd of beasts fighting tooth and nail wouldn't be easy, anyway.

The massacre boiled with groans and spilled blood all around me.

Something slithered my way.

A snake?

A tentacle?

There was no time to figure it out.

Grabbing one of the long claws that the scorpion-monster had sliced off the tall creature's paw, I stabbed the snake-tentacle with it. Leaving the thing wiggling in the sand, I dashed to the nearest pile of rocks next to a short, skinny bush. Neither looked like much of a shelter, but I had to keep moving to stay alive.

Crouching by the rocks, I searched for Greyx. Something had happened to him that had turned him into a feral beast like that.

He was nowhere to be seen now.

The bloody fight in the arena wasn't slowing down. The creatures fought each other for no apparent reason. Murder after murder took place all around me.

I took a closer look at the setup of this place. Dark, round devices were mounted on top of the wall at equal intervals.

Were they speakers? Cameras?

Were we being filmed? To what purpose?

Through the deafening cacophony of cries and blows, I recognized a sound. It stood out, being unlike anything else in here. A soft humming of the song "Over the Rainbow," of all things!

I must be losing my mind.

Spinning around, I searched for the source of the humming and spotted the white crochet cardigan on the other side of the rocks.

"Lucy!" Afraid to get up, I crawled to her.

Barely visible against the white rocks and sand, Lucy was curled into a ball. They'd gotten her, after all. Both hands pressed tightly to her ears, she hummed the old, familiar melody.

I touched her shoulder. "Lucy. It's me, Tessa."

Her eyes shut tight, she jerked away from my hand, humming louder.

Something raw and bloodied hit my shoulder—a torn-off body part. My stomach lurched. I clutched harder the long claw I'd snatched earlier, ready to strike if needed.

"We have to move to survive, Lucy," I panted, searching for the next hiding place. "If we stay in one spot for too long, we'll die."

She finally looked at me, her eyes wide like large, blue saucers.

"Are you okay? Can you move?" I asked.

She just stared at me, frozen in silence. Even her humming had ceased.

I realized she wasn't staring at *me*, but at something right *behind* me.

Gripping the claw firmer, I spun around, embedding it into someone's flesh.

A yellow-gray monster, a nightmarish cross between a snake and a crocodile with two jaws, one inside the other, hissed in pain. I twisted the claw out of his side. Ducking under the monster's jaw, I stabbed him again, right in his throat.

Pale yellow blood splashed warmly on my hand, churning my stomach again. I shook with terror and repulsion. But we had to keep moving if we wanted to live.

"Come!" I yanked Lucy up by her arm.

Dragging her along, I ran in a crouch, away from the serpent-croc that crawled after us, blood squirting from his wounds.

"Do you have anything to use for a weapon?" I asked Lucy, running to the next pile of rocks, a little larger than the ones before.

She shook her head.

"Fine. Then watch my back, will you?" My teeth clattered so much, I could barely pass the words through.

She nodded.

Reaching the rocks, I crashed to the ground, catching my breath. I tugged at Lucy's arm, dragging her down with me.

"Stay close—" The end of the sentence caught in my throat as I spotted both Greyx and Prug on the far side.

Even without my glasses, there was no mistaking them. Large and burly, like two rock golems, they crashed, smashed, and tore with the horns on their arms, head, and shoulders. Keeping back-to-back, they slowly circled the arena, leaving blood and devastation in their wake.

Should I try to get closer to them?

Or should I make every effort to keep away?

After my last encounter with Greyx, this wasn't easy to answer. He looked wild and dangerous—not the Greyx I knew. But I'd only known him for a short time. Not enough to really get to know a person.

A shadow covered Lucy and me. A skinny creature with pterodactyl-like wings descended on us from above.

"Duck, Lucy!" I screamed.

She crouched low, cowering with arms over her head.

I slashed with the claw, cutting one of the leathery wings of the creature. Losing balance, it crashed and rolled on the ground.

I grabbed Lucy again. "Run!"

Leaping over the dead, we ran.

The sand of the arena no longer looked white or pristine. Churned by feet, hooves, and paws, it was soaked with blood and gore.

Gasping for breath, I crouched by a copse of skinny bushes. Far fewer creatures remained fighting. By now, most lay dead or dying on the arena floor.

A sudden, deafening sound of a horn made my heart leap, sending a jolt of adrenaline through my body.

Now what?

I glanced around wildly, expecting another horror thrown at us. My muscles vibrated. My nerves were strung tight. Holding out the claw in my hand, I was ready to stab and slash through anything that came too close.

At the sound of the horn, though, all movement had stopped. Fights broke up. Music blasted from the speakers above, as if it'd been a peaceful sport event or something like it.

Several gates opened. Groups of green aliens marched in. Wielding their pronged spears, they strolled through the arena, stabbing the injured animals on the ground.

Shaken by all the horror and senseless violence, I barely stood upright. Suddenly, my stomach couldn't take it anymore. Doubling over, I retched.

"Oh, it hurts," I groaned, my knees shook. My stomach spasmed, and I crossed my arms over my belly.

Lucy started humming "Over the Rainbow" again, arms wrapped tightly around herself.

The green aliens were taking the corpses out and herding the survivors toward the doors. Two of the guards headed our way, their spears at the ready.

Greyx and Prug strolled to a door on the opposite end of the arena.

"Greyx…" I said softly. He wouldn't hear me over the upbeat music filling the arena, even if I yelled.

Longing squeezed my heart. Longing for the man who'd held my hand gently and smiled at me cheerfully and carefree. Here, in the middle of the blood-soaked arena, that man seemed but a beautiful dream. The roaring monster who ripped living creatures apart with feral violence was the reality.

One of the guards beelined for me. He swung his stick, slamming it across my legs and knocking me down.

I hit the ground hard, the claw fell out of my grip on impact. The guard kicked it out of my reach. With a sharp click of warning, he aimed the prongs at me.

Greyx walked through the door and out of my sight.

"LET'S STAY TOGETHER, Lucy." I gripped her hand when the green aliens herded us back inside the facility.

The greens had made no attempt to separate us yet. Using their stupid sticks to keep us in line, they shepherded Lucy, me, and the few surviving creatures from the arena down the same wide corridor inside the facility, then under a tall arch in the wall, and into a large room. There was absolutely no furniture here, just several rows of rings on the floor with pieces of chains attached to them.

One green alien clipped the end of a chain from the floor to the ring on my belt. I held on to Lucy tightly, and he attached the chain of the nearby floor ring to the belt around her waist. I exhaled in relief—for now, at least, they were letting us stay together.

Leaning against the wall, I slid down to the floor. Some of the tension drained from my muscles. There was no way to tell what awaited us next, but the immediate danger was gone. No one was trying to rip my chest open or bite my head off.

This had been by far the craziest, most intense experience in my life. A nightmare. I half-expected to wake up on the floor of my cabin on the shuttle to find that I'd fallen off the top bunk and banged my head.

Lucy joined me on the floor. Was I dreaming about Lucy, too? Or did her presence here mean she'd also lost her mind?

The thought was especially disturbing because there appeared to be something actually wrong with *Lucy's* mind. Ever since I'd found her in the arena, she hadn't said a word. Now she hugged herself, rocking back and forth and humming.

I wrapped my arm around her shoulders. "Are you okay?"

She drew her knees into her chest but didn't reply.

"We'll be alright," I said, both for her benefit and mine.

We had to keep hope alive. I needed to figure out what to do to get us out of there.

If my experience in customer service had taught me anything, it was that there always was a solution to any situation. Over the years, I'd dealt with mean bosses, unruly drunks, and deranged customers from hell. Solving problems was a huge part of my job.

Granted, this was a million times worse than anything I'd ever dealt with before, but there had to be something I could do.

The room where we were had no doors, just the high archway open to the corridor. There weren't any bars or cages either. The only thing that kept us in place were the chains and the belts that the green meanies used in lieu of collars on us.

I examined my belt. It appeared solid, the two ends fused together with no visible locks or even a wide enough seam to slide a blade of a knife in between. Not that I had a knife. I didn't even have the claw anymore.

The chain appeared to be attached firmly, too, impossible for me to remove.

Maybe, when they disconnected it the next time, I could make a run for it?

But where would I run?

I had no idea what planet we were on.

The animals from the arena that had come with us had also been hooked to the rings all over the room. The creatures seemed exhausted. All of them fell asleep quickly as soon as our green guards left.

Worn out by the stress of the day, Lucy had dozed off, too, sliding sideways until she rested against my shoulder.

My thoughts flew to Greyx again.

The guards had taken the two Aldraians through a different door in the arena.

Where did they keep them?

The image of Greyx and Prug rose in my mind. To be honest, they hadn't appeared to be "taken" at all. Both Aldraians had walked willingly. No one had forced them. Neither of them wore the metal belts, either. Both had been topless, wearing only their black uniform pants and boots, but no belts or chains.

The memory of the Aldraian behind the glass in the examination room came to mind again. Whether it was Greyx or Prug, he hadn't been tied or chained. Some of the green guys had been behind the window with him, but they weren't guarding him. He appeared to be there on his own accord. Free.

I inhaled sharply, fighting the chill of dread inside my chest.

What if the Aldraians were a part of what was happening around here? Did they act together with the nasty green aliens?

But why?

Both Greyx and Prug appeared to enjoy the slaughter in the arena today. Had something been done to change them? Or were they being themselves?

Even if I found my way to Greyx, could I trust him at all?

Chapter 9

Tessa

The next time the green aliens entered the room, they hauled a huge pot and a bucket of water with them.

It was hard to tell the time of day without windows, but the chained creatures started stirring. I felt like I'd slept for at least a few hours, too. The green men appeared to be dragging in our breakfast. Those were all signs of morning to me.

Chatting between themselves, the greens poured each of us a tin of water then dropped a few pieces of the same white-and-black fruit on the floor for each of the animals. At least they had the decency to deposit Lucy's and my portions in our laps, not on the floor.

The fruit was hard and unappetizing, like before. After I managed to chew and swallow a few disks, they pressed down on my stomach like gravel—more nauseating than nourishing.

The water was good, though. It had absolutely no taste, and I drank the entire tin quickly.

Shortly after the meal, the aliens returned. I wished so badly to understand what they were saying between themselves. It must be of some value since they'd gone through the trouble of disabling my translator.

The group of them purposely headed my way. And my heart dropped.

"Oh, no..." I mumbled. "What do they want, now?"

I hoped it was not another fight in the arena. My muscles still ached from yesterday. I had no weapons, and the dull ache in my stomach only got stronger after the meagre breakfast. I wouldn't last a minute out there in this condition.

The sickening feeling in my belly grew stronger as the greens approached.

Lucy's face turned as white as her cardigan. She scurried back to the wall and curled into a ball. Covering her ears with her hands, she rocked back and forth, faint humming coming from her again.

"No matter what, let's stay together," I hurriedly whispered to Lucy.

Neither of us had any control here, but Lucy nodded, not lifting her head.

One of the greens unhooked the chain from my belt.

"What's going on?" I demanded.

The one with the stick held it up, the prongs nearly touching my neck.

"Where are you taking us now? What do you want" If I threw all my questions at them, would they eventually answer at least one of them?

Nope. They just yanked on the chain, dragging me toward the exit.

"Hey! Wait! How about Lucy?" Gripping the chain with my hands, I tried to gain any purchase on the stone floor with the flat soles of my shoes.

Easily overpowering me, they dragged me out of the room and down the corridor.

"Tessa!" Lucy's voice rang under the high vaulted ceiling. The first word I'd heard from her since we'd been taken.

"Lucy!" I screamed back, fighting against the grip of the greens. "I'll come back for you. I promise!"

I had no idea *if* or *how* I'd be able to fulfill my promise, but Lucy needed hope to hold on to or, I feared, she would sink so deep into despair, she'd drown and suffocate in it.

God knew I needed something to hold on to, too.

The greens dragged me through corridors and tunnels. I lost all sense of direction. There were a few stairs here and there, all leading down as the walls and the ceiling gradually moved closer, making the space narrower.

The corridor ended with a door. One of the greens unlocked it, and they shoved me into a wide room with a low ceiling.

A large cage with thick, rusty bars stood in the middle. At least a dozen green aliens surrounded it. Every other one held the spear-stick in his hands.

And inside the cage...

"Oh my God..." I pressed both hands to my chest. My heart leaped high into my throat. "Greyx?"

He was even more terrifying than in the arena. His nostrils flared. His skin appeared darker, flushed with red. Chest puffing with shallow breaths, he threw himself against the bars, raging like a wild beast.

Prug was with him. The two shoved and pushed each other out of the way, clawing at the bars. No coherent word came from either of them. Just growls, roars, and snarls. This couldn't be natural.

"What happened to you?" I stared at them wide-eyed, struck by shock and horror.

At the sound of my voice, both Aldraians lunged at the bars with even more ferocity, rattling the cage dangerously.

A guard unclipped the chain from my belt. Two others grabbed me by my arms and dragged me toward the cage.

"What are you doing?" I dug my heels into the stone floor. "Don't take me to them. They'll kill me!"

Prug drooled, shaking and rattling the bars. With feral growls, he stuck his hands out as far as the horns on his forearms would allow. His light-brown skin turned reddish-hot with blood flushing to it.

It wasn't hard to guess his intentions. The pants over his crotch bulged, stretching so tight, his dick risked ripping through them.

My heart hurt to even glance at Greyx. He didn't look much better.

"No way. No!" I kicked one guard while elbowing the other.

Propped on four legs each, they were much more stable than me. The flat soles of my shoes slid along the stone floor as the greens dragged me toward the cage.

"No!" I thrashed in their grip.

The Aldraians' stares were on me. Their nostrils flared as they sucked in air hungrily, slamming against the bars with the force of a freight train. The horns on their arms and shoulders screeched against the metal bars. Their teeth bared, foam dripped from them.

A guard used his stick to slide open a door at the bottom of the cage. The opening was too small for the Aldraians to squeeze through, with their horns, spikes, and mile-wide shoulders. Still, Greyx lunged for it. He shoved an arm through, grabbing for me.

The green at the door jabbed him with the prongs. With a deafening howl, Greyx staggered back.

The guards shoved me inside.

"No!" Panic rushed me. Swinging around, I tried to get back out.

A green alien stepped in, poking me with his stick. Shock coursed through every nerve in my body. Screaming, I crashed to the floor and curled into a fetal position against the pain.

The guards shut the door, locking me in.

Shaking, I forced my body up to face the danger head on.

Prug pounced on me first. A loud roar erupted from his throat.

I lurched aside, but not far enough. There wasn't much space to move around, not with two tank-sized males here with me.

He grabbed me by the throat, squeezing a whimper out of my chest. Pinning me to the wall, he ground the bulge in his pants against my belly.

"Prug," I croaked through his grip on my neck. "Don't..."

He displayed no reaction to the sound of his name, slamming his body against mine with bone-crushing force.

"No..." I managed on the exhale, gasping for air.

He painfully bit into my shoulder, holding me in place. With deep grunts, he rutted into me, dry humping me through our clothes.

My chest compressed under his weight. I couldn't scream. I couldn't breathe. I struggled against his hold, but it only seemed to excite him further.

Suddenly, his head jerked back. His teeth clanked, yanked off my shoulder. Two hard-knuckled hands gripped the horns on each side of Prug's head. Greyx stood behind him.

With a sickening crunching sound, Prug's neck twisted at an unnatural angle. Skin split open. The muscles underneath tore.

Frozen in horror, I watched as Prug's head separated from his body. His hand fell away from my throat, letting me draw a desperate breath at last.

Prug's body crashed to the floor. And I was faced with Greyx, who was holding his friend's head by the horns.

My stomach roiled.

I screamed, blinded by terror.

Blood dripped from the torn blood vessels of the severed head, suffocating me with its nauseating smell.

Greyx stared at his buddy's head in his hands, as if wondering how it got there. He then tossed it aside, moving my way.

"Greyx," I pleaded, scrambling over the headless body on the floor to get away.

He looked nothing like the Greyx I knew, still I tried to break through to him. I had no other choice. There was no escaping this cage.

"Greyx, it's me, Tessa," I panted. "We danced, remember?"

Struggling to breathe, choking with fear, I hummed the melody we'd danced to on New Year's Eve. That night seemed to be centuries ago. In another world. Another lifetime.

I kept humming as if my life depended on it. Because it did.

"Remember, Greyx?"

He lurched at me with a snarl. Caging me with his body, he pinned me to the bars—just like Prug had done. Only with Greyx, it hurt so much more. It wasn't just the physical pain of him crushing me.

"We danced." My vision blurred with tears. "You kissed me. It was the best kiss of my life..."

He leaned closer, pressing his entire body to me. And I sensed him shaking. Every muscle of his appeared to be vibrating, strung tight with tension. The spasms seemed almost unnatural, like a strong electric current pumped through him.

"Greyx..." I lifted my face to his. "Say something. Please."

His irises turned black, not a speck of the sunny orange I remembered. Blood-shot, the whites were crisscrossed with thin, red webbing. His eyes roamed around, not focusing on anything.

It couldn't be him. He wasn't well. Something terrible was happening to him.

"What have they done to you?" I breathed out. Working my arm out from between us, I touched the side of his face.

His skin felt impossibly hot. He jerked at my touch, snapping his gaze to my face, and snarled, baring his teeth.

With a strangled growl, he slammed his hands at the bars above my head.

I shut my eyes and drew my head into my shoulders, wishing I could curl up and hide in a shell, like a snail or a turtle.

His chest expanded so wide it nearly crushed me against the bars. My ribs ached. I felt him shake violently and opened my eyes.

His hands on the bars above my head, Greyx pulled fiercely. His arms strained. The muscles in his neck bulged, veins popping thick under his skin. His facial features taut and distorted.

The bars behind me moved, giving in under his incredible strength.

Panicky chirps and clicks came from the greens.

Tossing his head back, Greyx roared. The deafening sound reverberated under the arched stone ceiling, bounced off the walls, and rolled through the room. The bars moved apart under his force. The gap widened enough for my butt to slip through.

With a thrust of his hips, he shoved me out of the cage.

I fell backward, bruising my tailbone on the stone floor. The greens rushed to me. And I scurried away from them on all fours.

A guard ran to Greyx, brandishing a pronged stick in his green hands. He stabbed through the air with it, aiming for Greyx, who kept pulling the bars apart, further widening the gap.

Greyx grabbed the stick and yanked it out of the guard's hands.

The green froze in shock, no longer brave without his weapon.

Holding the stick in front of him, Greyx slipped through the gap between the bent bars. His large body went through with only a clank of the horns on his shoulders against the metal. Then, he was out of the cage.

Forgetting about me, the guards lunged at him.

Greyx flipped the stick in his hand and stabbed the closest guard with the sharp prongs.

With a loud screech, the green collapsed and rolled onto the floor. His own weapon clattered away on the stones.

The others quickly retreated.

Crouching low to the ground, I swiped the discarded stick. My fingers curled around the weapon, immediately making me feel stronger and less afraid.

A new group of the greens barged through the door. Two in the front held devices that looked awfully close to firearms.

"Greyx! Guns!" I warned.

Whipping his head to face the newcomers, he threw his stick like a spear. Hurled through the air, the stick embedded in the neck of a guard with a gun. The green gurgled and fell, dropping his gun.

I ducked when the second guard fired.

Greyx leaped into the air and kicked the shooter in the chest.

Gripping my stick, I sprinted to Greyx, trying to stay close. There was no time to ponder whether or not to trust him. Right now, he was the one kicking the asses of my enemies, and I felt safer closer to him.

Two greens jumped in front of me, cutting me off from Greyx.

"Get out of the way!" I thrust my stick in their direction, hoping my frown looked more menacing than terrified.

One of them hopped around the stick to me. I jumped back and jabbed the prongs in his belly.

The alien howled in pain, doubling over and dropping to the floor.

"Ha!" I yelled triumphantly. "Not fun, is it? Serves you right."

Emboldened by my success, I swung my stick at the second one. He shuffled back on his four feet.

The bright flash of a gunshot lit up the room. The retreating green dropped to the floor, cowering. Another green fell next to him. This one had a smoldering hole in his head. Dead.

"What the..."

Where did the shot come from?

Greyx held the gun, firing wildly in all directions.

Dropping my stick, I dove to the floor.

He showered the entire room with fire, appearing to have no par-ticular aim. Bright rays—lasers or something like it—blasted from the gun like spray from a water hose.

The greens fell like flies—stunned or killed, I couldn't tell and, frankly, didn't really care.

I covered my head with my arms and closed my eyes, praying for it all to be over.

When the hissing sound of shooting finally stopped, the silence was deafening. My ears rang.

A rough hand grabbed me by my cardigan and hauled me up to my feet.

I opened my eyes, coming face to face with Greyx. He no longer foamed at his mouth, though his eyes remained dark and bloodshot—the expression in them dead. No longer raging, he still was far from the Greyx I'd first met. Now, he looked like a robot on a mission.

Without saying a word, he let go of me and strode to the door.

None of the greens in the room got up.

I rushed after him. Clearly, he was dangerous, but he hadn't harmed me yet. He also might have an escape plan in that big, horned head of his—a plan I'd had no chance to devise yet on my own. At the very least, I hoped he knew how to get out of this building.

I dashed after him down the corridor.

The place seemed deserted. Either all the greens in the building had rushed to the room with the cage where Greyx had mowed them down, or they hid, fearful of the gun still in his hands.

Either way, no one stopped us. Greyx moved swiftly on his long, powerful legs, and I tried to keep up.

We took a few turns and made it up a few stairs on the way. The corridor had grown bigger again, the ceiling was much higher, too. I recognized the space. We must be close to both the door to the arena and the room where the greens held Lucy and me.

Lucy!

I needed to get her. If there indeed was a way out of here, she had to come with me.

Greyx stopped in front of an arched entrance abruptly. With a quick glance inside, he stormed in. Catching up, I poked my head in, too.

It appeared to be a break room of the green guards, or something like it. The spear-sticks hung on the wall. Chains and metal belts, like the one I was wearing, were piled up in wooden crates.

Greyx swiftly moved to a metal box in the corner and grabbed something that looked like a brown bagpipe. Then he dug through a pile of rags in another corner, pulling out a long strip of material. Grabbing the bag under his arm, he started winding the material around his neck like a scarf.

"What are you doing?" I gaped at him, bewildered.

He glanced my way from under the heavy brow ridges, but said nothing in reply.

"Listen, we need to hurry," I urged him, nervously scanning both ends of the corridor outside of the room. "If you know the way out of here, we need to get going. There may be more meanie greenies around here."

I wondered if his translator might've been tampered with, too. He certainly didn't act like he understood what I was saying.

Instead of rushing to search for the exit with me, he approached the metal grate protecting the spear-sticks. With one hard yank, he ripped the grate off the wall, but instead of going for the spears, he took a wide leather belt from one of the hooks then started buckling it around his hips.

"Really? A belt!" I spread my hands in the air, shaking my head in disbelief. "A bag, a scarf, and a belt? This place may be crawling with greens. They'll be after us any minute, ready to pack you back in that cage. And you're...*accessorizing?*"

He cast me another glance but didn't stop.

Burning with impatience, I kept scanning the corridor. There was another archway up ahead, and I believed I recognized it.

I grabbed one of the sticks off the wall.

"Be right back," I tossed over my shoulder to Greyx, leaving him to search for whatever else he thought he needed—a pair of gloves to match his bag or a hat to go with that scarf, maybe.

I ran down the corridor to the next archway.

"Lucy!" I called, holding the stick in front of me, just in case there were any greens hiding in there.

Rattling of chains, hissing, and growling came from every direction. The chained beasts stirred. Some leaped at me, immediately yanked back by their restraints.

"Lucy. I'm back. Just like I promised." I found her where I'd left her. Curled in a ball by the wall, she had her hands over her ears, her eyes closed.

I rushed to her. "Come, Lucy. We may be able to get out of here, but we need to hurry."

I tugged at the belt around her waist, but it wouldn't budge. Sticking the end of the spear-stick through the ring on the floor, I tried to wrench it out. To no avail. The metal held.

My heart sank.

Lucy finally opened her eyes, staring at me silently. She didn't need to say it; I saw it in her terrified expression that she knew what this meant. If I wanted to get out of here, I had to leave her behind.

I fervently ran my hands along the chain, hoping for a weak link I could possibly snap. "I'm not going anywhere without you."

Heavy footfalls by the entrance snapped my attention to the archway. Greyx was running by.

"Greyx! Wait!" I yelled.

He skidded to a halt at the sound of my voice.

"In here." I waved. "Help us. Please."

He scanned the place, his eyes narrowing at the beasts.

"These are prisoners, just like us," I explained. "They're all chained. There are no greens here." At least not that I could see.

He barreled towards me.

Lucy shrank back as he approached.

"Help, please." I gestured at her belt. "Can you take it off?"

I had no idea if he could understand what I was saying, but he seemed to get what I wanted. Dropping his bag and the gun on the floor, he grabbed onto Lucy's belt. She squeaked, drawing her head into her shoulders.

"It's Greyx, Lucy," I said softly. "He's not going to hurt you." I had no authority to make these assurances. His darkened eyes rotated wildly in their sockets. A scowl appeared to freeze permanently on his face. For all I knew, he would smash my head and hers between those deadly forearms of his, any minute.

But what choice did Lucy and I have?

He tore his stare off me and inspected the belt and the chain, then got down on his knees to examine the floor ring closely. Next, he rose to his feet.

Was he leaving?

My heart plummeted with panic.

Lucy whimpered.

"We're not leaving her here!" I jumped up. "You didn't leave behind your bag and all these things..." I wildly waved my hands at the scarf around his neck. "We can't leave Lucy."

He glanced at the ends of the scarf hanging down his bare chest, then stared back at me, clearly unaffected by my distress.

I scoffed, throwing my hands up in frustration. Did I have any right to demand anything from him? The Greyx I thought I knew wouldn't leave either me or Lucy behind. But did I really know the man who was now standing in front of me?

He could turn around and leave without lifting a finger to help me, and I wouldn't be able to do anything to stop him.

Unexpectedly, he grabbed me by my arms and yanked me to his chest.

I yelped in shock.

He leaned closer and buried his nose between my neck and my shoulder, then took a long, deep breath. His body tensed around me, his hands shook as he pried them off me.

One glance at his face, and I stepped back in trepidation.

The wild expression returned to his eyes. His scowl grew deeper. Veins bulged out on his forehead, popping thickly along his neck, too.

Lucy trembled violently as he took hold of her belt again and yanked her to her feet. The muscles in his arms rippled and bulged as he pulled at the belt with force. The lock snapped. The belt broke in half, and he tossed it aside.

"Wow..." was all I could manage, breathless.

Without sparing me a glance, he grabbed his bag and the gun off the floor and stomped out of the room.

"Quickly!" I tugged at Lucy's arm. "We need to keep up. I think he knows the way out of here."

With a nod, she hurried into the corridor with me.

"There!" I spotted his back way ahead already. He was fast, even as he didn't appear to be terribly in a rush. "Come."

Dragging Lucy behind me, I ran after Greyx.

Seeing that we'd caught up, he sped up.

My heart thundered in my chest, beating so hard it felt as if it'd moved up into my throat after a while. My focus narrowed on that tall figure running ahead of us. I was determined not to let his broad shoulders and horned head out of my sight.

He turned around another corner.

"Hurry, Lucy!" I gasped, afraid to lose him.

The hissing of gunfire made me skid to a stop. Lucy bumped into my back at full speed.

White flashes bounced off the walls ahead of us, coming from around the corner where Greyx had just run.

I bit my lip. "Must be the greens."

Lucy grabbed my arm, her pale fingers digging into the sleeve of my cardigan.

I'd left my spear-stick back in the room with the archway entrance. Now, Lucy and I had no weapons on us. I flattened my back against the wall. Lucy did the same.

The shooting ceased as suddenly as it'd started.

I waited for a fraction of a moment, expecting the greens to show up at any moment. When they didn't, I took Lucy's hand. "Come on."

Quietly, we crept along the wall. When we reached the corner, I carefully inched closer to look around it.

Greyx stood in the hallway, his weapon raised. Green bodies piled up all around him.

Tension drained from me at the sight of him, safe and sound.

"He won." I squeezed Lucy's hand.

My gaze connected with his, and he held eye contact for a moment. With a nod, as if he'd just waited for us to join him, he took off again.

"Here we go again." I sprinted after him. Glancing over my shoulder, I made sure Lucy was following close behind me.

After another turn, the hallway narrowed, the ceiling lowered. There were no archways here.

A breeze fluttered my clothes, sending a shot of excitement through me. We must be getting closer to the exit!

After another turn, a splash of reddish light came from the distance, the same light I'd seen outside in the arena. I hoped Greyx had led us to the exit, not back to the arena. My chest squeezed with both fear and hope.

The red light was coming through a round window at the end of the corridor. The window seemed just big enough even for Greyx to fit through, except that a thick grate covered it, with bars nearly as thick as the ones of the cage down in the basement.

Greyx had been able to bend those, though. Maybe he could deal with these ones, too?

He stopped at the window. Lucy panted at my side, working on catching her breath after our mad dash through this place.

I gasped for air, too. My side pinched, and I rubbed it with my arm, trying to regulate my breathing.

"Can you break it?" I asked Greyx, gesturing at the grate.

Without saying a word, he tucked his gun into his belt and handed his bag to Lucy, then turned to me. Slowly, he dragged his gaze down my body, unabashedly taking in every dip and curve.

I shivered under his blatant perusal and wrapped my arms over my chest, shielding my breasts.

He growled, swiftly moving closer.

"Greyx?" My voice was thin.

He placed his hands on my shoulders, then slid them down my arms. Even through the material of my cardigan, I felt the heat of his touch.

"What are you doing?" I whispered as he leaned closer. "Greyx?"

At the sound of his name, a rumble vibrated deep inside his chest. He drew me to him, his hands sliding to my back and fisting into my clothes. His warm breath hit the side of my neck, sending a flock of tingles down my body. His scent rushed me. There was no other fragrance mixed with it this time, just the hot, spicy scent of a male.

My knees shook, but he held me too tight for me to fall or even sway.

I slid my hands up his bare chest. There was no hard plating there, just warm skin and firm muscles underneath. His heart beat wildly, fast and strong.

I hadn't even realized how badly I needed a hug in this place. I momentarily forgot all about the murders he had committed and the dark madness in his eyes. Basking in the warmth and strength of his large body, I couldn't let go, but I knew I had to.

"We have to get out of here," I whispered.

His nose pressed to my hair, he inhaled deeply then leaned back. His eyelids dropped slightly over his eyes. Heat flashed in his irises. His heavy brow furrowed, his hard features shifting into an even harder expression—fierce and dangerous.

His hands at my waist, he yanked at my metal belt, breaking it at once. He tossed it aside, then shoved away from me with enough force to make me stagger back a few steps.

He stomped to the window and ripped the grate out in one powerful tug.

My head was spinning from the rollercoaster of emotions this man caused in me. I stared at the discarded belt on the floor while understanding slowly rose in my head.

Every time Greyx broke or bent things, he was near me, breathing me in. He was a strong man, but something about me seemed to amplify his strength. He used me as a drug to make himself stronger.

He grunted—the sound meant to get my attention. I found him peering at me over his shoulder as he was about to climb out the window.

I nodded.

"Come, Lucy." I touched her shoulder.

Hugging Greyx's bag to her chest, she followed him through the window.

Poking my head out after her, I gasped. My breath caught in my throat at the view from the window.

We were high above the ground, on one of the top floors of this sprawling building. Everywhere the eye could see, the ground was covered with the same white sand like that in the arena. The peaks of the sand dunes were painted blood-red by the huge crimson sun hanging low in the sky.

If I had any doubts before, I had none left now. This wasn't Neron or Aldrai. This was most certainly not Earth, either. We were not on any planet I knew.

Far below ran a wide stream of milky-white water that took the shade of strawberry cream in the red haze of the sun.

Lucy and Greyx stood on the narrow ledge on the wall.

"You've got to be kidding me," I said under my breath, gripping the frame of the window.

The river seemed at least fifty feet below us. The wall was too smooth to climb down.

Greyx stared at me expectantly, obviously waiting for me to join them on the ledge.

I glanced back down the corridor. Noise echoed through the stone walls of our prison. There must be more greens in this place. Greyx hadn't killed them all. They would be searching for us, and it might not take them long to get here.

"Okay." I drew in a breath and hiked up my skirt.

Swinging a leg out, I turned to grip the window frame while carefully getting my second foot out, too. With my head and arms still inside the building, my belly pressed to the bottom part of the window frame, I felt with my feet for the ledge below.

My ballet flat slipped on the stone. A large, warm hand wrapped around my bare calf, guiding my foot to the ledge.

"Thanks." I blew out a breath, climbing out to stand next to Greyx.

He shifted away from me now. Other than searching for a body contact with me when he needed to break something, he appeared to avoid any closeness with me, even if it was just an accidental brushing of hands.

I inhaled, afraid to look down into the moving water. "Now what?"

"Jump," Greyx grunted.

The first word he'd said since...well since we'd been taken.

And I understood it! My translator was working.

Stunned, I almost missed Greyx jumping off the ledge and into the river.

"Greyx!" I shouted after him. "Are you insane?"

His hard, massive body arched rather gracefully before smoothly entering the cloudy waters below, head first.

"Did you see that? He jumped!" I turned to Lucy with my mouth hanging open.

She stared back at me for a moment—her eyes impossibly wide—then stepped off the ledge too, clutching the brown bag to her chest like a lifesaver.

"Shit. Lucy!" I flayed my arms to keep my balance.

Her white sweater opened on her back like a tiny parachute before she splashed into the river. Greyx had surfaced already, swimming down the stream in wide, powerful strokes.

"You both are crazy!" I screamed, but there was no one to hear me.

With a quick glance toward the window to make sure no one was following us yet, I pinched my nose closed with my fingers and jumped.

Chapter 10

Tessa

I hit the river feet first. Cool water knocked the air out of my lungs and flooded my senses. My lungs burned with the urge to take a breath. Letting go of my nose, I kicked my legs and arms, desperate to get up to the surface.

Breaking through, I sputtered and gasped, splashing wildly and fighting for each ragged breath. I'd taken some swimming lessons as a kid. Now, instinct and muscle memory helped me find the rhythm as I treaded water, staying afloat.

Turned my way, Greyx fought the current, watching me. After making sure I wasn't drowning, he swirled around and swam down the river.

About half-way between us, Lucy's blonde head bobbed in the milky water next to the shapeless bag she clung to. The bag appeared to have some buoyancy that helped her stay afloat.

I moved my arms, remembering what the swim instructor had taught me so many years ago. Either scooping the water in long strokes or doggy-paddling here and there, I made my way down the river, following Lucy and Greyx. My shoes got in the way, but I was afraid to kick them off. Sooner or later, we would have to get out of the river. If I lost my shoes now, I'd be walking through the sand barefoot for who knew how long.

The river took us away from the gray-brown building of our prison—an ugly construction, designed with no concern for aesthetics.

After a while, all I could see on either side of the river was just waves and swells of the white sand. It appeared to glow in the red lights of this planet. Its crystals shimmered, which looked almost magical. Except that the sinister red haze gave it the flair of *dark* magic.

Greyx took a turn to the left. The strokes of his arms grew stronger and faster as he fought the current, cutting across the stream to shore.

I turned left too, kicking and paddling.

But Lucy kept going straight, stuck in the middle of the river.

"Lucy!" I yelled, water splashing into my open mouth.

Clinging to the bag with one arm, she splashed with the other one, but she had no strength to combat the current. The river kept taking her farther and farther away.

Greyx saw her struggle. He turned sharply, swimming across the river back to her. Cutting across the stream, he caught her by grabbing to the bag with one hand. He used his other arm to swim back to shore, dragging Lucy and the bag behind him.

A lot of strength was in that guy, whether he sniffed me or not.

My strength, on the other hand, left much to be desired. My shoulders ached. My lungs burned. I struggled, fighting the current on my way to shore. When my feet finally touched the soft bottom, it was a relief. Climbing onto the sandy ground, I stumbled toward Lucy and Greyx, who waited for me down the stream.

"Thank you," I rasped, panting, then dropped next to Lucy into the warm sand.

Greyx got up. "We need to keep moving."

His voice sounded gruff. His expression was gloomy. But I was so glad he was speaking. And that I could still understand him. Whatever the greens had done to my translator didn't affect my understanding of Aldraian language.

Now, if only Lucy would say something, too. She remained silent, however, wringing the water out of her hair and clothes.

"Moving?" I groaned, the meaning of what he'd said fully registering with me. "Again?"

Every muscle in my body was in pain. It hurt to move, to breathe, to speak... The breakfast I'd eaten so long ago still refused to settle, my stomach twisting in knots. All I wanted was to lie down and sleep.

Greyx remained firm, though. Unyielding. He reached for his bag. "They will deploy drones soon. If they haven't already."

Lucy leaped to her feet, clutching the bag and refusing to give it up.

"Do you want to carry him?" Greyx asked.

She nodded, hugging the bag tighter.

"Fine," Greyx conceded. "But he's heavy. Let me know when you get tired."

She nodded again, tucking the bag under her arm.

He?

Did Greyx just call his bag a *he?*

I took a closer look at the thing in Lucy's arms. It had the appearance of a shapeless, lumpy, suede bagpipe in a lifeless taupe color. A cone-shaped tube was on one end, with short dark strips hanging in clusters of four on each side.

The thing was definitely an *it*, not a *he.*

Maybe Greyx got his prepositions confused? Or maybe it was my damaged translator acting up?

When he mentioned the drones, I peeled my ass off the soft, warm riverbank and forced my body into an upright position.

Giving our small party an assessing look, he nodded, then headed away from the river.

Despite the ache and exhaustion, I hurried alongside him. "Greyx, what is this place? Where are we?"

"Zoltu," he said, keeping a brisk pace.

"Is that the name of the planet?"

"Yes."

"I've never heard of it before. I thought I knew the names of all populated planets in this area."

He grunted. "Technically, this planet isn't populated. Zoltu is dying. It's not worth colonization."

He'd gone from a complete silence, to single word replies, to finally the whole three sentences. More importantly, he sounded almost normal when he spoke.

I had to keep him talking. "Why is it dying?"

"Its sun is cooling and expanding. It's only a matter of time until it'll grow to swallow Zoltu completely."

I nervously looked up at the giant red disk in the sky. Now it seemed even more menacing. "How long until that happens?"

"Not long." Greyx seemed to be heading toward the slim, dark line of the forest that appeared on the horizon. "Anywhere between several hundred and several thousand universal years."

All habitable planets in this sector of the galaxy were roughly the same size, very close to the size of Earth. The years on all of them were almost of identical length, for that reason. A universal year was calculated as the average between all of them.

Hundreds of thousands of years was long enough for me to breathe with relief. The sky wasn't crashing on our heads any time soon.

"So, the green guys aren't native to this place?" I asked.

"*Yirzi*? No. They're from the planet Tragul."

That was the same planet where Ravils lived. Earth had a military agreement with the Ravils. The name *yirzi* also sounded familiar.

"Weren't *yirzi* involved in the war that Voranians and Ravils fought a few years back?" I read something about it.

"Not officially. The war was between Ravils and *fescods*. It started on Tragul. Once *fescods* took over the Country of Ravie, they invaded Neron, intending to take over Voran, too. Then, Voranians joined Ravils in fighting them. Both Aldrai and Earth had a military alliance with Ravie, too, ultimately helping defeat the *fescods*. *Yirzi* had no formal agreements with either side. But they had attacked our allied forces often, helping *fescods*."

"Why?"

"For money. There's nothing they wouldn't sell." He shook his head. "Nasty, vile creatures."

From what I'd learned about *yirzi* while being held in their captivity, I totally agreed with Greyx's assessment of their species.

"What do they want with us?" I struggled to keep up with him, fighting for every breath, but I had so many questions, and now that he'd started talking, I was hoping to finally get some answers. "Why did they kidnap us?"

"For fighting in the arena. And..." He cut a glance my way. "And for breeding."

"Breeding?" I tripped in the sand. "Is that what they were trying to do? When they shoved me into your cage?" He had broken us out of there. I dreaded to think what would've happened if he didn't.

He said nothing to that, marching up a sand dune a little faster. I quickly fell behind, thinking about everything he'd said and about the fact that he spoke at all.

Greyx talked to me. He knew my name, which meant he remembered me. But he behaved as if we were complete strangers who'd just met. Something was off about him. His very nature had changed, so much so that I too felt as if he were an entirely different person now. A stranger indeed.

Unanswered questions gave me a mad rush of energy, spurting me to catch up with him once again.

"Why did they do that?" My voice shook a bit. "Why would they want to 'breed' us?"

He looked almost reproachfully at me and took a step aside, putting more distance between us. "For entertainment. The *yirzi* record and transmit the fighting in the arena, taking bets from the viewers. There's a lot of money involved. Now, it appears, they're branching out into illegal breeding, too."

I kept moving for a few steps in silence, shifting my legs mechanically. If we hadn't made it out of there... My mind refused to comprehend the horrors that could have followed.

"Breeding is cheaper than acquiring new fighters," Greyx explained. "It also provides an opportunity for genetic selection and manipulation. By taking the strongest female and breeding her with the strongest male—"

"I'm not the strongest," I mumbled, flabbergasted. To believe that things like that could be happening in our time and age...

He glanced at me again, studying my face for a long moment.

"You survived the fight in the arena, didn't you?"

"Right.'

They'd watched me. The nightmare in the arena had been part of a brutal selection process. A test. And I'd proven my "worth."

A chilling shudder rolled through me again.

"You saw me there." He'd saved my life by killing the giant scorpion-beast. But he had also looked ready to kill me himself. I recalled his feral expression and blood thirst in the arena.

He nodded silently, not sparing me a glance.

I wished to see him smile, to see a hint of the attention with which he'd showered me back at the New Year's party. It would mean the world to me right now. One friendly word and a hug would give me strength to keep going.

Yet he remained as cold and distant as the building we'd just escaped from.

Did Greyx even have any smiles left to give? I'd seen nothing but a deep frown on his face lately.

"Why didn't you say something to me back in the arena?" I tried to hold his gaze, but he kept shifting it away.

"You should stop talking," he said finally. "For better breathing control."

"But—"

He didn't let me finish. "We must get to the forest. We need cover from the drones."

With that, he mercilessly increased his speed. Hauling his bag on her shoulder, Lucy dutifully hurried behind him.

I winced, trying to keep up. My muscles protested with every move. My shoes sank into the sand, filling with it with every step.

After a while, Lucy started falling behind.

"Let me carry this..." I grabbed the bag from her. Reluctantly, she let me have it.

The bag felt warm. The material it was made of felt like soft suede. No wonder Lucy liked cuddling with it. Or maybe she associated it with safety now, after the bag had supported her in the water, allowing her to float. Regardless, it still had a considerable weight. My arms ached as if being wrenched out of the sockets by the time we finally made it to the forest's tall, skinny trees.

Greyx waited for us just behind the tree line. He'd been pushing us to the limit with the manic brutality of a boot camp trainer. With our lives being on the line, it was hard to be mad at him. However, it didn't stop me from utterly despising him and his long, fast legs.

He reached for his bag, and I was happy to shove it at him. "Here. Take back your stuffy."

I bent over at the waist, my hands propped on my knees, and panted hard, struggling for each breath.

Lucy collapsed into the sand beneath the trees, her face flushed, her blonde tresses slick with sweat.

"We need to keep moving," Greyx said calmly.

A swell of misery rose inside me at the idea of forcing my body into any kind of activity at this point.

Cruel, cruel Greyx. He seemed in excellent shape himself. Unlike us, he didn't even break a sweat after all the swimming and hiking.

He was right, though, the forest canopy wasn't thick enough to hide us. The pale, yellowish-green leaves of the trees were long but thin like pine needles. Some had black round fruit dangling on the thin, twisted branches. But there weren't that many of either the leaves or the fruit to provide a solid cover for us.

The bloated, red sun had dipped toward the horizon by now. The day was coming to an end.

"Do yirti drones have night vision?" I asked Greyx.

"*Yirzi*," he corrected. "And yes, the drones will be able to spot us at night, even under the trees."

Heaving the bag over his shoulder, he marched on, deeper into the forest. I fought a wave of resentment, watching him move so fast and effortlessly.

At the end of the day, though, it wasn't Greyx's fault that I'd preferred reading to running on a treadmill. I loved biking and even jogged occasionally back home on Earth. But sitting in my cabin for five months during our trip here had taken a toll on my physical shape. Now, I was paying for it.

I helped Lucy to her feet, then we both trudged after our guide again.

"Where are we going?" I yelled at the Aldraian's wide back.

Unlike his chest that was all smooth skin and planes of muscles, his back had hard plating. The plates descended from his shoulder clusters, covering his shoulder blades. A hard ridge ran along his spine, with a smooth, polished bump topping each vertebra.

"We're going to hide from the drones," he tossed over his shoulder, without slowing down.

"Where? Is there such a place?"

"Yes." He didn't elaborate.

"Is it far?"

"We still have a way to go. Spare your breath," he threw my way, speeding up, as if trying to get away from me and my questions.

Catching up was not an easy task. Whether I wanted it or not, I had to stop talking after all, to preserve my energy.

My brain, however, didn't stop working even as my mouth was shut.

Greyx used to put me at ease. When we met, he was talkative and smiled easily. I loved that about him, maybe because it was the opposite of my own reserved nature. I found his outgoing, down-to-earth personality irresistibly attractive.

Now, his gruff attitude put me off. While he used to seek my company before, now he appeared to be actively avoiding it. We might be running away from *yirzi* drones, but the way he always kept at least a few paces ahead of me made me feel like he was running away from *me*.

He'd broken us out of that vile place, but he didn't look like he was pleased about being stuck with us now. Come to think of it, he hadn't forced me to escape with him. I'd kind of tagged along on my own. Maybe he would've preferred that I hadn't?

Would he have cared if I stayed behind?

The image of an Aldraian watching me through the window in the examination room rose in my mind again, stirring doubts.

Why did *yirzi* target our space shuttle, out of hundreds or maybe even thousands of spacecraft out there? And how exactly was Greyx involved in all of this?

"Hey!" I called after him. "Where are you taking us, General?"

His shoulders jerked at the sound of his rank. He'd asked me to call him Greyx before. But first names were often reserved for friends, family, and lovers. Greyx and I were none of the three. And judging by how he'd behaved, he preferred it that way.

He didn't reply to my question, but slowed down, allowing Lucy and me to catch up. He then stopped so suddenly, I nearly bumped into him. It was a good thing I managed not to. Crashing full speed into his hard, solid body could cause serious injuries.

"There is an extensive cave system on this planet," he finally explained. "We need to get underground before the drones arrive."

He brushed his fingers along his belt. A compartment opened, and Greyx took a flat disk out of it. Pressing something on the disk, he made it light up with ink spot shapes and wiggly lines.

"The nearest entrance is that way." He gestured ahead.

I eyed the disk in his hand. "Is that your navigation device?"

"Yes." He nodded. "Among other things."

"Like what? Can you use it for communications, too? Can you call for help?"

"Maybe." He inserted the disk back into his belt and started on his way again. "We'll see."

'We'll see what?' I wanted to shout, but he'd taken off already, leaving me no choice but to hurry along.

Trudging through the sandy forest floor alongside Lucy, I focused on simply keeping up with the punishing pace Greyx had set for us.

After a while, he stopped. His focus seemed to be on a patch of low shrubs in front of us. Leaning in, he parted them, revealing a narrow crevasse in the ground. Less than three feet wide at the opening, it appeared to grow wider the deeper it went.

My hands on my knees again, I was laboriously catching my breath. "Is that it?" I panted. "No more running?"

He nodded silently, looking around. Walking over to the nearest tree, he plucked a few dark, round fruits off its gnarly branches, then stuffed them into the folds of the scarf draped over his neck and shoulder like a sling.

"Come." Hands propped on both sides of the crevasse, he swung his feet over the edge and jumped in.

Lucy stared at Greyx's wide back as he departed, then slipped into the crevasse after him.

I hesitated, but only for a moment. Greyx was the one with a plan and possibly the means to get us off this planet. Following him—whether he liked it or not—still seemed like a good idea.

"Okay then," I muttered under my breath before climbing down after them. "Great. I'm always the last one."

Chapter 11

Tessa

Only some of the dying daylight filtered into the crevasse from above. I walked carefully, trying not to bump my elbows on the smooth walls of the narrow canyon. The thought of Greyx's broad shoulders came to mind. The guy must be squeezing sideways through some of the narrower parts in here.

After a while, the space widened. We appeared to be moving downhill. Then, the opening above us disappeared completely as the crevasse turned into a tunnel.

"I can't see a thing." I followed the sound of the footsteps up ahead, relying on my ears rather than my eyes to guide me at that point.

A pale blue light flickered in the distance—Greyx held up the glowing disk in his hand, giving me a beacon to follow.

The light bounced off the walls of the tunnel, reflecting with a million iridescent sparkles in the facets beneath the smooth surface. I slid my hand along the hard rock walls. It was semi-transparent, like milky glass or quartz. Broken into tiny pieces, the rock produced the white sand that covered the ground above, I assumed.

A faint trickle of water came from up ahead. The light in Greyx's hand stopped moving, and I found him and Lucy waiting for me in front of a fork in the tunnel.

"This way." He gestured to the left.

The walls here seemed to glow on their own. After a while, Greyx flicked the disk off and slid it back into the compartment on his belt.

The glow of the walls continued to illuminate the place in a soft pinkish-white light.

After another turn, the tunnel expanded into a cave. The cloudy white water trickled from the narrow crack in the wall and down glistening quartz. Thin stalactites hung from the ceiling like light fixtures. Their blue glow was even brighter than the pinkish light of the walls.

"We'll take a rest," Greyx announced, easing the bag off his shoulder and setting it on the floor.

Lucy rushed to the waterfall, cupping her hands under the stream.

I stopped her with my hand on her shoulder.

"Is this water safe to drink?" I asked Greyx.

I had no idea why or how, but he obviously had some knowledge about this place.

He nodded. "It's safe."

Leaning in, he dipped his face under the stream, drinking in large gulps straight from the waterfall.

There was nothing special about this gesture, just a tired man quenching his thirst. Yet I couldn't take my eyes off him as he drank, the water dripping down his bare chest, milky rivulets running between the hard squares of his abs and soaking into the fabric of his pants at his trim waist.

"You're not thirsty, Tessa?" His voice snapped me out of my gawking. "Or do you prefer to wait a bit? To see if the water has some adverse effects on my body?" He tilted his head, lifting an eyebrow ridge.

Was he teasing me?

A spark of amusement in his expression made my heart skip a beat. For a second, I was swept back to the night when music reigned and this man held me in his arms. For just a moment, the old Greyx returned.

Then he blinked, and it was gone. A grim expression settled firmly in his eyes once again as he stomped away from me to the other side of the waterfall.

"Your body?" I repeated stupidly. Did I just dream that tiny change in him? It must have been just my wishful thinking. I missed even his teasing. "Sure... I mean no. Oh, whatever..." I gave up on talking for now. Silently, I shifted closer to the waterfall and cupped my hands under the stream.

The water felt cool and refreshing. I drank greedily, washing away the dust and sand that had lodged in my mouth and throat.

Lucy had a drink too, then made herself comfortable with the suede bag on the floor.

Greyx took out the fruit he'd picked off the tree outside, rinsed it, then sliced it up with the laser-like knife he had produced from another compartment on his belt.

He gave Lucy a thick slice of the fruit. "Eat."

I recognized the pale violet flesh of the "space turnip" the greens had fed to us. Greyx gave a slice to me as I sat next to Lucy, and my stomach roiled at the minty smell.

"Do they have any other kind of fruit or vegetable on this planet?" I couldn't help a grimace of disgust, already feeling the nausea-inducing heaviness of this nasty thing in my stomach before I even took a bite.

"From what I've learned about Zoltu, no." Greyx sat on the floor on the other side of Lucy and stretched his long legs in front of him. "*Dohmat* is the only edible fruit here. There isn't that much plant life left on Zoltu, as you might've noticed. The planet's climate has been changing as its sun moves closer. Long ago, there used to be seasons here, with snow and such. Now, only some life forms still remain near the poles. The equator belt is completely dead—scorched sand and nothing else."

From what I've seen, the planet certainly looked like it was at the end of its life.

"Where did you learn about this place?" I remembered my suspicions.

He looked at me as if assessing how much he should reveal to me.

"In school, some of it," he finally replied after a long pause.

"They teach you about Zoltu in school?"

"This planet is relatively close to Aldrai, less than a day away. Even shorter if you use a Voranian spaceship. Yes, they teach children in Aldraian schools about it."

"Do they teach about *yirzi*, too? And about the 'fun' entertainment facility they run here?" I asked sarcastically.

"No," he retorted calmly. My sarcasm bounced off him like an arrow probably would from his built-in body armor. "All information about the facility is classified."

Classified.

He'd used that word before, back on the shuttle.

"Does your job have anything to do with this place?" I halted my breath, waiting for his answer. I wanted to trust him with all my heart. But could I?

He shifted uneasily. "Like I said, it's classified."

"Right." My voice rang high with nerves. "But Lucy and I here..." I waved a hand between her and me. "We're kind of stuck in the middle of it now. Everything that's been happening to us here must be classified too, right? Are we not allowed to speak about what happened to us? What are we to expect if we ever get off this planet?"

He pressed his mouth into a thin line.

"What if the government or the Army of Aldrai lock us up to keep us quiet? Don't you think we should know what's happening here? What's happening to *us?*" I pleaded.

"No one is going to lock you up," he gritted through his teeth. "Not as long as I live."

The force with which he spoke made me breathe a bit easier. He appeared to be on my side on that, at least.

He heaved a heavy breath, visibly hesitating.

"Just tell me something, Greyx, please. Anything." I searched his eyes. "I can't follow you blindly. I need to know what we're dealing with here."

He seemed to consider it.

"We've only recently discovered the location of this facility," he said slowly, as if weighing every word carefully. "But we've known that something like it existed for some time. Transmitted footage of the fights has been intercepted on a few occasions. Rare and endangered animals have been reported stolen from zoos and sanctuaries. I've been leading the military task force with the purpose of locating and neutralizing this illegal operation."

"Was that the reason they targeted our shuttle? Did they know you were on it?"

He worked his jaw. His eyes glimmered dangerously from under his thick eyebrow ridges. "Our travel plans were classified. No one knew about it other than Alcus Hecear from the Liaison Committee and your crew. And even those who knew had very little time to act."

"What are you saying? That Alcus or someone from my flight crew had a hand in the attack on the shuttle?" I had a really hard time believing it.

"No, Tessa." He started unraveling the scarf from around his neck. "I'm saying someone from my own task force leaked the information."

"Oh... It was an inside job." I leaned back against the wall, processing what he'd just said. "So much for it being *classified*, huh?"

He tore a long piece of fabric from the scarf, then started wrapping it around his left forearm, padding and concealing the sharp peaks and hard ridges there.

"Do you always keep those covered?" I asked.

He nodded. "Unless I'm in a battle. It's dangerous to have the arm horns exposed otherwise."

I slid my gaze along the horns on his head and his shoulders. His entire body was dangerous—an armored weapon made for fighting. No wonder the *yirzi* wanted him for their arena.

He finished wrapping the left forearm, then started on the right one. Catching me staring, he tipped his head at the untouched disk of fruit in my hand—*dohmat* as he called it. "You have to eat."

Lost in thought, I obeyed, bringing the piece to my mouth and taking a bite. "So, you think someone from Aldrai betrayed you?"

He sighed, bending his legs and resting his now fully wrapped forearms on his knees.

"*Yirzi* are a species with no morals or values. They are largely motivated by money and led by herd mentality. They lack creativity or organization. It's highly unlikely they would be able to organize and operate the facility on this level without the involvement of other species."

"Aldraians? Someone from Aldrai must be helping them."

He exhaled a humorless laugh. "I think someone from Aldrai is *using yirzi* to run this place for them."

"Who?" I asked and added quickly. "Or is that also *classified*?"

He shook his head. "Not classified, but unknown. We have a few leads. None have been confirmed yet."

I took another bite of the fruit and chewed while mulling over his words.

"Where were you held while in the facility?" I asked.

A flash of anger crossed his features. "In the fucking cage."

That explained his lack of a metal belt in the arena. If he wasn't chained like Lucy and me, he wouldn't be required to wear it. That still didn't explain his behavior in the arena and later in the cage. He appeared even less himself back then than he was now—killing, raging, violent.

"Did you spend *all* the time in the cage?" I asked again. "Were you there from the very beginning?"

He looked at me closely. "Yes. Why?"

I worried my lip with my teeth, briefly considering if I should tell him. He appeared guarded with me, but I didn't think he'd lied.

I chose to be honest in return.

"I saw someone in the window of the examination room. Where the *yirzi*..." I swallowed hard.

The phantom memories of the unwanted touch crawled along my skin. The examination must have something to do with the *yirzi's* intentions to breed me. The few bites of *dohmat* I'd swallowed stirred in my stomach, bile rising to my throat at the thought of the "tests" the *yirzi* might've done on me.

"Where I was before they took me to the arena," I finished, carefully avoiding any details.

"Who did you see?" Greyx was watching me closely.

"An Aldraian. I lost my glasses. Without them, I couldn't see his face—he stood too far—but it was an Aldraian, without a doubt. You guys are hard to mistake for anyone else." I gestured at the crown of horns on his head and the clusters on his shoulders, then paused, contemplating just how open I wanted to be. "I thought it was you."

"Me?" He frowned in confusion.

"The person wasn't chained or bound. The greens didn't appear to guard him. I tried to call your name, but they gave me something that knocked me unconscious again..."

"So, you thought I'd be just standing there, watching them abuse you?" His hands fisted, his biceps bulging thickly. Rage appeared to pulse through his entire body.

"I... I don't know what to think, Greyx. I really don't know you, do I?"

What little I thought I'd learned about him had changed so drastically, I didn't recognize him anymore. How could I say with any certainty what he would or wouldn't do?

"I wasn't there, Tessa. If only I were, I'd..." He glared at me. "Did they hurt you?"

"No..." I had no pain or scars when I woke. "They kept me under most of the time. I only woke up that one time. And only because, I think, they'd tampered with my translator and wanted to make sure their tampering worked. I believe they didn't want me to understand their language."

He nodded. "Right. They did the same to mine, too." He rubbed his forehead, looking extremely tired. Maybe all the running and swimming took a toll on him, after all.

We all could use some rest.

Lucy was already snoring softly, Greyx's "bagpipe" propped under her head.

"Do you think we're safe here?" I asked him.

"The drones can't see us underground," he said confidently. The way he let the end of that sentence hang, though, might mean that there were other means the *yirzi* could use to find us.

I nervously glanced at the entrance to the cave.

"Rest, Tessa," Greyx assured me, his voice softening. "Sleep for a couple of hours. I'll stay up while you sleep."

Was it fair that we slept while he stayed up watching over us?

No, it wasn't. He was tired too. But I had no strength to argue.

"Not for a couple of hours..." I stifled a yawn. "Just a ten-minute nap... Please, wake me up soon. Okay?"

Adrenaline had finally receded, leaving me feeling like a deflated balloon.

Taking off my sweater, I rolled it into a ball to use as a pillow. The air was warm in here, thick with humidity from the waterfall, but my clothes had almost dried after the plunge into the river. Running through the heat outside had sucked most of the moisture out of them. I felt comfortable enough.

Shifting closer to Lucy, I pressed my back to hers and let sleep claim me.

Chapter 12

Greyx

He cut another slice of the *dohmat*. It tasted disgusting.

The women slept, cuddled together into a bundle along with the *brahlu*. The animal remained in a catatonic state, which actually made things easier for now. That creature could cause a lot of damage when awake.

With any luck, Greyx should be able to get all of them out of here, and soon. Thankfully, whatever drugs the *yirzi* had been keeping him on started to wear off. Some clarity of thought had returned.

The urge to keep going overpowered his tiredness, but he knew the women needed a break. He'd pushed them too hard, rushing to make it to the caves as fast as possible. Neither of them complained, but it was obvious they were at the end of their endurance.

He knew he shouldn't be watching Tessa sleep, but his gaze drifted to her again and again.

Why did she take off that dull gray sweater? At least it had concealed her arms from view before. Now, the expanse of her bare skin appeared to glow in the illuminated cave.

Worse was that he knew exactly how her skin felt under his palms. He remembered those arms wrapped around him. Her lips sliding softly against his. She tasted like sweet desire itself...

His cock obviously remembered all of that, too. Blood rushed to his groin, swelling his member with pressure and heat. So much heat, it burned.

His physical reaction to her was amplified tenfold by the remaining mating drugs in his system. Another thought about Tessa's soft skin or the taste of her luscious lips, and his pants would surely catch on fire.

He groaned, shifting his hips and spreading his legs wider to make space for his swollen erection. The heat came with throbbing pain as his cock hardened to the limit. Lust took over, clouding his mind.

Damn *yirzi* and their drugs!

They had pumped rivers of untested, experimental, illegal substances into his veins. The chemicals coursed through his body, swelling his muscles with unnatural strength and his cock with a frantic need that was nearly impossible to fight.

Yet he'd been fighting his desire to pounce on Tessa.

When he'd found her in the arena, surrounded by the most dangerous predators of the galaxy, all he could do was to get away from her. The drugs, mixed with the stench of spilled blood, had turned him into a raging beast, capable only of fighting or fucking. Murdering other monsters was the only thing that distracted him from ravaging and brutalizing her.

Killing the deranged Prug had helped him stave his feral hunger for Tessa's body when the *yirzi* had shoved her into his cage, expecting them both to rape her.

Fighting his lust for her had taken everything he had. It also proved far more exhausting than swimming, or running, or even all the fighting in the arena he'd done.

With a low grunt, he forced his stare away from Tessa and got up. He stomped far away from where she was sleeping and sat with his back to her. He could no longer see her, but his memory supplied plenty of images.

His brain had documented every detail of her taking her sweater off—the way her chest had pushed against the front of her dress when she'd brought back her shoulders. The small plastic buttons in the front of her dress that struggled to hold the two parts together, straining to contain her full breasts.

He wished to release them both as well as to discover everything else her clothing was hiding. His imagination could only go so far since he'd never seen a human woman naked before. But he didn't need much for his arousal to torture him. Everything about her made him want her.

The way she squinted at him, as if searching in his eyes for something or someone she'd lost and now wanted back, badly.

How that one stubborn strand of her hair refused to be tamed into her bun. It hung on the side of her face, a dark wavy curl he itched to touch.

The way she drank from the waterfall, her lips bright and glistening afterwards, just like after their kiss—the only time he'd ever kissed her.

Unable to sit still, he got up.

Pacing made things worse. The material of his pants rubbed against his throbbing cock, the seam in the middle feeling like it was cutting it in half.

His tail tingled and itched, begging to be stroked.

Carefully avoiding another glance at Tessa, he stepped around the sleeping women and went into the adjacent tunnel.

All seemed quiet. Ensuring someone took the watch while the rest of the team rested was a long-standing habit from being in the military for most of his life. Maybe it wasn't necessary tonight?

Maybe he could lie down next to Tessa, let her snuggle against him, wrap her in his arms...

He stomped determinedly, getting farther away from her and the temptation she presented.

If he touched her, he wouldn't stop until he fucked her. And if he fucked her, it wouldn't be pretty. It'd be what Prug had been ready to do to her before Greyx had stopped him.

Only who would stop *him*? He'd have to rip his own head off.

The throbbing ache in his groin quickly grew from being uncomfortable to unbearably painful. The effort to control this had been wearing him down. The thought of another torturous day of hiking tomorrow with a swollen cock between his legs made him groan.

Turning a corner, he figured he'd made it far enough from the cave not to wake the sleeping women.

Unable to hold back any longer, he yanked his pants down, freeing his engorged cock—hard, hot, and pathetically needy.

"Make it quick," he mentally ordered his appendage.

Leaning back against the wall, he slid his palm along his bumpy length. The swollen nodules tingled at the contact, making his toes curl in his boots. A rush of pleasure rippled along his tail, pressed to the wall. He groaned and let his thoughts run wild. Of course, they immediately rushed to Tessa.

He fantasized about letting her hair out of the tie that held it in a knot at her nape and wondered how long it'd be if he spread it down her bare back, strand by strand.

He tried to imagine what she looked like naked, with only two breasts high on her chest.

Two...

One for each of his hands.

So perfect.

He imagined kneading them while pounding hard inside her. A moan tore out of his throat, his fist closing tighter around his throbbing length.

He wondered what her skin would taste like if he licked it.

What little noises she'd make if he sucked on her nipples. Would they be as sensitive as those of Aldraian women? Did women of Earth like their men to play with their breasts? Would Tessa enjoy him playing with hers?

Would she let him use his tail on her?

The glide of his hand along his length turned jerky. His breathing broke into ragged, shallow grunts. The overwhelming pressure erupted in fireworks of intense pleasure, swallowing him whole.

His legs shook as the tight spurts of his release hit the floor of the tunnel. His ass pressed against the wall, he curled over his cock, weakened by the onslaught of ecstasy.

Trembling, he slid to the floor along the wall, then blankly stared at the puddle of his release on the ground between his feet until his senses had finally returned to him and his head cleared.

"That's enough." He got up, tugging his pants in place in one determined movement. "No more."

Making himself come left him with a feeling of shame. He'd given into the weakness he should've been able to control and conquer. *Yirzi* and their drugs had done this to him. And now it felt like the nasty creatures had won.

When he returned to the cave with the waterfall, however, he realized he could look at sleeping Tessa without his cock fighting to rip through his pants.

And that was true relief.

Chapter 13

Tessa

"Time to get up," a male voice said.

The voice was low, with a vibrating note that reached deep inside me, tingling in my chest. The sensation trickled down to my belly... I squirmed at the touch of a large, warm hand on my bare forearm.

"Do I have to get up?" I moaned. The idea of this low, rumbly voice reading me a romance novel while I stayed in bed made the tingling sensation in my lower belly grow.

"Yes. We need to keep going." The voice sounded far less dreamy. Going where?

"Tessa, we need to get out of here."

The dream was gone, and reality hit me. We'd escaped an alien arena and breeding facility and were on a run. There was no bed here. We needed to keep going or the greens would catch us again, lock us in chains and cages, and make us kill each other...or worse.

"Right, right..." I groaned, rubbing my eyes. "I'm up."

My shoulders ached, and my legs protested when I tried to gather them under me. Waking up felt like climbing out of a well—impossible.

"It's been more than ten minutes, hasn't it?" There was no way I could've slept this deeply in that short time. Greyx must've let me sleep longer. Much longer.

"You needed to rest," he replied unapologetically.

He held out his arms, as if ready to catch me if I fell. The moment I stood fully awake and steady on my feet, he moved away.

Lucy was sitting nearby, also rubbing her eyes.

"How long did we sleep?" I asked Greyx.

"Two hours."

"That's a long time," I gasped. My body disagreed. It wanted at least five times as long to keep resting.

I forced my body to move, bending over to grab my sweater off the floor. I tied it around my waist. This place was too warm for a cardigan. I found my shoes nearby. How did I not remember taking them off? I must've been so tired. I still was.

Lucy got up, too, brushing dust off her jeans.

"Are you okay?" I asked her.

She nodded, still not saying a word.

I worried about her. Had the greens done something to her, more than what they had done to me?

Lucy had never been much of a talker. She often acted shy around strangers. It took me weeks of our months-long journey to Neron for Lucy to finally have a real conversation with me. Before that, all I'd gotten were one-word replies and brief polite smiles.

Lucy bent to pick up the suede bag off the floor. She winced, heaving it up.

She had said my name once, back when the greens were taking me away, which meant she *could* talk. She also responded to questions and followed instruction, which meant she heard and understood me.

Maybe her silence was the way she'd been dealing with stress and trauma of our kidnapping and captivity? If so, it might be best to just let her be.

Greyx produced a thin-walled bag from yet another compartment on his belt and filled it under the waterfall.

"I'll carry him." He tried to take the suede bag from Lucy, but she refused to give it up, holding it in a death grip.

"Lucy." I stepped closer. "It's heavy. Let Greyx take it. He's stronger than you."

She stood her ground, refusing to budge, her blue eyes fixed on Greyx in challenge.

"Okay." I placed a hand on her shoulder. "What about if I carried it? Would you let me?"

"Tessa—" Greyx started, but I lifted my hand, stopping him.

Lucy was smaller than me. She looked more fragile, too. I didn't want her body to suffer more than it could take. Neither did I want to cause any more damage to her mind. If she trusted me to carry the bag more than she did Greyx, then I would have to carry the damn thing.

"We'll walk together, okay?" I gently eased the bag out of her fingers. "You, me and...well, whatever this thing is."

A flotation device?

A body warmer?

I looked up to ask Greyx, but he was already by the far wall, checking the tunnel outside the cave. He broke off a long stalactite from the ceiling.

"There is no light after the next turn," he explained. "We'll use this to light the way."

The glowing residue smeared his hands. The rock wasn't what glowed blue. A fluorescent organism—a mold or algae—coated it.

"Ready?" Greyx asked.

Both Lucy and I nodded.

Holding the stalactite like a torch, he walked ahead, leading the way. His broad shoulders barely fit through the tunnel in places; the clusters of short horns scraped the smooth, glassy wall every couple of steps, sending shards of quartz-like rock to the floor and leaving deep grooves behind.

Thankfully, he'd wrapped up the serrated, harpoon-like horns on his forearms. Those things looked even more dangerous than the horns on his shoulders.

Lucy and I followed Greyx, trying to stay close. Not having to worry about the navigation, my mind wandered. My gaze did, too.

For whatever reason, my eyes kept resting on Greyx's firm backside, no matter where I tried to focus instead. Watching his hard glutes roll and flex under the black material of his pants was mesmerizing. I remembered Bree had mentioned that Aldraians had tails. And now, I was trying to make out the outline of it in the middle of his butt. Bree had said their tails were sensitive. I wondered what Greyx would do if I stroked his...

I tore my gaze away from his ass once again, trying to focus on the ground under my feet instead. A few paces later, however, my attention was firmly on his buttocks again.

I groaned in frustration.

"Hey Greyx?" I asked quickly to distract myself from ogling him. "How come *yirzi* kept your belt for you, nicely intact and stoked with all those handy things inside?"

"It was not a favor on their part." He snorted. "*Yirzi* are not the most intelligent beings out there. They've only managed interstellar travel because they steal technology from others. This is my tactical belt, programmed to be opened only by me. They obviously had no idea how to use it and couldn't loot the contents." He slid his hand along the belt. "Thankfully, they had enough common sense to realize it was valuable and not throw it away."

"Couldn't they just cut the leather?"

"*Shuczat* leather can't be cut. Neither by metal nor by laser. There are special tools used in production, but *yirzi* obviously don't have them on Zoltu."

I remembered how annoyed I had been with him when he had retrieved his "accessories." His determination to have the belt and the wraps on his forearms made so much sense now.

"Sorry for snapping at you for getting your stuff," I said. "I didn't realize how important the belt was. The scarves, too." I gestured at his wrapped forearms. "What would you do if those things weren't there when you came for them?"

He shrugged. "I would still run the first chance I got. I had to get out of there. *Yirzi* used drugs on me..." He paused, glancing at me as if to gauge my reaction.

I frowned. "What kind of drugs?"

He didn't reply, so I asked another question.

"How long did we spend in that place?" It felt like just a couple of days, but they kept me under at the beginning.

"Three days. We escaped on the fourth," Greyx said.

I remembered just the day of the fight in the arena, the cage, and the day of our escape. Oh, and I had that one shred of the memory of lying on the examination table. A shudder of chill seized me at that again.

"Where you conscious all that time?" I asked.

"They knocked me unconscious back on the shuttle, but I woke up during the landing of their craft here on Zoltu. They had me wrapped in chains." Wincing, he rubbed his neck as if a chain was still there.

"Did they start giving you the drugs right after?"

"Yes."

"What for?"

He seemed strong and healthy, yet different. I hoped whatever they'd done to him wasn't permanent.

"Is it the drugs that gave you your super strength?" *Yirzi* wanted him to fight in the arena. It made sense that they would enhance his natural abilities in that area.

"Something like that," he replied evasively.

I thought back to him hugging me every time before he broke something.

"Do you need to...um, sniff someone to activate your superpowers? You...smelled me, remember?" Now, when I said it out loud, it sounded even weirder than when I thought about it.

"Yes."

"Soooo—" I needed an explanation.

He stopped me by raising a hand, then tipped his head to the side, as if listening to something ahead of us.

I strained my hearing, too. A faint sound of water current reached my ear.

"Another waterfall?"

"Possibly." Greyx increased his pace. "We can stop to eat there."

A meal sounded lovely. Being on the move made me hungry. Except that the only things this planet had to offer for food were those awful black-and-purplish-white fruits I was beginning to hate with passion. The two bites I'd eaten last had been weighing in my stomach like a brick.

The noise of the water grew louder. The air turned pleasantly cool when we came upon a mountain stream that ran across the tunnel. It cut us off our way. However, translucent rocks stuck out of the stream, creating a path across it.

Greyx frowned, looking concerned. He crouched by the stream. Hovering his hand over the surface, he stared into the water.

He then took a critical look at Lucy's and my shoes. Lucy's white runners got a nod of approval. But his brow furrowed as he stared at my black ballet flats.

"Wrong shoes," he muttered under his breath.

I shifted awkwardly. These were perfect for working on a space shuttle. But I had to agree, my cute flats were a horrible choice of footwear for this entire adventure. I struggled to keep them on when swimming. They got full of sand out in the dunes. I felt every single rock of the tunnel floor through the thin soles. And they painfully rubbed my feet in many places during the entire hike.

Greyx straightened his back, rising from the crouch.

"We'll cross, using the rocks." He pointed at the ragged pieces of the quartz-like stone sticking out of the water throughout the stream. "Keep to the wall and whatever you do, do not get your feet wet."

He took the bag from me.

"Wait until I'm on the other side before you start crossing." He jumped over a few rocks at a time, his long legs eating up the entire width of the stream in a few long leaps.

Once on the other side, he set the bag on the floor.

"Now you, Tessa," he ordered, and raised his arms as if ready to catch me.

Carefully holding on to the wall, I stepped on the nearest rock, then shifted my weight, placing my foot on another one. I wasn't exactly following Greyx's steps. My legs were shorter than his, and I needed almost twice as many rocks to get across.

Greyx waited for me on the other side.

"Careful," he said softly, keeping his gaze on me, as though it were a lifeline that connected me to him.

I had almost made it across when my foot slipped on a patch of slime covering the rock I'd stepped on. I yelped as my foot splashed into the water. It was barely knee-deep here.

"Out! Now!" Greyx's sharp command cut through the air.

I hopped onto another rock.

He grabbed me by my arms and hauled me to him. His terrified expression scared me.

"It's not that deep here—" I tried to calm him down.

A sudden stab of pain in my ankle made the rest of the sentence stuck in my throat. I screamed, doubling over.

The burning pain intensified, rapidly spreading up. Crashing to the ground, I grabbed my leg with both hands.

Greyx dropped to his knees at my side. In one quick movement, he hiked up my skirt to my waist.

Howling in pain, I didn't protest.

Horror struck me when I looked at my leg.

A thick, dark line wiggled its way up under my skin. Agony zigzagged through me as the thing swiftly moved up to my crotch.

"What's this?" I screamed, blinded by terror and pain. "Greyx. It's inside my leg!"

Greyx pressed firmly into my inner thigh with his thumb, stopping the progress of the ugly black thing moving through my flesh. Leaning in, he bit into my skin just below his thumb.

The sharp pain of his bite made me scream again. A warm trickle of blood ran down my thigh.

"Get it out! Please, please, please," I begged, half-paralyzed with panic.

He sucked at the wound. I grabbed on to the horns on the side of his head, arching my back, my muscles spasming with a new stab of pain.

With a twist of his head, he wrenched his horns out of my grip and leaned back.

My throat tightened with shock, cutting off my screams. A long black body wiggled in his teeth as he slowly pulled it out of the wound in my leg.

"Oh, God, it's gross... So gross," I whimpered, shaking from head to toe, tears streaming down my face. "Please, please get it out of me..."

The last of the disgusting creature emerged from under my skin. Its tail lashed across Greyx's face with a sloshing wet sound. I crabwalked backward, scurrying away from it until my shoulders hit the opposite wall of the tunnel.

"W-what is that thing?" I sobbed.

Greyx grabbed the black snake with his hand, smashed it against the ground, then took the laser knife and cut the black slimy length in three equal parts. Even separated, each part continued to wiggle on the floor of the tunnel.

"*Iszel*, the water snake," he explained, turning the blade off and putting the handle back into his belt. "Can be deadly, but a good source of protein."

"A-are you going to eat *that?*" I stared at the wiggling pieces, unable to look away.

He gazed at me with concern.

"Are you okay, Tessa?" His voice turned unexpectedly soft—gentle.

Had he asked in his gruff, almost mechanical tone of voice he'd been using with me lately, I would've just brushed his question off with a canned "I'm fine." But the tenderness in his voice disarmed me. Tears swelled in my eyes, and I blinked, glancing away.

I was not okay.

I'd been abducted, made to kill deadly creatures for entertainment. I'd seen a person die, his head brutally ripped off by the man I really, really liked. I should be terrified of Greyx after that, but I just wanted to feel his strong arms around me at least one more time.

My body hurt, my stomach ached, and my heart longed for a hug. I wanted him to take me in his arms and tell me it all would be okay.

He scooted a little closer. Taking a small bottle out of his belt, he sprayed liquid on the wound left by his teeth on my thigh and on the one at my ankle where the snake had first burrowed under my skin.

"It'll sterilize and seal the wounds," he explained. His voice remained gentle, but there was clearly no hug coming my way any time soon.

I nodded, stifling a sob. "Thanks."

He lowered my skirt carefully, covering the wound and my underwear. His right hand lingered, hovering over my knee. It appeared he was about to stroke it, as if in reassurance. But he didn't, withdrawing his hand instead.

I took a long breath, putting myself together the best I could, completely on my own.

"We need to help Lucy cross," I said, getting up on my shaking legs.

IT TOOK US A WHILE to get Lucy to cross the stream.

At first, she refused to move at all. After some coaxing, though, she made the first tentative steps across the rocks. Reaching the spot where I'd slipped, she froze and wouldn't move again.

I talked her into taking a step. Then Greyx hopped onto the nearest rock and reached for her across the remaining distance, carefully guiding her to safety.

On our side, she collapsed to the floor, hugging herself. Soft humming came from her again, worrying me more than her screams would have. Why did she hum that song, over and over again? Why wouldn't she speak?

"You made it." I sat at her side and wrapped my arm around her shoulders. "We're together again. You did well, Lucy."

Her slim body shuddered, the humming getting louder. I wished she'd just cry or scream, to let it all out. But she just hummed and rocked back and forth, keeping it in.

"Here." I grabbed Greyx's bag and put it into her lap. The silly thing seemed to comfort her.

She hugged it, pressing her face into the soft material.

I stroked her back.

"It'll be okay, Lucy. We'll be okay. Greyx will get us out of here." I looked up at him for confirmation.

He nodded grimly.

"What's your plan, Greyx?" I kept my voice soft for Lucy's sake but slipped a harder note when I added under my breath, "And don't you dare tell me it's *classified*."

He glanced over his shoulder, scanning each end of the tunnel as if *yirzi* would be hiding there, listening. "The plan is to get to the meeting point for one of our ships to pick us up."

"What? Someone is coming for us?" This was the best news I'd heard in a while. Relief lifted the worry in my chest. We weren't forgotten or abandoned here. There was a way off this dying planet. "Thank you." I then turned to Lucy. "Did you hear that, Lucy? I told you we'll be fine."

She kept hugging the bag. But the rocking and the humming had thankfully stopped.

Greyx crouched in front of us.

"It's a long way to the meeting point still—there aren't many places where shuttles can land and most of them are watched closely by *yirzi*. The place where we're heading is about two days away. You'll need your strength."

Two days.

It was a long way away.

He shoved a piece of the black snake in Lucy's hands. "You need to eat."

She shook her head, wide-eyed with horror. I couldn't blame her. The thing was repulsive, ink-black blood dripping from its both ends.

"Sorry, Greyx. This is just..." I shuddered, my insides twisting at the thought of eating *that*. "Here, Lucy." I took a thick slice of *dohmat* from my pocket instead.

The fruit didn't agree with my stomach, but Lucy seemed to have no trouble eating it. She took it from me, then bit into it with a crunching sound. The toothpaste-like smell of the *dohmat* wafted through the air, making me nauseous. I shifted away from Lucy, trying to fight it.

I was sure Greyx was judging me. I felt his displeasure. He must be worried about having to schlep my malnourished ass on his back all the way to his ship when I ran out of energy to keep walking.

He was right, of course. We had to eat to keep moving.

Stifling a sigh, I took the remaining slice of *dohmat* from my pocket. This was the same one I'd tried to eat last night, but had to give up after just two bites. I took another bite of it and chewed slowly, trying to ignore the sickening, minty smell.

Then I made the mistake of glancing at Greyx.

His heavy stare firmly on me, he lifted the piece of the snake to his mouth. He was actually going to eat the creature that had burrowed a tunnel under my skin just a little while earlier.

My stomach spasmed.

Dropping the *dohmat*, I dashed up the tunnel and around the nearest bend before dry heaves sent me to my knees. My hands shook. My head ached as my stomach roiled again and again, trying to get rid of every trace of *dohmat* I'd ever had. There wasn't much. It was mostly empty already.

Soft hands brushed my hair away from my face, tacking it back into my messed-up bun.

"Lucy?" I glanced back over my shoulder, my hands propped on the floor, my arms shaking.

Concern spread across her lovely face.

"I'm okay." I drew in a shaky breath.

Greyx stood just a step or two behind her, his feet parted wide, his hands fisted at his sides. He looked like he'd rushed in, expecting to fight something or someone.

Instead, he'd found me...puking.

Mortification heated my face. Of all the people in the universe, Greyx was the last person I wanted to see me in this state.

Lucy handed me the bag with drinking water.

"Thank you," I rinsed my mouth, then took a long drink and heaved myself up, holding on to the wall.

"You're ill," Greyx stated. His expression remained murderous, like he was ready to punch someone, but had no enemy to fight.

"I'll be fine," I dismissed, smoothing down my skirt. "Just a little indigestion, that's all. The *dohmat* thing doesn't agree with me."

"Why didn't you tell me?"

"What for? It's not like there's any choice of food on this planet."

"You need to eat to have energy," he said in that grim, slightly robotic tone of voice that was beginning to grind on my nerves.

"Don't worry. I've lots of energy stored." I slapped my hip. "Right here, see? I'll be fine."

He snapped his stare to the place where my hand had connected with my hip. His eyes darkened, clear appreciation sparkling in his expression. I'd never had a man stare at my hips with so much hunger.

Did he really like what he saw?

The thought made me blush.

"Let's just keep going, shall we?" I mumbled, heading back to the tunnel.

Chapter 14

Tessa

After another day of hiking through the endless tunnels, we stopped for the night.

Greyx stretched his back. "The exit is close now. We'll wait until the morning to leave the caves."

Sitting down after hours of walking felt incredible. I stretched my legs in front of me. A fresh breeze caressed my skin—we must be really close to the exit here. As tired as I was of the endless tunnels, I felt apprehensive about leaving the cover they provided.

Lucy plopped next to me, arranging the bag in her lap.

Greyx wandered off without saying a word. Maybe he wanted to make sure the area was safe. Or maybe he simply needed a bathroom break?

Using the moment, I lifted my skirt to inspect my injured leg. It throbbed a little, but not too badly. The puncture wound on my ankle where the water snake had entered my leg was tiny. It was hard to believe the creature as thick as my thumb had squeezed through it.

The wound high on my inner thigh had the distinct shape of a bite mark, with Greyx's teeth clearly imprinted in my skin. A wiggly, purplish line of a bruise stretched between the two wounds.

Greyx had treated them both, and they seemed to be healing well. The pain didn't bother me much, not even after all the hiking today. The horror of the creature slithering inside me had faded away.

I circled the bite mark with my thumb. This was not how I would've imagined having Greyx's head between my legs with his teeth on my skin and his horns keeping my thighs open for him...

A warm, tingling sensation trickled through my chest and down to my lower belly. I recalled gripping his horns, their surface hard and rough in my hands.

I glanced in the direction where he'd left, wondering what was taking him so long. Before I had a chance to get worried, the stomping of his boots announced his return. I hurriedly yanked down my skirt.

He carried a flat slab of the quartz-like rock.

"What's that for?" I asked.

He put the slab on the floor by the wall, making sure it was leveled properly. "Cooking."

Taking the glowing stalactite we brought with us, he scraped some of its fluorescent slime onto the rock.

"What are you going to cook?" I cocked my head, intrigued by his ministrations. "And how?"

He raised a brow ridge, glancing at me.

"You'll see," he said mysteriously, with a hint of his former playfulness in his eyes. It was but a faint echo of his former self. Still, my heart leaped and fluttered, latching onto that tiny part of him I recognized.

The old Greyx was there somewhere. His lively, sunny personality hadn't been killed off completely. Deep inside this gruff stranger, the Greyx who'd charmed me on New Year's night was hiding. I hoped with all my heart I'd see more of him with time.

I stilled, watching him quietly.

He flicked the flame of the laser knife on, then thinly sliced one of the *dohmats* we had left.

I didn't believe anything could make those things tolerable. But I said nothing, curious what he was going to do with them.

Greyx adjusted something on the knife's handle until the thin flame turned from the cool blue to a hot red. He then placed it under the quartz-like plate.

Before long, the glowing slime turned into a clear liquid that siz-zled as the rock heated.

Greyx arranged the *dohmat* slices on top of the rock. The slices curled at the edges, reminding me of potato chips or miniature taco shells. A whiff of appetizing aroma reached my nostrils, making the hollow emptiness in my stomach more acute.

"Smells nice." I swallowed as my mouth watered.

Next, Greyx tossed a handful of what appeared to be tiny white mushrooms onto the slab. They melted in the heat, forming a thick creamy substance that coated the curled *dohmat* slices.

Greyx switched the knife off, then tipped his chin at the slab. "Try it."

I didn't need to be asked twice. The scent was pleasant, with a hint of roasted nuts and fried mushrooms. And it was the best thing I'd smelled since being taken.

Carefully, I lifted one hot slice with my fingers. It had soaked in some of the white mushroom liquid. Mindful that it was still the freaking *dohmat*, I took a small bite.

Cooking had turned the hard fruit mushy and starchy. It was definitely more pleasant to eat now. Each bite descended, soft and warm, into my stomach, lining it with comfort for the first time in days.

"Boy, is it ever good," I moaned, reaching for another slice.

Lucy shifted closer, taking one too. She stuffed the entire slice in her mouth, then turned to me...smiling.

She *smiled* as she chewed.

My throat tightened, at the same time my chest expanded. I grinned back. "You like it?"

She nodded.

I turned to Greyx, gratitude bursting from my heart. "Thank you."

What he'd done was more than provide us with our first warm meal in what felt like ages. Sitting by the little hearth he'd made felt like a family dinner, almost like a picnic or a camping trip—such a normal thing, when I'd feared I might never feel "normal" again.

For the first time since they took us from the shuttle, I felt free.

"You have no idea what it means to me, Greyx." I swallowed hard, overwhelmed by gratitude. "I could kiss you right now."

On impulse, I leaned over and placed a peck on his cheek. There simply didn't seem to be a better way to express the flood of emotions that rushed through me.

He shrank away as if I'd bitten him. A grimace of pain distorted his hard features when I pulled away. Suddenly, he leaped to his feet and stormed out without saying a word.

Confused, I stared after him. The warm, cozy feeling inside me dissolved, as if flushed away by a cold shower.

"Did I do something wrong?" I looked at Lucy. "Was the kiss too much?" It could hardly be called a kiss, just a quick press of my lips to his cheek.

Did it offend him somehow?

There once was a time when Greyx didn't mind kissing me. In fact, he'd left the impression he'd wanted to do more of that.

Now, a tiny peck on the cheek sent him running.

I dropped my gaze to the floor, feeling deflated.

We ate in silence. Every bite was still as satisfying as before, though I paid little attention to the food now. In my mind, I kept going over everything I'd done and every word I'd said, wondering what had set Greyx off.

Back on the shuttle, he'd been the one willing to talk things over, to clear any misunderstandings between us. He seemed to know what he wanted, and he went for it. Now, he clearly avoided me.

He'd spoken about being drugged. Could that have affected his personality?

When compared to the way he was in the cage, Greyx had made an improvement. I could only hope the drugs would work their way out of his system. And I wished he'd tell me if there was anything I could do to help him cope.

"He didn't sleep at all." It occurred to me. "Didn't eat anything, either."

I glanced at the rock-griddle he'd made. Lucy and I had left a few curled *dohmat* slices for him. They were slowly cooling off in his absence.

Where did he storm off to? Having some food and getting some rest might make him feel better.

Lucy made herself comfortable by the far wall, wrapping her arms tightly around the suede bag.

Just before I started seriously considering going to look for Greyx, he came back.

I gestured at the cold leftovers. "We left you some dinner."

"Thanks." Avoiding eye contact, he sat on the other side of the grill and swiftly polished off the remaining food. He didn't look like he was in the mood to talk. So I kept quiet, too.

"I'll take the first watch tonight," I said when he was done with his dinner.

He stared at me. "The first watch? You?"

"Yes. You can't always be the one to watch over us. You need to sleep, too."

"I'm fine." He jerked his head, swaying his horns.

I bit my lip, thinking about the best way to convince him.

"You see, it's in our interests—mine and Lucy's—to have you well-rested." He made a gesture with his hand, ready to protest, but I didn't let him. "People make mistakes when they're tired. You're our guide. The only one who can get us out of here. We can't afford to have you tired and making mistakes."

He narrowed his eyes at me.

I met his stare straight on and even batted my eyelashes innocently. "I insist."

"Fine." He yanked the gun from under his belt. "Here." He handed it to me. "Shoot anyone who comes through that tunnel."

I eyed the gun in my hand. "Anyone?"

"There're no friends on this planet, Tessa. Whoever finds us here could only be an enemy. Promise you'll shoot, or I wouldn't be able to close my eyes, let alone fall asleep."

I'd never shot a weapon before. But if it was a *yirzi* coming for me, I was confident I'd pull the trigger without hesitation.

I inspected the smooth white gun in my hands. "Do I press here?"

He gave me another look. "You've never seen a gun before?"

"Of course I have. In the movies. I've never shot one, though."

"All right." He moved closer. "Hold it like this." He adjusted the weapon in my hands. "Then press here." He pointed at a smooth level on the side of the handle. "Short, one-second blasts. Understood?"

"Sounds simple enough."

"It's never hard to kill," he muttered under his breath, heading to the corner where Lucy was sleeping. "It's *saving* a life that requires much more skill and character."

The image of him ripping Prug's head off flashed through my mind.

"Could Prug's life have been saved?" I blurted out.

He snapped his stare back to mine. "Only at the expense of yours."

Cold prickled the skin on my arms.

"It's true, then. He would've raped me to death if you'd let him." It wasn't a question.

He frowned, nodding silently, and I drew in a shaky breath. He stared at me for a long moment, studying my face.

"I have reasons to believe Prug was the one who led *yirzi* to your shuttle," he said suddenly.

"What? It was him?"

"I'll need more evidence of his involvement, but I'm confident I will find it once I'm back on Aldrai because I know where to look now."

"Wow..." I plopped on the floor where I stood.

I never liked the guy, but learning that he could be the one responsible for our troubles and his own death blew my mind.

"Prug wasn't there when I woke up. Neither was he in the cage with me at the beginning," Greyx continued. "I believe he worked for the people who run the facility. They used him to get to us, to me. Then, they betrayed him by imprisoning him, too."

"Do you think Prug was the one watching me through the window, then? While I was being examined?" Unpleasant feeling crawled up my arms like creepy little spiders at the thought of Prug seeing me on the table with my skirt up while the greens poked and prodded me.

"He very well could be." Greyx nodded. "Tessa." He crouched in front of me, holding my gaze with his. "I was...not entirely myself when I killed him, but I don't regret what I've done. I'd do it again under the same circumstances. If I hadn't..." He heaved a breath, shaking his head, as if trying to shake off the images of what would've happened had he let Prug live. I didn't want to imagine that, either. "Prug died a traitor," he said resolutely. "It'll be enough for his family to deal with. But I stopped their son from becoming a rapist, too. The dishonor of that would've been even more devastating."

That was one way to look at it.

"Will you be prosecuted for his death?" I asked.

"There will be an investigation. I'll tell the truth and present the evidence. The law is on my side."

I felt relieved. "Good. I wouldn't want you to go to jail for saving me."

He gave me one of his intense stares, not moving away.

"You should get some rest, Greyx," I reminded him.

He nodded, getting up. "Just for a couple of hours."

I shook my head. "You'll need more than that. A human being requires eight hours a night to feel rested."

He rolled his shoulders back, tilting his head. "But I'm not a human." A corner of his mouth twitched up.

Was it a smile?

I all but stopped breathing, afraid to spook it away, as if it were a rare, beautiful butterfly. I hadn't seen his smile since the shuttle. And God, did I miss it.

"*Six* hours, then?" I said, somewhat breathlessly.

He shook his head, the ghost of a smile playing on his firm lips. He clearly enjoyed the negotiation. It was like a game, which must appeal to the playful side of Greyx, the side that had been buried under so much pain and responsibility lately.

"Okay. Four. And this is my final offer." I moved my eyebrows into a stern expression. "You sleep for four hours while I watch. Then I'll wake you up for another four hours while I sleep. This way, we'll each get a decent amount of rest before another day of hiking."

"This woman," he murmured under his breath. "Always the voice of reason." There was a warm note in his voice.

He took out the navigation disk. "I'll set the alarm for you. Four hours." He punched in the disk something, making blobs and lines on it move.

Once he finished, I took the disk from him and slid it into the pocket of my dress. "Sweet dreams, sir."

He exhaled sharply, his lopsided half-smile got wider for a moment.

"Go to sleep, Greyx. The time is ticking." I patted the pocket with the disk in it.

He stretched his neck and shoulders before sinking to the floor. Now that he'd relaxed a little, he looked outright exhausted.

"Take this." I untied my cardigan from around my waist. The night chill had entered the caves, but I could use it to help me stay awake.

I rolled the cardigan, then placed it on the floor for him.

"Use it as a pillow," I explained. "It must be uncomfortable to lie on the floor with the horns."

He glanced at my sweater hesitantly but didn't argue. Lying on his side next to Lucy, he bent his arm, hugging my cardigan, then placed his head on it. He looked comfy like that, and I smiled.

His eyes remained open, focused on me.

I walked over to the exit from our little cave and out of his view. He needed to rest, to close his eyes and try to get some sleep, not to stare at me as if I were the most amazing thing in the Universe.

Moving as quietly as possible, I sat on the floor with my back to the wall and placed the gun in my lap. From this spot, I got a good view of both ends of the tunnel outside of the cave and of the two people sleeping just a few feet away from me.

A minute or two later, Greyx's breathing deepened, then a soft rumble of his snoring announced he'd fallen asleep.

That was good. I hadn't lied when I said we needed Greyx in his best shape. Everything depended on him. He was the only one who could lead us out of these tunnels and to the ship. I couldn't even read the navigation device without him—the blobs on the disk made no sense to me.

Taking my shoes off, I massaged my sore feet. They were red and swollen, rubbed raw by the edge of the shoe and the sand that had gotten in there.

With a small whimper, Lucy shifted in her sleep, turning Greyx's way. She threw her leg over his hip and pressed her face to his back.

Great. Now she was closer to him than I'd ever been. The thought came with a pinch of envy.

I got to my feet and padded barefoot around the cave for a while. When the sight of Lucy and Greyx cuddling in their sleep got too annoying, I left to explore the nearby tunnels, watching and listening for any sign of danger out there.

All seemed quiet. And after wandering the tunnels for some time, I went back to the cave.

Greyx sprawled over the floor in his sleep. Lucy snuggled into his side with her cheek on his arm. At least it kept them both warm, right?

Even asleep, Greyx exuded unstoppable power, like a dragon at rest. There truly was something of a rhino in Aldraians. Must be all those horns, the wide shoulders, and the thick, strong limbs. The hard, bumpy plates on their shoulders and forearms also fit the image. But mostly, it was in their physical strength and in the way Greyx tackled all obstacles, fiercely and head on.

I thought back to him fighting in the arena—his head tilted forward, forearms crossed in front of his face, the massive shoulders rolled out. His body was biologically designed as a perfect fighting machine—hard plates, horns, and spikes—meant to crush an enemy like a tank.

All of that was on the outside.

But I knew what it was like to be *inside* those arms, pressed to his chest. There were no hard plates or bumps, just warmth of his body and spice of his scent. When his arms were wrapped around me, it seemed nothing bad would ever get to me.

Longing threatened to take over.

Then, a sudden movement behind Lucy caught my attention.

The "bagpipe" behind her head undulated and squirmed. The clusters of curved sticks wiggled and the long "pipe" shifted from side to side.

What was that thing?

"Lucy," I called in a loud whisper, carefully inching closer. "Come here, please."

I touched her leg, needing to get her away from the squirming bag that had suddenly come to life.

She blinked her eyes open and gasped, finding herself practically wrapped around sleeping Greyx. Her eyes wide open, she scurried away from him and from the "bag."

Greyx came awake instantaneously. One moment he lay still as a log, the next he was up on his feet, his fists raised, ready to punch.

"What's going on?" He glanced around.

"It's moving!" I pointed at the "bag."

It gathered its short protrusions under itself and rose a few inches above the ground.

Greyx dropped his fists and crouched by the "bag."

"It's alive," I warned him, stating the obvious.

He nodded, carefully inspecting the soft sides of the chubby body.

The creature was the size of a medium dog, fat and round, like a short chubby sausage, with eight equally chubby legs. It had no neck and no shoulders; the round puffy head seemed to be just another bump on its shapeless body.

There were no eyes that I could see, either. If the creature had them, they must be hidden somewhere deep between the numerous rolls and folds of its face. The long, cone-shaped tube stuck out in the middle, in the approximate location of a nose for people and most animals.

Scurrying away from it, Lucy pressed to my side.

"Is it dangerous?" I asked Greyx.

He stroked the creature's back. "It could be."

The sound of an alarm pierced the air. It came from my pocket. I grabbed the disk but couldn't figure out how to shut it off.

The chubby bag-animal snorted nervously, trotting on its short legs in a circle on the same spot.

"Shh." Greyx kept stroking its back soothingly. With his other hand, he gestured to me for the device. I handed it to him, and he shut the noise off. "It's all good, little buddy," he cooed at the creature, with tenderness and patience. "It's all good."

"What is it?" I tilted my head, studying the curious thing.

It snorted a few more times, then settled down. Greyx's voice and caress seemed to calm it.

"It's a *brahlu*," Greyx explained. "One of the rarest animals. There're only a handful of them left in the Universe. They come from a dead planet."

"Like this one?"

"No. The *brahlus'* home world is long gone. A giant asteroid destroyed it. These animals don't breed well outside of their world. That's why there are so few of them left."

I eyed the creature with compassion. "What's one of them doing here?"

"It was stolen from a sanctuary on Aldrai."

"Why?" The thing appeared more comical than aggressive. It wouldn't accomplish much in the arena.

"When irritated or scared, *brahlus* emit energy waves that can cause serious damage to people and animals alike."

"What kind of damage?" I shifted away from the thing now.

"The waves can pop ear membranes, burst eyeballs, cause internal damage, too."

"Wow. Really?"

It was hard to imagine this chubby little puff ball that was now sniffing the cave floor with his long tubular nose was dangerous.

"When threatened, they also often just fall into a trance-like state," Greyx continued. "Like this one had been."

"So, if you scare him, he may kill you or he may just fall asleep?"

"Pretty much."

Now, I wished the creature would go back to sleep. Who knew what things it'd find irritating or threatening, and what it'd decide to do then?

It sniffed its way around, slowly heading Lucy's way. She squeaked when its nose touched her knee.

"*Brahlus* are cuddly, affectionate creatures," Greyx assured her.

Cuddly, unless they were startled, felt threatened, or irritated—then they might kill you. Great. I sucked in a breath, fighting the fear of the chubby "suede bag."

Lucy tentatively hovered her hand over the *brahlu's* head. As if sensing a pending pat, the animal jerked his head up, shoving it against her palm.

A smile quivered Lucy's lips. She lowered her hand, connecting with the short, suede-like fur of the creature.

Brahlu snorted, happily this time, and climbed into her lap.

"He likes you," Greyx said with a short laugh.

Lucy's smile stretched wider as she petted the chubby thing. Maybe even in his trance-like state, the *brahlu* had felt her hugging and cuddling him?

"Mittens," Lucy said softly.

I jerked my gaze to her. Did she just say something? Out loud?

She kept looking at the *brahlu*, petting him gently. The animal appeared to relax completely, all eight of his chubby legs spread around his blob of a body.

"We used to have a cat when I was little," Lucy continued quietly, not addressing anyone in particular. "His name was Mittens. He ate way too much and was almost as round as this little guy. Come here,

Mittens." She hugged the creature, scooting closer to the wall. Lying down, she curled her body around her newfound friend.

"Did she just call him mittens?" Greyx squinted at the two.

As far as I was concerned, Lucy could call him anything she wanted, as long as it made her speak again.

"She spoke," I said. "She hasn't spoken in days."

He glanced at me with understanding.

"Why did you take him?" I asked.

"When I saw a *brahlu* in the crate in the *yirzi* room, I couldn't leave him there. It'd be like leaving a weapon of mass destruction in their hands."

Right. Now, we had the "weapon." I just hoped it wouldn't turn against us.

"He's not going to harm her, is he?" I asked, staring at Lucy hugging her *Mittens*.

Greyx swung his head their way, watching the two for a minute. "They seem rather fond of each other."

It certainly looked that way.

"Well, maybe they'll keep each other from having meltdowns," I muttered under my breath.

While Lucy's meltdowns broke my heart, the *brahlu's* could cost us our lives.

"They'll be fine," Greyx decided.

Coming closer, he took the disk of the navigation device out of my hand.

"Your four hours are now ticking." He lifted the disk. "Your turn to sleep."

My body was sore, but I didn't feel sleepy. The excitement of watching the suede "bag" suddenly come to life had ruffled me too much to sleep. This might be my last chance to get some rest, though.

"I'll try." I lay on the floor next to Lucy and fitted the cardigan roll under my head. Still warm from Greyx's body heat, the sweater had retained some of his spicy scent, too. "It smells like you," I mumbled, nuzzling it.

With my eyes closed, I felt the vibrations of his footfalls and opened my eyes to find him gone.

I sat up, forgetting all about sleep.

Why did he run away again? Was it something I did? Or said?

I stared at the gray cardigan on the floor.

Reading Greyx used to be so easy, even when I barely knew him. But now...

I hated this planet for what it'd done to all of us.

Chapter 15

Greyx

She didn't need to kiss him or to undress in front of him. All she had to do was lie down to sleep, or look in his direction, or simply *exist* to make him all hot and needy, and running for the nearest side tunnel to prevent his cock from exploding in his pants.

Gods...

He leaned against the wall for support, his legs shaking. His fingers trembled, fumbling with the buckles of his pants. Sweat beaded on his forehead. Waves of sweltering heat alternated with bone-chilling cold, racking his body.

He could blame it on the *yirzi* drugs. But Tessa had always had this effect on him. It had just been a little easier to manage before. He used to be able to focus on other things, not just physical.

From the moment he'd laid eyes on her, her no-nonsense manner appealed to him. Tessa was straightforward, independent, and frank, which was refreshing. She didn't play games. She'd proven capable and protective of her friends.

At the same time, he saw a feminine vulnerability in her that she tried to hide. It made him want to wrap her in his arms and keep her safe, away from any harm.

She was the first woman who caught his interest in the past seven years, ever since most of his family perished. From that horrible day on, friends, parties, and yes, the occasional encounters with females, had been his way of dealing with the overwhelming loneliness.

Never before had he wanted to keep a woman for longer than a night, though. Of course, the fact that he admired Tessa as a person only made him want her more.

The dress she wore was the opposite of seductive. Dark and rather starchy in appearance, it reached to her knees, with short sleeves almost down to her elbows. The front was also cut high, with the first button of her neckline somewhere right below her collarbone.

Yet somehow the dress made Tessa even more desirable. He couldn't stop thinking about what that dull material was hiding underneath. He'd give his left testicle to see just a sliver more of her skin of that delicate shade between creamy beige and light brown.

When he bit her thigh, his mind had been on fire from the horror of potentially losing her. All he could think then was stopping the snake from reaching her vital organs.

Now, he wished to replay that scene without the fucking snake. Just Tessa and him. His head between her legs. His mouth on her inner thigh, so close to her sex...

A pained groan erupted from his chest as he whipped his erection out. It throbbed and was so impossibly hot, another degree hotter, and he'd probably burn himself.

Closing his eyes, he wrapped a shaking hand around his length, roaring from pain and need. Another groan reverberated through his chest, echoing with a shudder throughout his entire body.

"Greyx?" His name, said in a soft feminine voice, thundered like an explosion through his brain.

His eyes flew open in shock.

Tessa.

What was she doing here? She was supposed to be asleep.

She stared at him, wide-eyed. Her gaze flicked to his red, engorged appendage fisted in his hand.

"Oh!" she gasped softly, retreating a step. "I—I'm so sorry." She blinked, diverting her eyes.

Mortification doused his lust like a cold shower. He hated for Tessa to see him like this—shaking, sweating, and out of control.

He expected her to turn and run.

She looked like that was exactly what she wanted to do. Yet, she lingered, lifting her shoulders awkwardly and shifting her gaze between the tunnel walls and the floor.

Unsure what to say—what the fuck *could* he say here—he stuffed his straining cock back into his pants. Sharp pain made him suck in a breath through his teeth. His fingers shook too much for him to even attempt closing the buckles of his pants. He left them open.

"I—I heard a noise," Tessa said hesitantly. "It sounded like someone was in pain..." She let the end of the sentence hang between them. As an invitation for him to explain? To open up?

Could he really open up to her?

Not about *this*. Shame burned through him.

Yet she hadn't run, standing there, staring at him expectantly. Would she understand? Or would she be disgusted?

Did he have a choice, after what she'd already seen?

He drew in a breath and took the plunge.

"I *was* in pain," he rasped. "Still *am*." He fisted his hands at his sides. It did nothing to stop them from shaking.

"Your eyes..." She swallowed, then cleared her throat. "They're dark again. Even the irises are darker than normal. They do that when...when you're like this. Like back in the cage. Is it *yirzi*? Their drugs?"

"The drugs..." The words stuck in his dry throat. Every part of his body seemed to be burning dry.

"Right." She nodded, shuffling her feet in those useless shoes of hers. Slippery soles that had no grip to keep her on the rocks when crossing the river. "They drugged you to make you stronger."

"They pumped me full of mating drugs," he confessed.

"Mating drugs?" Confusion spread across her lovely face. Gods of *Yeseera*, she was so pretty with bright patches of blush over her paled skin.

He forced himself to remain where he was, his back pressed to the wall, his hands fisted at his sides.

"They forced me to mate with you," he snarled. "Whether you wanted it or not. Even if you fought me. Even if you pleaded with me—"

Now she would run.

But no, she stepped forward, jerking her chin up.

"Yet you didn't." Pale and trembling, she took another step toward him. "Even drugged out of your mind, you chose not to hurt me. You killed one of your own to keep me safe." Her voice was firm, determination etched hard in her delicate features. "They did their worst, but you're stronger, Greyx." She stopped right in front of him. "You won, but it cost you. Is there..." She hovered her hand at his chest, so close, he could feel the warmth of her palm, but she wouldn't touch him without his permission. "Is there anything I could do to help you?" she asked.

A growl vibrated in his throat.

Did she even realize what she was offering?

She had the power to end it all. If only...

Could he trust himself around her? He'd ripped Prug's head off without giving it a second thought. And he barely remembered it. What if he did something to her? What if he hurt her?

He couldn't risk it. He had to send her away.

She slid her hand between them, hovering it in front of his crotch. "Where does it hurt?"

A man could only take so much. There was an end to his endurance.

He snapped, shoving his hips forward. Grabbing her hand, he pressed it to his barely contained bulging cock through his pants.

"Fuck!" he growled, blinded by pain and pleasure.

She pressed her forehead to his chest. "Let me help you."

Her soft, slender hand slipped behind the open waistband of his pants. Her cool fingers connected with his heated flesh. He hissed in both agony and ecstasy.

Her fingers stilled. "Does it hurt?"

"Everything hurts," he said through clenched teeth. "But you're making it all better."

She placed a tender kiss on his chest, then sunk to her knees.

Oh, all the great gods and the deities below them! She tugged his pants down, freeing his cock completely.

"Wow," she exhaled. "This is...something."

He was afraid to look at her, scared of what he would find on her face. Disgust? Pity?

"What are these?" She gently pressed on one of the raised bumps on his cock. Just a tad softer than the rest of his shaft, the round nodes were porous. When she touched one, it secreted a clear, oily substance meant to ease the slide into a female's passage. Aldraian females produced no lubrication on their own.

Was that how it worked between humans, too?

He knew nothing about their mating habits. Now, he wished he'd listened to Prug when the male had bragged about having sex with Tessa's friend. He'd cut Prug off then. But he could use some of that information now.

"Does it hurt?" Compassion warmed her voice, the sound like a balm against his pain. "Would you rather I didn't touch these?"

"No." He shook his head adamantly. "Nothing hurts when you touch it."

She trailed her fingers along his length, sending a shiver of pleasure up his body.

"More," he begged.

She tentatively wrapped her fingers around his girth.

He gripped the rock wall behind him, struggling to stay upright and ready to fall at her feet. Sticking her little pink tongue out, she dragged it around his swollen tip. Warm, slick, and so tender, her tongue was the one single thing that could bring him to his knees.

But he needed more.

Lust rushed through him in a torrent of heat. His mind blanked. Grabbing Tessa by her upper arms, he yanked her to her feet.

She yelped in surprise. He swung her around, pressing her back to the wall.

"More." He wrapped her hand around his cock tighter. "Much more."

He pumped his hips into her hand. The oil from his nodules made her palm slide easily, no matter how tight he pressed. Pain warred with pleasure, but he knew which one would win when Tessa was with him.

Her lips parted. She breathed heavily, her eyes full of shock and...want? Did she want this? Did she fucking want *him?*

The thought spurred his arousal to astronomical heights. He fisted his other hand into the messy bun on the back of her head and claimed her mouth in a kiss.

Heat exploded through his chest—pure, undiluted hunger. Pain receded. Only intense desire remained.

Devouring her mouth, he thrust into her hand, trapping her between the wall and his body. She wasn't going anywhere. He wouldn't let her. From the moment he saw her, she was his.

He roared, the sound rolling through the tunnels like a rockslide.

His cock spasmed. Release pumped through him in hot, blinding bursts. And with every shudder of pleasure, the achy pressure let go. Madness ebbed. His senses returned.

He could feel the softness of her body pressed to his. The sweet taste of her lips. The scent of a woman, warm and...

Aroused?

Gods help him.

He let go of her hand around his cock and of her hair. Hand over hand, he hiked up her skirt.

Startled, she tensed when he slid a finger into her undergarment.

"Hush, sweetheart," he murmured against her lips. "Don't be afraid. You can stop me any time now. One word from you, and I'll stop."

She'd helped him bring his lust under control. Now, he wished to do something about her desire.

"Stop me," he challenged, but she only kissed him harder in reply.

He grinned against her mouth. Taking her kiss as an invitation, he let his fingers explore.

She was almost as hot down there as he had been. He was shocked to discover her slick and wet between her legs.

Were human women self-lubricating?

His heart thundered at that discovery—something new. And exciting. So exciting, in fact, that a charge of tingling heat rushed to his cock again.

It wasn't about him this time, though.

He kept exploring her—sliding his fingers between her silky, slick folds; letting his digits dance around her opening; skimming a hard, swollen bud at the very top.

And as he explored, he took note of her gasps, her soft moans, the tightening of her muscles. Through his body pressed to hers from the hip to the chest, he studied her shivers, trembles, and spasms—all in response to what his fingers did to her between her thighs.

"Greyx...I..." She bent her leg, hooking it around his hip. Her arms twined around his neck, just missing the horns on his shoulders.

He leaned back to see her face.

Her lips parted, swollen and red like the ripest berries from his kisses. Her long eyelashes shaded her clear, gray eyes. Her breathing grew shallow, ragged, just like his own. She pumped her hips, riding his hand. And it was the most beautiful thing he'd ever seen.

She exhaled sharply and dropped her head to his chest. Her hips jerked, her slick core pressing into his fingers.

"Oh, God…" She gripped his neck.

He made her gasp again and again, until her trembling body slacked against his.

Reluctantly, he removed his hand, and she dropped her leg from around his middle. He refused to let go, though, holding her in his arms.

She released a shaky breath, making no move to pull away from him, either.

The throbbing returned between his legs, but he ignored it, not wishing to break this moment. How wonderfully the things had worked out between them. How well she responded to him.

He knew she was made for him. He had always known.

"So good," she breathed out.

"I told you I'd give you a night to remember," he murmured above her ear, grinning smugly. "This is just a taste."

She threw her head back, catching his gaze. Her eyes shone like precious gems in the darkness of the tunnel.

"Greyx." A smile slowly spread across her face. "There you are." She traced his bottom lip with her thumb. "You're back."

"Back?" He raised his eyebrow ridges, confused.

"You haven't been yourself lately," she explained. Her light fingers skimmed his jaw, dancing along his cheekbones and up his side horn. "I've missed this smile. And this bright, sunny orange in your eyes."

He blinked. Ever since the *yirzi* had started tinkering with his system by injecting him with who-knew-what, he really hadn't felt himself. His focus had narrowed to two basic instincts—breed and fight. Fight the need to breed. Fight for a chance to escape.

Thankfully, the drugs must be wearing off, allowing his mind and his emotions to return. He could hold Tessa in his arms again, without the feral desire to ravage her...

No, not true. The desire to ravage her simmered hot just under his skin. All he had to do was unleash it.

Right at that very moment, though, he wished for nothing more than to hold her—something he'd feared he might not get to do for a long while yet.

He nuzzled her hair. "You didn't get any sleep, did you?"

"I was going to, but your growling and howling wouldn't let me," she retorted, not skipping a beat.

He chuckled, loving how quick she was with a comeback.

"I promise not to *howl* anymore."

She cupped his face. "Are you feeling better now?" Compassion floated, light and warm, in her eyes. "No more pain?"

"What if I said it still hurts?" he teased. "Would you lick it again?"

"Greyx," she reprimanded, tilting her head. "I'm serious."

She frowned, but her lips quivered in a smile, betraying her.

"Nothing hurts, my sweet girl." He kissed her again, then murmured against her lips, "You made it better. You make everything so much better."

Tessa

HE TOOK ME BACK TO the small cave where Lucy was sleeping.

"To bed with you, now." His expression might be stern, but affection clearly softened his voice. "I'll lie down with you until you fall asleep to make sure you don't wander off again."

His chest to my back, he curled his large body around me. He placed one arm under my head, hugging me with the other. I noticed he angled his lower body away from me, keeping a distance between his pelvis and my butt.

Mating drugs.

Was that all there was in his wild desire earlier?

I thought back to our dancing at the New Year's party, his orange eyes setting my body on fire with need. Back to the way he'd looked at me in the elevator, his passion warring with his respect for my wishes.

Greyx was a true gentleman. He'd let me go when I insisted. But I believed he always wanted me, even before all the drugs.

I pressed my nose to his arm and took his other hand in mine. Here, on this planet from hell, I'd found a piece of paradise. It happened to be right next to Greyx.

Chapter 16

Tessa

"I'll go first," Greyx instructed, standing at the exit from the cave system. "Once I reach the trees, wait for my signal. You remember what it is?"

Lucy nodded. But he stared at me expectantly, obviously waiting for me to repeat it out loud.

"One finger, I go. Two fingers, we both go," I said quickly.

We'd been sitting here all morning, after another breakfast of fried *dohmat* with the yellow sauce made from the fungus Greyx had collected inside the cracks between the rocks in the tunnel.

Greyx had been watching the sky for any sign of drones all this time. I'd watched, too, wary of any movement or sound. Though without my glasses, I couldn't see too far.

There had been no signs of life. Zoltu was mostly dead already.

Despite the stillness of our environment, Greyx insisted we remain cautious.

Keeping low to the ground, he ran to a small patch of short skinny trees about thirty feet from the exit from the cave. He slowly turned around, scanning the sky for drones and the sand dunes for any sign of *yirzi*.

Once satisfied there weren't any, he lifted two fingers in the air.

I adjusted the *brahlu* under my arm. Even awake, the creature probably wouldn't keep up with us on his short chubby legs and had to be carried this part of the way. He was rather heavy, too. I took Lucy's hand.

Together, we dashed across the sand to Greyx. Standing close to each other, we all tilted our heads back, searching for any threat from above.

All remained quiet.

"Do you think they've stopped looking for us?" I asked.

Greyx shrugged his hard-plated shoulders.

"That'd be stupid. Whoever is behind their filthy little operation knows I will put an end to it when I get back to Aldrai. I expect them to do everything in their power to try and stop me from ever making it back home. They're searching. They just haven't found us yet."

Yet.

The word made me shiver with dread. Greyx was brutally honest. I sighed, squinting into the sky.

There was nothing. Not even a bird or an insect. Just the bloated, red sun hanging over us, painting the world the color of blood.

I remained vigilant as we abandoned our cover behind the scrawny trees and headed up a sand dune, away from the caves.

I set the *brahlu* down, and he managed to keep up with us. I caught up with Greyx then walked side by side with him.

"We should reach a river sometime in the afternoon," Greyx said as we trudged ahead. "Then we'll be moving along the stream all the way to the mountains. The meeting point is on the other side of the first mountain ridge. The shuttle will be waiting for us tomorrow."

Was it really happening?

Could we all get off this planet, and soon?

It was hard to believe when all that surrounded us was the pristine white sand glowing blood-red under the oppressive sun.

Greyx appeared serious this morning. Focused. But when I caught him glance my way, affection shone in his eyes, warming my heart.

My thoughts shifted forward into the future. What would happen once we'd been rescued? Our return trip to Earth was coming soon. I'd have to leave this part of the Galaxy. And Greyx would stay...

The thought pressed heavily on my shoulders. My feet slowed down as if on their own, allowing Greyx to get ahead.

I stared at him, trying to imagine what it'd be like to say goodbye and...couldn't. Sadness shrouded me, dark and heavy. I could barely breathe in the suffocating heat of the sun-scorched sand.

Realizing I was no longer next to him, he whipped around, searching for me.

"Am I going too fast?" His eyes focused on my face. "Is everything okay, Tessa?"

I blinked rapidly, thwarting the impending tears. "Sure." I nodded.

He didn't appear to buy it, watching me carefully.

"Are you tired?" he asked. "Hungry?"

I managed a wavering smile.

"I'm fine." I caught up with him and took his hand in mine. Large, warm, and rough like a sun-heated boulder, the touch of his skin grounded me, keeping my head from spinning in the storm of my worries.

"You look...sad," he said softly, his expression troubled.

I scrambled for a distraction from my troubling thoughts, lest they poison his mind too.

"Oh, I am sad." I slipped a teasing note into my voice. "You know what I've just realized?"

"What?"

I wiggled my eyebrows. "That I still haven't seen your tail."

His eyes widened. His cheeks grew darker and warmer in color. I loved making him blush. Except that it made me want to kiss him, too, to feel the heat that came with that color.

He was quick to combat his unease, giving me a lopsided grin.

"You're right to be sad, sweetheart," he murmured seductively. "My tail is a sight to behold."

HIKING IN THE OPEN proved much harder than in the shelter of the tunnels. As warm as it'd been in the caves, the rock had shielded us from the sun. Being trapped between the hot sand and the red monstrosity in the sky felt like being cooked alive.

Hot winds blew across the dunes. They appeared to change their directions with every blast, attacking exposed skin with the sharp stings of tiny grains of sand from every direction. The erratic blasts of hot air brought no relief. There was nothing refreshing in this wind.

I had my sweater tied around my waist and had all the buttons of my dress open. In this heat, the dark, polyester-blend material of my dress felt like metal armor, stifling and unbreathable. The only reason I kept my sweater with me was that this ordeal wasn't over yet, and ditching any supplies or resources didn't seem wise, no matter how useless they might appear at the moment.

We stopped briefly for a drink of water and a quick meal of sliced *dohmat*. Without the luxury of time or the caves to collect the fungus to fry the nasty fruit, Greyx simply switched his blade's ray from blue to red again and slowly cut a thin slice off *dohmat*, searing the pale flesh. It wasn't the same as frying it, but my stomach accepted it as food.

Chewing on another slice, I kept scanning the sky for the drones. I noticed Greyx doing the same. The feeling of hidden danger was hanging over us like the red haze from the sun—almost palpable.

"Not long, now," he assured me when we started on our way again. "We should see the river soon."

The heat grew heavier, muddier somehow. It clung to my skin, making it clammy. In a few minutes, the water glinted on the horizon. It looked bloody in the setting sun.

"The river should make the trek easier," Greyx exhaled. His skin flushed on his face, neck, and chest. Perspiration beaded on his temples, his breathing rugged. Hiking in this climate had taken its toll on him, too.

Lucy dragged her feet in the sand, her blonde curls plastered all around her face, wet with sweat.

The *brahlu* was the only one who seemed completely unaffected by either heat or exhaustion. His pace—though not overly fast to begin with—never slowed down. He trotted steadily next to Lucy.

Humidity grew thicker around the river. A few gangly trees with wiry branches and skinny pale leaves grew along the riverbank, but there was no grass, algae, or bugs that usually accompanied a body of water back on Earth.

Lucy dropped to her knees, stretching her hands to the cloudy liquid. I stopped her by pressing down on her shoulder.

"Are there any dangerous things in there?" I asked Greyx, cautiously surveying the water's edge.

"No. There's hardly any life left on Zoltu," Greyx kicked his boots off, rolled his pants up and walked knee deep into the river.

Bending over the stream, he splashed some water on his chest and neck, then cupped his hands, scooped some water, and drank.

After a day of trudging up and down the dunes, it felt like I had sand covering me everywhere. It grated between my teeth, mixed with sweat between my breasts, and even chafed inside my underwear. I wished for nothing more but to join Greyx in the river and wash at least some of it off.

But I remembered the bluish line running down my leg, where the water snake had burrowed itself under my skin. The memory sent a shudder down my back.

"How about the water snakes?" I asked, staying on shore.

I removed my hand from Lucy's shoulder, but with the mention of the snakes, she stayed away from the water, too.

Greyx shook his head.

"The snakes can't live in sunlight. Surface rivers are too hot for them. They're only found in cool underground streams." He splashed his hand in the water at his knees, as if to demonstrate that it was safe. "Come, have a drink, wash off a bit, then we'll have to be on our way again."

Satisfied with his assurances, I toed off my shoes and waded into the river. The water felt cool after the heat, soothing the pain in my sore feet. I bunched my skirt in my hands, lifting it higher to keep it dry, then walked over to where Greyx stood.

By twisting and tucking my skirt to keep it dry, I freed my hands from holding it. I washed the sand off my face, then splashed the water on my neck.

"Oh, it's so good," I moaned, washing my arms and as much of my chest as I could reach through the neckline with the buttons open.

Lucy splashed in the river beside me. She hadn't bothered to roll her jeans up, just had taken off her shoes before getting in.

The *brahlu* stayed on the dry land, only dipping his tubular nose in the water to drink.

I wished I could take off my clothes completely and wash off the grime of the days in captivity. But lingering in the same spot for too long made me nervous. Greyx was right, we had to keep moving.

Instead, I just slid my dress off my shoulders and splashed some more water on my neck and chest. "How long until we get to the mountains?"

The faint outline of the ridge glowed in the red haze of the sunset on the horizon.

Greyx stared at me, his eyes following my hands as I tried to wash the sand out of my bra.

"A few more hours?" I prompted when he didn't reply.

His throat bobbed with a swallow. He licked his lips.

"Um..." He blinked, glancing aside and scratching the horn above his ear. "Yes, a few more hours."

Getting out of the water, I dried my feet with the hem of my dress and put my shoes back on. My feet had swollen in the heat after so much walking. And no matter how many times I shook the sand out of my shoes, it found its way back in.

A few more hours.

Having the end in sight was the only thing that kept me going once we started hiking up yet another sand dune.

I pulled a foot out of the fine, glistening sand just to plunge it right back in, a step further. Then I did the same with the other foot. Step by step.

"Tell me about Aldrai," I asked Greyx, in an attempt to distract my mind from the misery my body was going through. "Please tell me it's nothing like Zoltu."

He scoffed, swaying the crown of his horns with a shake of his head.

"Gods, no. Not in the populated areas. Not anymore. We've spent generations terra-forming our deserts. The process is still ongoing. But where I come from, the vegetation is lush, green, and abundant. It takes an effort to control it in living areas."

"So, no sand?"

He dragged his foot out of the dune, the sand streaming off his boot like fine, dry sugar.

"Not like this, no."

I managed a smile. "Lucky you."

"The suburbs of Arqa, our capital city, are beautiful. We have flowers of every color of the rainbow. Some grow as big as half of the *yirzi* arena."

"What? Really?" I almost forgot all about the heat and the sand, trying to envision a miracle like that—giant flowers.

He nodded. "You can sleep in one. People do. There're hotels that rent flowers instead of rooms."

Now, I wished for a holiday on Aldrai, if only to find out what it was like to sleep in a flower. Cutting my eyes to Greyx, I wished he'd come on such a holiday with me. Sleeping anywhere would be so much more pleasant if Greyx were with me.

"Some birds are even more colorful than flowers," he continued. "I've seen valleys where the ground appears to rise into the sky when the birds and large, brightly colored insects fly into the air from below. Then, the entire valley looks like one large garden, up and down and all around you."

His voice drifted through the hot air, painting the most wonderful pictures in my mind. It was impossible to believe something so beautiful could really exist.

"It sounds like a fairy tale, Greyx."

"It's my home," he said with a wistfulness that could mean he simply missed it, but it appeared to be more than that.

"Do you have someone to...share your home with?" I prodded carefully.

He'd been open with me about many things, even his "classified" assignment. His family was the only thing he'd been quiet about. He'd shut down when I'd bought it up before, but I sensed it had nothing to do with me. It felt like he simply didn't know how to talk about it with anyone. Like he hadn't spoken on this topic at all.

"No. I live alone." He shrugged his shoulders, as if trying to shake off the uncomfortable subject. "But I hardly spend any time at home. I rent an apartment in the city."

"What? Why?" After all the beauty he'd described?

He rubbed the back of his neck, avoiding my eyes.

"Work, travel, missions..." he replied evasively. "It's easier that way."

Chapter 17

Tessa

The sun had almost entirely hidden its bloated mass behind the horizon when we finally reached the mountains. There were no rolling hills before that, no gradual increase in ground elevation. The pinkish quartz-like ridges and peaks just stuck out from the sand dunes like humongous rock candy.

The river cut right into the rock. Its stream had carved a cave, with a few feet of dry space along the bank for us to enter.

"So," I said cautiously, staying as far from the water as possible. "Since we're underground again, there might be snakes?"

Greyx was busy with his navigation device, scrolling through it in circles.

"Right," he replied, somewhat distractedly. Lifting his eyes from the device, he saw the horror on my face and shook his head quickly. "Farther down the stream, most likely. It's too close to the outside for them to be here, Tessa."

His words comforted me a little. I was not going anywhere near the water, though. No matter how much sand had packed into my clothes on the way here.

Greyx put the device away.

"We won't go deep into the cave. We just need to find a safe place for the night. First thing tomorrow morning, we'll have to cross the mountain to meet the shuttle on the other side."

About a hundred feet farther, the cave around the river widened. Several smaller tunnels ran from its banks on either side. This must be where the river cut into another one of Zoltu's cave systems.

"Here." Greyx turned into the second tunnel on our left and switched his device on to illuminate our way.

After a few minutes of walking, a faint glow came from the ceiling. The cave here was streaked with fluorescent green and blue. The tunnel widened a little, cutting to the right.

"Stay here," Greyx ordered Lucy and me.

Leaving us in the small cave, he disappeared in the tunnel to the right.

Lucy immediately sat on the ground by the far wall. Rolling her white sweater into a bundle, she stuffed it under her head, laying down on her side. The *brahlu* promptly trotted to her. She wrapped her arm around him, and he pressed his nose to her shoulder.

"Don't make yourself too comfortable," I warned. "We may have to walk more when Greyx comes back."

She nodded but didn't get up. Stroking *brahlu's* meaty side, she started singing again. The same damn song, "Over the Rainbow." I bit my lip, hating the sound of it. The song had become a reminder of the damage Lucy had suffered, and I feared for her mental state.

Then I realized she wasn't simply humming it. She sang it, with proper lyrics.

I turned to face her, and she met my gaze with a smile. She wasn't rocking or covering her ears. For once, she looked peaceful. Stroking the *brahlu*, she sang the lullaby to him.

Maybe we would all be okay, after all?

One day.

I breathed a little easier, wondering if I should sit and rest as well. My feet ached inside my shoes. I couldn't wait to take them off. But I feared if I did it now, I wouldn't be able to put them back on again if Greyx wanted us to keep walking.

Heavy footfalls sounded in the distance. Alarm cut through me—the sound came from the direction where we'd just come from, from the river, not from where Greyx had left.

"Shhh." I signaled Lucy to stop singing, hating how her eyes widened with fear again.

I had nothing on me that could be used as a weapon. Taking one of my shoes off after all, I flattened myself against the wall.

With the shoe in my right hand, I inched a little closer toward the footfalls and away from Lucy.

A tall, wide figure appeared from the shadows.

I lunged at it, my shoe raised in my hand.

"Tessa?" Greyx grabbed my wrist, thwarting my attack. With a glance at my face, then at the shoe in my hand, his eyebrow ridges shifted into a frown. "I should've left you the gun. I didn't think I'd be gone for long."

"You weren't." I released a breath in relief. "You weren't gone long at all. I just didn't expect you to come from this direction..."

My voice trailed off as my attention shifted to where his thumb started stroking the inside of my wrist. His eyes glistened in the darkness.

He cleared his throat, not letting go of my arm.

"There is a hot spring that way." He tipped his chin toward the tunnel behind me. "The path to it circles back to the river. We won't be cornered if they come here. We'll stay here for the night."

I nodded, waiting for him to release me and wishing he never would.

"Are there any snakes in the hot spring?" There was no usual pang of fear or revulsion when mentioning the snakes. My attention remained on Greyx who took a step closer.

"The water is too warm for the snakes." Letting go of my wrist, he slid his hand up my arm. "Perfect...to have a bath."

He leaned over me, his grip tightening on my upper arm. With a sharp breath, he suddenly released me, stepping back.

"That is if you want a bath," he said, taking another step back.

Would he join me?

I didn't have the courage to ask.

"I brought some water." He lifted the full bag in his hand. "It'd be just *dohmat* for dinner tonight."

Couldn't there be *anything* else on this planet?

AFTER EATING A FEW slices of *dohmat* scorched by Greyx's knife, Lucy and I left the cave for a quick bathroom break. Greyx waited just around the corner for us, watching out for any danger. The sun had fully set, but the heat remained, maintained by the sand heated during the day. I was glad to return to the caves right after. The air here was more humid but a bit cooler.

"Lucy," I said when all of us returned to the small cave for the night. "Greyx says there is a hot spring here. Do you want to wash up before going to sleep?"

She yawned, her eyelids drooping.

"No." She made herself comfortable on the floor again. The *brahlu* snorted happily, snuggling against her. "Maybe tomorrow."

I nodded, glad to hear an actual reply from her—a whole three words.

"Okay. Would you mind if I left you with Greyx for a little while, then? I really need a bath."

"You both go." She waved me off, closing her eyes. "I'll be fine."

From being terrified of simply breathing, she'd gone to being almost too careless in a span of a few hours.

"Someone should stay with you," I insisted, even as Greyx had already leaped to his feet, ready to show me the way. "You can't be alone."

"I'm not alone," she murmured through another yawn, without opening her eyes. "Mittens is with me." She cuddled the *brahlu* to her, her expression peaceful. "Mittens will kill anyone who'd want to hurt me. Greyx said so…"

My jaw slacked, I moved my stare to Greyx.

He cocked a brow ridge. "See? *Mittens* is going to watch over her."

"Can he, really?" I lowered my voice as Lucy's breathing slowed. She appeared to be asleep already.

He stared at the puffy, shapeless body of the animal in Lucy's arms.

"Well, he will be able to hear anyone approaching from much farther away than you or me. If he raises the alarm, we'll have time to come back and get them. The hot spring isn't that far away."

"All right," I conceded, leaving Lucy to sleep by the wall of the cave. "Let's make it quick, then."

I didn't bother putting my shoe back on, limping after Greyx without it.

The ceiling glowed brighter the further we walked.

"Here it is," Greyx said, circling around a large pile of rocks.

My jaw dropped at the sight in front of me. The tunnel had hollowed into a grotto. Blue, dark-pink, and violet stalactites hang from the ceiling, illuminating the semi-translucent rock walls.

The opaque water streamed down a wall, shimmering in the glow from the ceiling. The perfectly round pool glowed and shimmered, too. Milky water bubbled along its edge, with iridescent ripples spreading along the surface in concentric rings.

"Wow!" I paused, taking in the gorgeous sight. "This is so beautiful. Like…like a dream."

"I agree." His voice sounded directly behind me. "This is probably the most beautiful place on this entire planet."

I heard the rustle of clothes and turned to find Greyx…naked save for the wraps on his forearms. He stepped out of his boots, a smirk on his face.

Sliding my gaze down, which couldn't be helped, I took in his thick, muscled thighs, the hard-plated shins, and that magnificent bumpy dick of his. I could only guess how it'd feel inside a woman—and the guess was glorious.

His marvelous member was up. All the way. Pointing straight at its master's chin. Darkness already swirled in Greyx's eyes, despite the playful smile on his lips.

The sight of him—naked, expectant, gorgeous—took my breath away. It was so incredibly overwhelming, it hurt my chest. I heaved a breath.

"W-well..." I stammered, waving my hand toward the water. "You go ahead, then. I'll be right there."

With a wicked smile, he turned around.

And I saw it. His tail.

Its wider base fit snuggly against his backside. The rest of it stretched and curled as he sauntered to the water.

His tail wasn't that long, maybe about a foot-and-a-half—the tip didn't reach his knee. It was slimmer than his other appendage in the front and seemed exceptionally flexible.

Slimmer and longer.

Suddenly, I found myself wondering what places it could fit in and how far it could reach. A charge of desire shot through my chest, then pooled in my lower belly with liquid heat.

Did I just get turned on by seeing...a tail?

I turned away, hiding my blushing face.

A splashing of water let me know Greyx went in.

"Are you coming, Tessa?"

I turned around to find him standing waist deep in the water, his burly arms folded across his wide chest.

Only now I realized that by sending him in first, I'd given him the opportunity to watch me undress.

"Would you...um," I twirled my hand in the air. "Could you turn around, please?"

He lifted an eyebrow ridge, tilting his head a bit, but turned around as I'd asked.

I swallowed, taking a minute.

I desperately needed a bath. Greyx had tagged along with me here, and I didn't really mind. I wanted him with me. He'd touched me already. Heck, I'd held that very dick of his in my hand.

Yet he hadn't seen me naked. And...well, frankly, I wasn't ready to flaunt my stuff in front of him like this, in the multicolored lights of this fairy tale grotto. I wasn't a freaking fairy princess, after all.

Making sure he wasn't peeking over his shoulder or anything. I unbuckled the fabric belt of my dress then pulled the scratchy garment off over my head.

It felt good to be rid of the stuffy dress. The warm air of the cave brushed pleasantly against my bare skin. Glancing furtively Greyx's way, I shimmied out of my underwear, kicked off my one remaining shoe, and removed my bra.

My arms over my breasts, I padded to the water's edge.

The pool was even warmer than the air. Yet the water felt refreshing when I stepped into it. Soft ripples sloshed lazily around my legs as I waded deeper.

The sores on my feet stung, and I gasped through my teeth.

Greyx was by my side at once. "Are you hurt? Is anything in the water?"

He grabbed me, lifting me out of the pool.

"I'm good," I protested, grasping the horns on his shoulders for balance. "It's nothing, really. My feet are just sore from all the hiking."

"Sore?" He glanced at my feet dangling to his left as he held me in a cradle hold in his arms.

"It's nothing," I insisted.

He sat me on the rocky edge of the pool. I crossed my arms over my breasts and my legs in front of me.

Grabbing my right ankle, he inspected my foot.

"See?" I said. "Nothing to freak out about. The skin isn't even broken anywhere."

He placed my foot on top of his palm. His hand was bigger.

"Are these red lines normal?" He traced with a finger the spot where the back of the shoe had rubbed the most. "How about the spots here?" He pressed on the side in the front where the sand had been especially challenging to get out of the shoe.

"Just some chafing. From the sand, and stuff." I mumbled. "It'll be better by tomorrow."

He gently rubbed the sole, massaging my foot, pressing on every single toe from its base to the very tip. Tension was draining from each tiny muscle in my foot, taking the pain with it.

I swallowed a moan, afraid it'd sound like I was coming already. It felt so good. At that moment, I would gladly forgo an orgasm for this—his hands kneading my sore, achy foot back to life.

"It amazes me how strong you are, Tessa," Greyx murmured. "So resilient for a civilian."

Strong? Resilient?

Was he making fun of me?

"You're literally tending to my injuries, Greyx. What's so resilient about wrecking one's feet during a hike?"

"You're not a warrior," he retorted, unfazed. "You haven't been trained for this. Yet here you are, bearing it all without a word of complaint. You're doing great, Tessa."

"Great? I've been barely keeping up with you. Look at all the fuss it took just to feed me. Even Lucy seems to be faring better than me. You guys would've been better off without me, really."

He lifted his eyes to mine, his smile shifting into a hard line.

"If Lucy has done better, it's only because you've made it easier for her."

"Me?" I blinked.

"Lucy could afford to lose herself in her head completely because you took all the worry, stress, and planning for both of you."

I opened my mouth to protest. Greyx was the one who stressed and planned for all three of us—four if I counted the *brahlu*. All I'd done was follow him.

He wouldn't let me say it, though.

"You care about those you love, Tessa, and you shift their burdens upon your shoulders. If it wasn't for you, Lucy wouldn't be here. She only survived the arena because of you. *You* made sure she escaped that place. I didn't even know Lucy was there, and I sure as fuck couldn't worry about anything but my throbbing cock and my itching fists back then. I still wonder how I managed to escape at all, to be honest. The memories of that day are nothing but a blur."

I refused to minimize what he'd done for us. "You got us all out," I argued.

He brushed it off with a shrug. "You even carried the fucking *Mittens* for Lucy." He smiled again. "Lucy is a sweet person. The one thing that really worked for her for the past couple of days is that she's wearing the right shoes."

He gently placed my foot on the stone edge of the pool, and I turned aside to keep my legs closed.

Massaging my other foot, he kept talking. "You're an amazing woman, Tessa. Strong, fiercely loyal, and breathtakingly beautiful." The last two words came out with a soft groan from him, as if he lost his breath for a moment. He masked it with a smile. "A pair of right shoes, sweetheart, and there'd be no stopping you."

Curling my shoulders in, I just sat there, unsure of what to say in reply. I had no words. No one had ever looked at me with this much adoration before.

He surely was mistaken. I simply couldn't be all those things.

Nevertheless, pleasure glowed warmly inside my chest at his praise. I might not be what Greyx thought I was, but I wanted to be that person. More than anything, I wished to be worthy of that warm affection and reverence in his eyes.

"I didn't need to drag you all the way across the desert of Zoltu to figure out what kind of a person you are, Tessa, or how I feel about you." He put my other foot next to the first one on the edge of the pool and stepped closer. "I knew all I needed to know about you back at the party."

"What do you mean?"

"I learned you weren't afraid of taking chances and trying new things even if those things were a silly dance with a strong prospect of public humiliation. I saw you were protective of your friends. And by the time I kissed you..." His gaze caressed my face, sliding to my lips. "I wanted you more than I'd ever wanted any woman."

That kiss...

I wanted more of that, too.

He stood right in front of me, his mouth a little lower than mine because I sat on the edge of the pool while he stood in the water. All I had to do to kiss him was to lean down a little.

"I wanted you too, Greyx. From the moment you kissed me."

Desire flared in his eyes—a flush of fire in the darkness of his dilated pupils.

"I knew I couldn't have you for life, though," I added in a half-whisper. "And a night wasn't going to be enough. With you, it never would be enough."

A wide smile spread on his face. Greyx smiled with his entire being. The radiance of his grin seemed to illuminate the room brighter than the stalactites.

"You want to keep me for life?" He leaned against the edge of the pool until his chest pressed to my arm.

"Well..."

What was one supposed to reply to that? What did it matter what I wanted if we couldn't possibly...

Sitting sideways, I pulled my legs to my chest. My position might be defensive, but his smile disarmed me, leaving me no choice but to grin back.

He grabbed my ankles and rotated me to face him.

I lost my balance from the movement. Arms flailing in the air, I slid off the edge and into the water. Then I slipped on the smooth rock of the bottom and went under.

The warm water closed over me, rushing up my nose. Strong hands grabbed me, lifting me out of the water.

"Are you trying to swim away from me?" Greyx chuckled, holding me around my waist.

I wiped my eyes, shoving away the wet hair that had come loose from my band and plastered to my face.

"Does it really look like I *planned* this?" I sputtered.

"No!" He laughed. "That was the least coordinated dive I've ever seen."

I huffed and grabbed onto his shoulder horns. And because I couldn't come up with any other way to stop him from laughing, I pulled myself up and kissed him.

It worked. His laughter cut off. A deep rumble thrummed in his chest instead. His arms went around me, his hands sliding down my back and cupping my ass. He lifted me higher, his erection rubbing against my lower belly then nestling neatly in the middle of my closed legs.

My body stretched flush against his, my toes skimming just below his knees. I let go of his shoulder horns and wrapped my arms around his neck.

He pulled back, breaking the kiss.

"That's when I knew..." he panted. His eyes were wild, not a hint of a smile, just pure hunger and...longing. A longing so strong, it floored me. "The moment I kissed you, I knew you were made for me. I wasn't going to let you go, Tessa."

"You did let me go." I cupped his face. "You left. And you will leave again, once—"

"No." He turned, twirling me through the water. "I had to leave, but I was going to come back for you. I would've found you anywhere, and I was going to do anything it took to convince you we belonged together."

"But how?"

We couldn't be together, could we? He belonged to Aldrai, and my life... Well, my life was everywhere else but there.

"I don't care how," he said resolutely. "If you feel about me at least a little bit the way I feel about you, we'll find a way. I never want to see you leaving me again, like in that elevator. It nearly broke my heart."

I knew my heart was not safe around Greyx. I just never expected I'd be able to break *his*.

"We'll find a way," I echoed, wishing to believe with all my soul. "I can never leave you again, Greyx. I just can't."

Chapter 18

Tessa

He peppered my face with light, tiny kisses, walking me back to the edge of the pool.

"God, I want you so much," he groaned.

I smiled against his lips and teased, "It's the mating drugs."

Darkness flared in his eyes, slashing through the warm, easy feeling in my chest. He lifted me on the rocky edge again.

"The drugs weren't meant to make me do this." He yanked my legs apart.

With a startled noise, I tried to close them again, but he fitted his head between my knees, wedging his horns in to keep me open for him. He trailed his lips on the inner side of my right thigh, along the bluish line left under my skin by the water snake.

When he reached the bruised bite mark left from his teeth, he placed a soft kiss on the same spot. "Does it hurt?"

"Not really." I spread my legs wider Right now, the only thing that hurt was the ache low in my belly, the need for him.

He kept kissing higher and higher until I felt his tongue slide between my folds.

My inner muscles spasmed. I whimpered, bucking my hips. My foot slid down, nudging his shoulder. He caught it and shifted it over to his back, keeping it away from the sharp horn on his shoulder.

I leaned back, propped by my arms behind me. He dragged his tongue over my opening, slowly and firmly.

My arms shook, my elbows buckled, sending me down flat. Gripping my hips, he yanked me closer to his mouth. His tongue explored with the same enthusiasm his fingers had done before. And every stroke sent ripples of pleasure through my body.

He dipped his tongue inside me, stroking my inner walls with the tip.

Sweet pleasure rippled and rose. I arched my back, moaning. The sound echoed under the glowing ceiling. He shifted higher, nibbling, stroking, sucking.

Digging my heels into the hard plates over his shoulder blades, I raised my hips, grinding against his mouth.

It'd been so long since I'd been with a man, and nothing any man had ever done to me could compare to the way Greyx was doing it.

I gripped the horns on his head as pleasure swelled and ebbed. An orgasm teased me, dancing on the tip of Greyx's tongue.

With another firm stroke, he released it. Climax crested, setting me free.

He held me close, flicking his tongue to rip every single shudder of bliss out of me.

Feeling completely boneless, I dropped my feet from his back and he helped me slide back into the water.

I didn't get to touch the bottom this time. Greyx held me up. I wrapped my legs above his waist, and he kissed between my breasts.

"Your skin is so soft," he murmured, licking drops of water from my right breast. "I want to taste all of it. Everywhere." He sucked my nipple into his mouth, his dexterous tongue playing with the pebbled tip.

I shuddered with sensation.

His erection prodded me from below, demanding attention.

He shifted his focus to my left breast, lapping at the nipple. I squirmed in his arms. The faint tingle between my legs grew stronger, bringing back the needy pressure. I rubbed myself against his hard abs.

He growled against my nipple—a feral, intimidating sound.

"Greyx…"

Holding me tight, he waded out of the pool, then placed me down on my back. Lowering himself over me, he held his large body above mine, propped on his outstretched arms.

Darkness flickered in his bright eyes, in and out. As if he was trying to fight it.

I wasn't frightened. Even back in the cage, when his mind had been hardly his own, he had found the strength not to hurt me. I trusted him fully.

Grabbing on to his horns, I lowered his head to me.

"Do your worst, Greyx." I lifted my hips to him, trapping his hard-on between us.

He snarled like a wild beast. Reaching down, he slid one thick finger inside me and circled my opening, stretching me from the inside. He had a massive dick to prepare me for. I spread my legs wider, bracing for the invasion.

"I won't hurt you," he whispered in my ear, his breath a cool caress against my heated skin. Fisting his length, he slid his hand along it, coating it in the clear slick that seeped from the spongy bumps on its surface.

The thick, blunt point of his erection pressed against my opening. Greyx caught my mouth in a kiss before pushing in.

He swallowed my gasp, stretching me wide, inch by inch. Despite his incredible size, he slid in painlessly, slick and snug.

I moaned, cradling him between my legs.

We were a perfect fit.

"I told you, you were made for me." He grinned happily.

Shifting his hips, he pulled out a little. The firm nodes along his length tugged at the rim of my opening in the most delicious way.

Pressure mounted low in my belly with a sweet, needy ache. With a loud moan, I shifted my hips up to meet his next thrust.

He groaned, echoing me.

"I said I wouldn't hurt you," he snarled in my ear. "But I *will* fuck you, Tessa. Hard."

He slammed inside me.

I curled my toes and gripped the horns on his shoulders.

"Oh yes...Greyx." The tingling between my legs turned to hot throbbing need, and only he could help me satisfy it.

"I dreamed about fucking you." He slammed into me again and again. "Just like this."

"Greyx..." I whimpered when it all got too much and not quite enough at the same time. "I need..."

A gentle prodding tapped around the place where our bodies joined. I jerked, startled, then relaxed. It was the tip of his tail. It found my most sensitive spot and pressed, rubbing in sync with Greyx's pounding into me.

Breath caught in my throat right before the orgasm crested and crashed over me, hard and violent like his thrusts. I trembled, wild shudders of pleasure rippling through every nerve ending. He pumped his hips into me relentlessly, making the ecstasy go on forever.

With my legs wrapped around him, my foot slid down. My toes touched the base of his tail, making his whole body jerk. I stroked with my toes along his tail, this time on purpose.

Tossing his head back, he roared, shuddering from his own climax.

As the spasms through his muscles subdued, he buried his face in the side of my neck.

"This was fucking incredible." He moaned against my skin.

"It's the drugs." I chuckled, caressing the back of his head.

He rolled over to his back, flipping me to his chest. "You're my addiction, Tessa, and drugs have nothing to do with it."

I pressed my nose to his throat. Without the hard plating he had on his back and shoulders, his chest and belly were warm and comfortable. He slid his hands up my back and speared his fingers through the disheveled bun on the back of my head. Tugging at it, he worked out the thick hair elastic I used to keep my hair back.

"What are you doing?" I asked.

"Setting it free," he murmured, spreading my long, wet hair down my back, strand by strand. "I dreamed about doing this, too. And it feels even better than in my dream."

"When did you manage to dream about all of it?" I smiled. The slight tickle of his fingers on my back sent ripples of pleasure down my arms. "There haven't been many nights to dream since we met."

"You have no idea," he groaned. "I dream about you day and night. Every single minute, you're on my mind. I think about what I'd do to you, from simple things, like running my fingers through your hair, like this. To...well, things I probably shouldn't talk to you about until we get to know each other a little better."

He chuckled softly. His chest vibrated with his laughter under me.

"Until we get to know each other a little better..."

Would we ever get the chance to do that?

If we made it off this planet, safe and sound, I'd be heading back to Earth soon. I heaved a long sigh at that thought, my smile slipping away.

"We'll find a way," Greyx's words sounded in my head, giving me hope.

Propping my hands on his chest, I rose over him. Cupping his face, I stroked the hard ridge of his cheekbone with my thumb. I slid a tip of my finger up the wide bridge of his nose then along one of the heavy eyebrow ridges. They had no hair, but their darker color made it look like they did.

His face—strange and different when we first met—had become dear and familiar to me. His eyes shone with appreciation as he slid his gaze down my front. Lifting his hand, he skimmed the underside of my breast.

"Do I look strange to you?" I asked as he splayed his hand on my flat belly.

He moved his hand to the left, gliding it down my ribs and exploring the unfamiliar.

"A little," he confessed. "But in a very thrilling way." A naughty twinkle sparked in his eye as he cupped both my breasts with his hands, his thumbs flicking my nipples. "I love the idea of playing with *all* your nipples at once as you ride my cock like this."

Desire tugged in my lower belly anew in response to his touch. Unbelievable. How many times could this man make me excited in one night?

The impression in his eyes left no doubt he was infatuated with me. Which in itself was new and exciting. I never thought of myself as the one to sweep men off their feet. But Greyx looked and acted smitten. And I loved it. I loved the warm tingles in my chest when he looked at me like that, like I was the most gorgeous creature in the whole of the Universe, with all my faults and flaws.

What would the rest of the Aldraians think of me, though?

The things Prug had said to Bree echoed in my head unbidden.

"What would your sister say if she knew about me?"

He grinned. "Linai will love you."

"But wouldn't she rather you found an Aldraian woman?" There was no shortage of females on his planet.

His smile dimmed somewhat, making me worried.

"She..." He glanced aside. "Trust me, my sister will be happy I found someone at all."

"Why?"

He wouldn't reply and wouldn't meet my eyes.

"How about your parents?" I asked. "What will they think?"

With a grunt, he heaved himself up into a sitting position, making me slide into his lap.

"My parents are dead, Tessa," he said bluntly, as if ripping off a band-aid.

"I—I'm so sorry."

"As are eleven of my siblings, their spouses, and my thirty-seven nieces and nephews."

"What?" Horror slid through me with icy sensation. "How?"

He still wouldn't look at me, focusing his stare somewhere behind my left shoulder.

"Seven years ago, Aldrai survived the biggest accident in centuries," he said in an odd, detached voice, sounding as if he was reading a news report. "A leisure spacecraft, carrying fourteen hundred tourists on a two-month journey through our part of the Galaxy—a once-in-a-lifetime vacation for some—exploded, killing everyone on board."

I held completely still, afraid of what I sensed was to come.

"Out of the fourteen hundred lives lost that day," he continued, "sixty-two were my closest family."

He moved his gaze to mine, his features hard as if chiseled from stone, but the look in his eyes was soft, raw, and vulnerable.

"Greyx," I whispered, taking his face between my hands.

"They were gone in seconds," he said. "All of them. Linai and her husband were supposed to join the ship on the next planet. That's how they survived. And I..." He heaved a breath. "I survived because I had to work. I had a mission I couldn't cancel or postpone, which had greatly upset my mother. My parents had been planning this trip for years. I knew the dates well in advance, yet when the mission happened, I chose work over them."

"You survived," I tried to console him. Greyx staying behind seemed like a lucky coincidence to me.

Judging by his grim expression, he didn't see it that way.

"We had an argument. The last words I said to my mother were, 'My job comes with responsibilities. It's more important than a trip. I'll see you when you get back.' I never saw her again. None of them came back. And I've regretted not coming with them every single day since. Trust me, Tessa, nothing in life is more important than family. Nothing."

I never had a real family. I could only imagine how Greyx's great loss felt. I didn't know the best thing to say or do to console him, but I knew what it felt like to be completely alone in the Universe.

I wanted him to know that I understood.

"I... I never knew my parents," I said. "I don't know who my dad was. My mom left the hospital shortly after giving birth to me, wanting nothing to do with me. I was given my name by the agency that ended up being responsible for my care—Tessa, because "t" was the letter of that month."

His eyes focused on me, the intense pain in them giving way to compassion. I didn't care even if he pitied me, as long as his own hurt receded.

"New Year's Eve is my favorite holiday," I continued. "You know why? Because that's pretty much the only holiday back home that you're not expected to spend with your family. The only one I can celebrate just like everybody else."

He gave me a faint smile. "I make sure I work every holiday and stay at the rented apartment in the city. It's so much easier than being at my family's place, with all those empty spaces where their beds used to be. It's my parents' garden. Seven of my siblings lived with them, including two of my brothers with their families. The place used to be so full of people and noise. Children laughing, running. And now... it's quiet, like a cemetery."

"How about your sister?" I asked.

"She lives in Arqa, with her husband."

"Do you get along?"

"Oh, yes." He nodded. "Linai is great. She's been trying so hard to carry on with all our family traditions. But it doesn't work with only the two of us, you know. It's not the same. Sometimes all I see when I look at her is everyone else who isn't there." He closed his eyes, rubbing his forehead. "So, I've been avoiding her, too. And since I couldn't stand being on my own, I've been working or partying with friends for the past seven years." He glanced at me and stroked my face. "I'm getting really tired of all the partying."

"I'm glad you came to the last party, though." I slid my arms around his neck and ran my fingers up the back of his head, along the middle row of horns.

"I'm glad I did, too." He lowered his face to mine.

His length hardened under me, and I moved my arms from his neck to his waist.

With each stroke of my hands, sadness receded from his eyes. Heat flamed in them again.

Splaying my hand on the small of his back, I slid it lower, past the firm rise of his butt cheek to the middle.

He stilled, his erection swelling thicker.

"Is it true that there's tail porn on Aldrai?" I whispered in his ear.

He cleared his throat, shifting somewhat uncomfortably. "Yes."

I blinked in surprise. When Bree had mentioned that, I'd only half believed her. It sounded so much like a joke.

"Oh. And...what do they do in that porn?"

He chuckled, his awkwardness melting away. "Would you like to watch it together sometime? We can make a date out of it."

"Hmm. I think it may be fun to figure it out on my own." I brushed by the base of his tail with my fingers, and his hard-on jerked higher. "So far, your tail appears to work like a remote control for your penis." I laughed, running my fingers down the length of the appendage on his back.

Just like the rest of him, his tail was furless. It felt slimmer than his erection but longer, and smooth without any bumps.

"What will happen if I take it in my mouth?"

With a growl, he flipped me to my back. "This." He shoved my legs open with his knee, fitting himself between my thighs. "This will happen, sweetheart."

Something nudged at my opening. Since his hands were propped on the floor on each side of my head and his erection was pressed to my belly, it could only be his tail probing me.

"You can move it so deftly?" I gasped in amazement.

"Oh, I have a much better control over my tail than I do over my cock. There're thousands of ways I can make you scream my name, Tessa." He shifted on top of me. "How about this one?"

The tip of his tail flicked rapidly, gently rubbing between my legs.

"Ohhh," I exhaled with a moan. "Greyx..."

"That's right," he purred with a rumble in his chest. "Let's see how many times I'll make you come before the night is over."

Chapter 19

Tessa

Six. Greyx made me come six more times that night. He promised he could double that number, and I believed him, but we needed to get some rest. We had a long day ahead of us. Our ordeal on Zoltu was far from over.

We slept in the small cave next to Lucy and her "Mittens." Like the night before, Greyx lay down with me. And I found sleep so much easier in his arms.

But when I woke later, Greyx wasn't there.

Lucy was sitting in the corner, finger-brushing her blonde hair. It was damp. She must've taken a bath in the hot spring.

"Good morning," she said brightly.

Mittens snored softly at her side.

"Morning." I winced, sitting up. My muscles ached from hiking all day yesterday...and from all the positions Greyx had bent my body into last night. My cheeks heated when I thought about that.

"Greyx went out," Lucy informed me before I had a chance to ask about him.

"Why is he out?" I adjusted my dress, remembering putting my clothes back on before going to sleep. My shoes stood nearby. But none of Greyx's things were there.

An appetizing aroma drifted into the cave from the exit tunnel. It smelled like grilled meat—a scent I never thought I'd smell on Zoltu.

Lucy drew some air through her nostrils. "What's that smell?"

"I don't know, but I hope it's something good." I put on my shoes and got up to my feet. "I'll go look."

"Be careful," Lucy warned.

I nodded. "I need to go to the bathroom, anyway. Do you want to come?"

"Sure." She got up promptly. "I'll come too. Why would I stay here alone?"

She sounded so normal again. No humming, no rocking. Even the perpetual fear in her eyes had receded.

I glanced back at the *brahlu*.

"Oh, he's fine," she assured me. "Let him sleep a little longer. Those short paws of his need some rest."

We headed down the tunnel, back toward the river. The farther we went, the stronger the pleasant aroma grew, though there wasn't any smoke.

At the exit of the side tunnel, I paused and raised my hand to signal Lucy to stop, too. It never hurt to be cautious. What if the amazing smell was a trap?

"I hope you're hungry," the familiar deep voice sounded from the main tunnel.

I froze, not expecting Greyx to hear or see us.

Lucy didn't seem startled, however.

"How did you know we were coming?" She stepped around me, walking out into the tunnel by the river.

I quickly followed, finding Greyx crouched by a slab of rock with something that resembled sausages sizzling on it.

Lucy sat next to the rock. "We were so quiet."

Greyx squinted my way, a smile dancing in his orange eyes.

"I recognize the shuffle of those shoes anywhere." He tipped his chin at my flats. They looked a hundred years old after all the trekking, hiking, and swimming they'd endured in the past two days.

He got up and greeted me with a quick kiss on my lips. "You need new shoes, my love. Badly."

My love.

My stomach fluttered with butterflies.

How was I supposed to reply? How did a *loved* woman act? I had no idea. I breathed faster, my chest expanding with a feeling I never had before.

He cupped my face gently. "How did you sleep?"

"Good," I mumbled, finally finding my words again.

Then, following more an impulse than any conscious thought, I splayed my hands on his chest and rose on my tiptoes for another kiss.

He eagerly obliged, taking much longer this time before breaking the kiss. I smiled, squinting at him like a cat in sunshine.

"Is he the alien Bree wanted you to meet?" Lucy's voice floated into the bubble of the warm, fuzzy feeling surrounding Greyx and me. "Was Greyx your blind date?"

"He was." I nodded.

Who knew blind dates worked out sometimes?

"You got lucky, then," Lucy concluded pragmatically. "He's much better than the other one."

The mention of Prug made me wince. One shouldn't hold ill feelings against the dead, and I was no longer angry with Prug. Thinking about him was still unpleasant, though.

"I'd better go to the bathroom," I said quickly.

Greyx walked me to the exit of the tunnel and made sure all was quiet before he let me out of his sight.

When we returned to Lucy and the frying sausages, Mittens was also there.

"See?" Lucy scratched his round head. "I told you he'll find us. He's a smart *brahlu*, aren't you, Mittens?"

The *brahlu* shifted on his eight paws eagerly, looking very intrigued by the meat on Greyx's makeshift grill.

"What are those, by the way?" I shook my head in disbelief. "Where on earth... I mean on Zoltu, did you find sausages?"

Greyx snorted. "These aren't sausages. I found some mollusks behind the waterfall of the hot spring—one of the few remaining life forms on this planet."

He poked at the meat with a stick, turning it on his rock grill.

"These species are both male and female at once," he explained. "Their male genitalia comprise about eighty percent of their body mass—"

"What did you just say? Their *what*?" I choked on a laugh.

He looked straight at me.

"Their cocks are bigger than the rest of them. It's the meatiest part of their bodies." A smile danced in the corners of his mouth, ready to burst into a laugh. "The tastiest part, too, I've heard."

"Well..." I stared at the "sausages," lost for words.

Lucy giggled.

And Greyx lost it. Laugh erupted from his chest, unstoppable like an avalanche.

I chuckled once, then twice. Finally, faced with Greyx's contagious laughter, I couldn't hold back, bursting out, too.

"Are you saying," I squeezed out between the bouts of laughter, "that you're literally frying us some dicks for breakfast?"

He tossed his head back, howling at my words.

"Talk about eating dicks," Lucy muttered under her breath, causing another eruption of laughter.

I couldn't remember when I last laughed so wholeheartedly. Definitely not on Zoltu. At this point, it didn't even matter if the "dicks" turned out tasting like garbage. By lifting our spirits, they'd already served their purpose.

Greyx poked one with the stick. "Well, they're ready. Are you brave enough to try one?" He flicked his gaze between Lucy and me.

My stomach twisted with hunger. Thanks to Greyx, I'd been able to eat the *dohmat*, but if there was an alternative to that nasty fruit, I wasn't going to pass on it.

"I'll have one, please," I said. "It smells delicious."

He pierced one of the "sausages" with the stick, then offered it to me. Grabbing another one from the grill, he took a huge bite, giving me a teasing look.

I took a cautious sniff of the meat in my hand. Up close, it smelled even better. I stuck my tongue out and licked it.

Greyx groaned, shifting in his sitting position on the floor.

"Really, Tessa, please just bite it. The licking makes me..." He stretched his shoulders with another groan. "Just don't lick it. Please?"

I arched an eyebrow, baring my teeth before taking a bite.

He winced, shielding his crotch with his hand.

"Like this?" I smiled, chewing.

The taste exceeded my expectations. Tender like butter, the texture reminded me of cooked scallops from back home, though the flavor was meatier than that of seafood.

"And? How is it?" Lucy asked, eyeing the remaining "sausages."

Staring straight at Greyx, I said, "Great. But it's not the best dick I've ever tasted."

His deep laughter thundered under the ceiling of the tunnel again. "That's the first one I ever did!"

Lucy took one from the rock carefully and bit off the tip. "Mmm, it is good. Thank you, Greyx."

"Thank you," I echoed, finishing one and reaching for another one. "For the...um, *sausages* and for the laugh, too. It was good to have both this morning."

A smile still played on his lips, but the expression in his eyes turned serious. "We need to eat well. If all goes as planned, this will be our last meal on Zoltu. I'd rather not make any more stops."

"If all goes as planned."

We had one last trek ahead of us. This one would be straight up the mountain, in the open, for all the drones to see.

"When do you want to leave?" I asked.

"As soon as we're done here." He handed another "sausage" to Lucy, and she fed it to Mittens. The *brahlu* eagerly sucked in the entire thing through his long nose.

Greyx checked his gun. "When we're out there, make sure you stay close. If we're attacked, we'll have to fight. Don't let them catch you. I'll keep them at bay with this." He tipped his chin at the gun. "But if anyone gets too close…"

He handed me his knife handle.

"Press here to flick the flame blade on." He demonstrated. "Twisting this will make the blade longer. And switching this button will turn it from cold to hot. Cold is better for fighting. It won't cauterize the wound. They'll bleed longer."

I tried to listen carefully. Shoving the fear aside, I prayed it wouldn't come down to me stabbing someone and making them bleed. The world would be a better place without the nasty *yirzi*. But I'd never killed anyone before, and I wasn't sure I could do it if it came down to it.

Then, I thought back to *yirzi*'s attack on our shuttle. I'd been so scared back then. But I was also furious. I hadn't hesitated when stabbing my attacker with the corkscrew, and I had no regrets about it. Maybe when the time came, I'd do it again to defend myself, and Lucy, and Greyx. Heck, I'd stab any *yirzi* who'd want to hurt Mittens, too.

I nodded with more confidence, hiding the laser handle in the pocket of my dress.

Lucy dragged the *brahlu* into her lap.

"We'll be okay," she whispered softly, either for him or for herself, or maybe for all of us.

"We'll be okay," I repeated, hoping with all my heart for that to be true.

Chapter 20

Tessa

A loose rock rolled from under my foot. I tripped, nearly losing my balance.

"Careful!" Greyx grabbed my arm, steadying me.

I gave him a reassuring smile. "I'm good."

Firm and solid, his features seemed to melt with a warm grin in response. "Watch your step," he said softly, stroking the bare skin on my upper arm with his thumb.

I nodded, brushing sweat-soaked hair from my face.

The sun had been climbing in the sky above us, lazy but steady, the heat rising with it. The air felt fresher here in the mountains than in the sand valley, and not as muggy. But the higher we climbed, the harder it was, and the more sweat we'd worked up. Even Greyx had a few beads of perspiration on his temples, right below his horns. His breathing had gotten more ragged, too.

"Not far, now." He tipped his crown of horns at the ridge above us. The crest of it was clearly visible. It seemed so close, but the smooth, rocky ground under our feet kept rising at a sharper angle with every step we took.

Giving up on walking, Lucy dropped to all fours, climbing like a monkey. A few steps further, I did the same, hauling my body up with my hands to help my legs. My legs shook from strain. And after a while of moving this way, my arms started to ache, too.

Yet there was no time for taking breaks or getting some rest. This was it. The last push on our way to freedom. And there was so much at stake.

I glanced up at Greyx's large figure ahead of me. He was picking the path for the rest of us to follow.

"We'll make it work," he'd said. And for the first time in my life, I really wished to give it a try. I still didn't know how, but I wanted it to work between us.

By the time we finally made it to the crest of the mountain, I was completely out of breath.

"How are you feeling?" Greyx asked, when all of us sat in the shade from a sharp peak jolting out.

"I'm fine." I panted, catching my breath.

Lucy nodded, wiping sweat off her forehead with her sleeve.

"Down should be easier, right?" I attempted a smile, though it probably looked pathetic because Greyx's frown didn't ease at the sight of it.

"Climbing down requires more concentration." He unhooked the water bag from his belt and passed it around.

I took a long drink. The water had warmed up in the sun, but it still refreshed my dry tongue and my parched throat.

"Be careful," Greyx instructed as we started the descent. "Watch your step and pay attention to your surroundings."

I tried to do as he said, listening for any noise from the sky and carefully choosing every rock I stepped on. Keeping on high alert for hours wasn't easy. My mind wandered.

If *yirzi* wanted to recapture us, they'd try to do it now, before we left the planet. Right here, on the side of the mountain, open to view of drones and everyone, we were at our most vulnerable.

The Aldraian spaceship that had come to pick us up would be in orbit by now. The crew was supposed to send a shuttle for us.

Would *yirzi* spot the ship? Could they trace the path of the shuttle, predict its trajectory and landing point? What if they were already here? Hiding, ready to recapture us?

Squinting in the red sunlight, I wished I had my glasses. So far all I could see was the pink rock under my feet, the white sand not far below now, and the valley of dunes beyond, where our destination lay.

"There!" Greyx touched my shoulder.

A bright spark high in the sky glistened red, reflecting the sunlight. It descended steadily.

"Our shuttle." His expression tightened with concentration. He, too, realized the danger of making a run for it. Having the escape, literally, in sight now, made any thought of a potential recapture that much more devastating.

Greyx eyes widened suddenly.

"*Yirzi*," he said sharply.

My heart leaped with a jolt, then plummeted into the abyss. I followed Greyx's gesture with my eyes, seeing nothing in the red, hazy sky.

Lucy whimpered softly at my side, dropping into a crouch.

A little while later, I saw them, too—a group of dark dots moving across the sky from the opposite end of the valley.

"Drones?" I gasped, afraid to draw another breath.

Greyx shook his head. "Aircraft."

He kept climbing down, and I followed, even as everything inside me froze. Fear turned my blood to ice at the idea of being captured and locked in chains again. The fear brought anger as the large group of *yirzi* aircraft approached.

Then, the defiance flared.

My chest puffed out, and I patted my pocket, making sure the knife handle was still there. I was not going to make it easy for them to take me.

"Run or fight?" I asked Greyx as the two of us reached the valley.

Lucy remained higher on the mountain, crouching next to a piece of rock, her eyes wide, her arms wrapped tightly around the *brahlu*.

Greyx stared at the approaching dots intently. His eyes flickering between them, he appeared to count them.

"These are individual aircraft." He reached for his gun. "There aren't that many. We'll fight."

I took my knife handle out, not sure how useful it could be in a fight against the aircraft.

Holding his gun under his arm, Greyx untied and unwrapped his arm coverings, baring the sharp horns on the back of his arms.

"Stay behind me," he ordered, placing the long gun on his forearm and taking aim.

As the group of dots came closer, growing in size, I could make out the shape of them. Each looked like a flying air bike, with a *yirzi* sitting on top.

Shoving my knife back in my pocket, I lifted a piece of rock instead and wrapped my fingers tightly around it.

"Stay close," I shouted to Lucy over my shoulder.

She didn't move. Her large eyes were open wide, with her face turning as white as her sweater.

"Lucy, come on," I tried to coax her into climbing down. "We need to stay together. You'll watch my back, I'll watch yours. We're a team, remember?"

Obviously terrified out of her wits, she didn't even nod, clutching the *brahlu* with white-knuckled hands.

Greyx fired. The bright blast softly hissed out of the gun. Flash exploded through the chest of the first *yirzi*. He jerked. His bike jolted off course, then crashed to the ground, sand spraying out on impact.

Greyx smoothly moved his weapon, adjusting his aim. He shot again, and another *yirzi* joined his buddy on the valley floor.

The vehicles got close enough now for me to see the riders' yellow eyeballs swaying on the antennae on top of their heads. They brandished the dreadfully familiar pronged sticks in their hands. The fact that they fired no guns meant their orders were to capture not to kill us.

Greyx shot again and again, taking more of them down.

I tossed my rock. It hit a rider in the shoulder. He swayed but stayed on his air bike, balancing the long stick in his hand. A curved metal strip was attached to the end of the pole.

The belt!

All the *yirzi* had to do to trap one of us was to snap that belt on. Swerving off course, he flew to Greyx from the side, aiming the belt at his middle.

My stomach hollowed with dread.

Lucy cried out behind me.

Greyx ducked then kicked his foot out, knocking the stick with the belt away from him. Next, he shot the *yirzi* in the head.

More vehicles circled us from both sides.

I grabbed another rock and hurled it, hitting a rider straight in his chest.

Greyx kicked one who got too close. Knocked out of balance, the rider fell out of his seat. As the *yirzi* rolled on the ground, Greyx leaped on him and crushed his skull with his forearm. Green blood splashed his arm and face.

The driverless vehicle lurched up, then crashed into the mountain some distance above us. Hot sparks and pieces of burned metal showered us from above.

Another vehicle flew to me. I dropped to the ground, letting it fly over. It swerved sharply. The rider leaned over, reaching for me with the belt on the end of his pole.

I frantically searched around for another rock, then threw it at him. It bounced off his shoulder, not slowing him down at all.

Spinning around, I scurried back up the mountain on all fours, away from him. But I wasn't fast enough. The belt clicked around my waist. Prongs of the stick pierced through my dress and skin. I screamed in agony, paralyzed by pain from the shot.

Greyx dashed my way. He grabbed the pole with his bare hands. With a deafening roar, his face distorted with rage, Greyx yanked at the pole, dragging the *yirzi* off his vehicle. He then bent his head forward, spearing the *yirzi* on his crown of horns.

The green alien screeched, then stilled. Jerking his head, Greyx tossed the lifeless body aside.

I scurried out of their way, the belt still around my waist, the pole dragging behind me. But the pain was gone now that no one was holding the other end of the pole.

Another *yirzi* snuck up on me from the side. Jumping off his bike, he went for the pole.

"No, you don't!" I kicked him in the head as hard as I could.

His head jerked from the blow. Screaming in rage, he lunged for me. He grabbed me by the throat and squeezed hard.

I struggled to breathe, scratching with my nails at his hands. I kicked at him, but the *yirzi* sat too high on my chest. My kicks didn't reach him.

His yellow eyes focused on me. My vision narrowed to a tunnel with black fuzzy walls and his face in the center.

Desperate for air, I threw my hands up and grabbed his antennae. I yanked them down as hard as I could.

The *yirzi* shrieked. He tossed his head back, loosening his grip on my throat. Gasping for air, I wiggled from under him, then kicked him in the chest, sending him rolling down the rocky slope into the sand.

Only then I remembered about the knife in my pocket.

Still screaming, the *yirzi* leaped to his feet and lunged at me.

I flicked the blade on—blue, not red. It sliced smoothly through his neck. Gurgling, he stood upright, propped by his four legs, then sank down to the sand. Green blood marred the stark whiteness of the valley floor.

A blast exploded behind me, sending me to the ground. Sand and shards of rock showered over me.

"Tessa!" Greyx's deep voice broke through the ringing noise in my ears.

His large, strong hands grabbed me by my arms, helping me up.

"Are you okay?" Greyx gripped the pole attached to the belt around my waist and broke it off, leaving the belt on.

I tried to focus on his words, his face, but everything swam, floating in a swirl around me.

He gave me a small shake. "Tessa!"

I blinked, staring at the splashes of green on his horns and face. His arms were green too, as if he had dipped them in paint up to his shoulders.

Not paint. *Yirzi* blood.

"Greyx..." I finally managed to utter.

A scorched, shallow crater was smoldering right above me in the pink rock of the mountain. Must be the site of another air bike exploding.

"Are they all gone?" I turned around, searching for more *yirzi* and air bikes.

As the smoke of the latest explosion cleared, only wreaked pieces of metal and dead bodies littered the ground.

One of the bodies was the green *I* killed. I did it, I took a life... My hands shook, dropping the blood-covered knife handle.

"More are coming. We need to run," Greyx urged.

Run.

I understood that word perfectly clear. Running was all I'd done lately.

"Lucy?" I looked around.

She was sitting in the same place under a rock up the mountain, hugging Mittens and rocking back and forth. I couldn't hear over the ringing in my ears, but I would swear she was humming again.

I climbed up to her and grabbed her arm.

"We need to run, Lucy. Now!"

Keeping her head down, she followed me into the valley, clutching the *brahlu* to her chest.

Greyx shoved his gun into his belt.

"Come!" He grabbed Lucy and me by our arms and ran, dragging us along on each side of him.

Far in the distance, the Aldraian shuttle was landing, aiming for a flat rocky plateau slightly to the right of us.

From the left, however, a much larger group of black dots approached. Like a swarm of locusts, they rushed across the valley, obviously intending to cut us off from the shuttle.

There were so many of them. We could never outrun them.

I pumped my arms and legs harder than ever. But my feet sank and tripped in the sand. It was like trying to run in a bad dream where no matter how fast I wanted to move, I went nowhere.

Yet *yirzi* whirred through the air effortlessly.

"Come!" Greyx urged, dragging Lucy and me along.

"We won't make it," I wanted to scream, only my breath was stolen by the running.

Greyx was stronger, faster. If he let go of Lucy and me, he could probably make it on his own. I just had to convince him to go for it. And I had to do it fast.

Lucy tripped, dropping the *brahlu* from her arms.

He landed on all his legs and snorted, shaking his head. Then, he suddenly took off, running away.

"Mittens!" Lucy yelled hysterically.

Wrenching her arm from Greyx, she dashed after the *brahlu*.

Shockingly, the creature moved fast, much faster than I'd ever seen him go before. His short, chubby legs scurried swiftly, the sight of them a blur. Instead of running to the shuttle, though, the *brahlu* beelined toward the approaching *yirzi*.

Did he want to return to their dungeon?

Maybe he preferred it there, hibernating in his quiet cage, rather than being dragged through everything we'd taken him through.

"Mittens, no!" Tripping over her feet, Lucy scrambled after him.

I dashed after her. "Lucy, come back!"

Greyx beat me, getting to her first. He grabbed her across her middle, swerving her around. Running back to me, he hooked his arm around my shoulders and swept me off my feet, too.

"Down!" He dropped to the ground, taking Lucy and me with him.

"No!" Lucy thrashed in his grip. "Mittens!"

She fought to get up, to look back. With a hand on the back of her head, he shoved her down again.

"You do *not* want to face his way," he snarled and ordered, "Close your eyes and cover your ears."

Blood pulsed in my ears, my heart thundering. I covered my ears, shut my eyes, and drew my head into my shoulders.

A sound rolled through the valley. It was weirdly deafening, without actually making any noise.

Then I realized it wasn't a sound at all, but a sudden absence of any noise completely. The roar of the aircraft stopped. The shouting. Even the blow of the wind and the soft noise it made by shifting the sand across the dunes also ceased.

Against Greyx's orders, I lifted my head and peered back over my shoulder.

The *brahlu* stood on his hind paws, with his back to us. His tubular nose opened like an umbrella, ribbed and membranous. Red sunlight filtered through it with deep burgundy.

A wide groove in the sand moved from the *brahlu* in an expanding arch. The vacuous silence appeared to roll from him, like a swell, in the direction opposite from us—and toward the fleet of the *yirzi* aircraft.

The greens and their vehicles shook violently, coming to a stop. Then...they broke apart.

The vehicles and the bodies of the *yirzi* riding them disintegrated into equal particles. They hovered above the sand like a swarm of insects before raining down and bouncing all over the valley floor.

I was unable to tear my eyes from the jumping, rolling balls littering the valley. "What's happening?"

Greyx gaped. Judging by his expression, the *yirzi* splitting into a million of bouncing balls was a shock for him, too.

Lucy twisted out from under his arm.

She got up and dashed to the *brahlu*. "Mittens!"

The animal didn't seem to notice that the *yirzi* were gone. He remained upright, his umbrella-nose open. His chubby body vibrated.

Another groove formed in the sand, indicating a new wave of devastation forming. The *brahlu* turned, and the direction of the wave shifted. It inched closer to the shuttle that had just landed on the plateau.

If he kept turning, the next wave would hit the shuttle directly in its path. And the wave after that one would be coming our way. Lucy would be hit by it first.

"Lucy!" I leaped to my feet.

"No!" Greyx grabbed me. "We need to run back to the mountains. Away from him."

"I can't leave her!"

"And I can't let you die."

He held me in a deadly grip, refusing to budge. And I couldn't fight him, watching in horror as Lucy approached the *brahlu*.

Stumbling in the sand, she reached the deadly creature. She came from the back, avoiding the murderous wave in front of him. Dropping to her knees, she wrapped her arms around him.

"Look, Greyx!" I nudged against him with my side, since he held me with my arms pressed to my body. "Look!"

Dragging me back to the mountains, Greyx glanced over his shoulder and paused.

Hugging her Mittens, Lucy rocked side to side. His nose, wide and smooth like a satellite dish, started collapsing. The membrane had slacked, then folded into a cone, slowly taking its usual tubular shape.

"He stopped, Greyx." I tried to shake his arms off me. "Please, please let me go to her."

He loosened his grip around me and took my hand. "We'll go together. Slowly," he warned. "No loud noises. No sudden movements."

I did what he said. Though everything inside me screamed to run to Lucy, to get her away from the danger. After all we'd been through, she'd become like a sister to me, a sister I'd never had. It'd kill me to see her hurt.

"Lucy," I whispered loudly, coming closer.

A sound reached me—the painfully familiar melody of "Over the Rainbow."

She was humming again.

"Oh, no..." I groaned, dropping to my knees at her side. "Please, not that song again... Please, Lucy, please look at me."

I wrapped one arm around her. Her slender body was trembling. She lifted her eyes to me. Tears filled them.

"It's not for me," she said softly. "It's for him."

She pointed at the *brahlu* in her arms.

The poor thing cuddled against her, pressing his nose to her neck. I realized Lucy's trembling came from the *brahlu* shaking violently. She kept singing, and slowly his chubby shape relaxed, his paws slacked, hanging along his sides.

Greyx picked up a ball off the ground. It was a little smaller than a ping-pong ball, perfectly round and one of the millions littering the valley all around us. It was green, the exact color of *yirzi* skin and blood.

"The flesh coagulated," Greyx muttered, with a long glance at the *brahlu*.

Lucy gently petted the head of the animal. "Seeing them attacking us stressed him out."

Greyx nodded with understanding.

"I don't know what they've done to him to make him able to do...this." He tossed the green ball away. "But it must've been bad enough for him to remember." The ball bounced off the packed sand, then rolled away.

Tears streamed down Lucy's cheeks, creating dark paths down her dust-covered face.

"The bad guys are gone now," she cooed gently, petting the *brahlu's* back. "You're safe. No one will ever hurt you again."

Chapter 21

Tessa

The Aldraian shuttle looked much larger up close. A panel opened on its side when we approached. It molded into a set of stairs as soon as the end of it reached the ground.

"Hi there, General," a melodious female voice sounded from the top of the stairs. It was the first time I ever heard Greyx being addressed by his rank, other than by Alcus Hecear.

A woman leaned into the door opening, back-lit by the soft yellow light from inside the shuttle.

"Greetings, ladies." She waved at Lucy and me. "Come on in!"

The woman's friendly manner drew me in. The warmly lit shuttle felt like a true sanctuary from the blood-red menace of the world outside. Greyx gestured for us to go ahead. Lucy climbed up the stairs, and I followed her.

The woman was Aldraian. She smiled at us as we boarded. "Welcome."

She was dressed in black, loose pants and a tight, sleeveless top, similar to the uniform of Greyx and Prug. Her golden-taupe skin was exactly the same color as her long, straight hair tied into a high ponytail, the ends of it reaching down to her waist.

"I'm Thuhai Xann, the captain of this fine flying machine," she introduced herself, splaying her right hand over the left side of her chest. "Welcome to my shuttle."

Her top was held together with wide leather straps at the sides and shoulders. A golden blob and some swirls decorated each shoulder strap, indicating her rank. She had hard plates on her bare shoulders, too, but only with a cluster of a few raised bumps, no horns or spikes. Neither did she have any horns on her head or her forearms, which were uncovered.

The females of the Aldraian species appeared to be a much gentler version of the males, visually at least.

I noted the six bumps on her front—three pairs of breasts. The first set was a little higher on her chest than that of humans. The belt of her uniform sat low on her hips to accommodate the lower pair of her breasts just above her waist.

Once Greyx got in, Captain Xann punched something on the wall by the door, closing it.

"Glad to see you're well, Greyx," she said with emotion, enclosing him into a hug.

Careful not to hurt her with the horns on his forearms, he embraced, too.

"We were so worried." She held him tight. "I nearly lost my mind when I saw the *yirzi* gaining on you. And I couldn't do a thing to stop them without accidentally shooting you, too. I couldn't even get any closer. Can't land on this damn sand."

He leaned back, holding her shoulders. "I know, but it worked out fine. We've got a weapon of our own, as it turned out." He glanced at the *brahlu*, who snorted softly, snuggling into Lucy's legs.

"That was phenomenal!" Captain Xann let go of Greyx and crouched by Mittens, gently patting his head. "I've never seen a *brahlu* before. That's what he is, right?"

"Right." Greyx nodded, then gestured at Lucy. "This is Lucy, she is with the Liaison Committee."

Captain Xann swiftly enclosed her in an enthusiastic hug. "So glad you made it," she said to the stunned Lucy, who just blinked in reply.

"And this is my Tessa." Greyx wrapped his arm around my shoulders, drawing me into his side.

My Tessa.

I blushed as warm pleasure spread inside my chest. I'd never been "anyone's Tessa" before, and I didn't argue against being *his*.

Captain Xann smiled, shifting her curious gaze from Greyx to me then back again.

"Welcome aboard." She hugged me next, wrenching me from Greyx's one-armed embrace.

"Thank you for coming for us, Captain," I said as relief and gratitude overwhelmed me.

She winced at my mentioning her rank. "Just call me Thuhai, please. I only call him 'General' to tease him." She winked, tipping her head at Greyx.

"We're long-time friends," he explained with a grin. "We've known each other since we were kids."

"Well, take your seats." Thuhai gestured at the long, cushioned benches that lined the walls of the narrow shuttle. "We'll take off as soon as you're ready." She patted one of Greyx's forearms. "And wrap these up, will you? There're some spare bracers in the compartment in the tail."

Lucy and I took our seats as Thuhai went to the cockpit in the front.

"Come, Mittens." Lucy dragged the *brahlu* into her lap.

Greyx found a couple of bracers made from soft, silicon-like material and slipped them over the sharp horns on his forearms.

"That's better." He sat next to me and placed his hand on my knee.

"Don't forget about your seatbelt." I pointed with my gaze at the straps at his shoulders, then added in my best professional tone of voice, "It's for your safety, sir."

He gripped the back of my head, lowering his face to mine. "You were so infuriating, refusing to hear me out, back on your shuttle. Then strapping me in my seat." He flicked his gaze to my lips, and I darted out my tongue to lick them. "Call me 'sir' one more time," he growled, fisting his hand in my hair.

I sank backward onto the seat under the weight of his body over mine. His growl resonated through my chest, heating my belly with a charge of arousal. "Please remain seated in an upright position during take-off..." I murmured, batting my eyelashes at him, then added innocently, "...sir."

He groaned, slamming his mouth over mine in a wild kiss.

"Hey, seat up, Greyx!" Thuhai called out through the open door of the cockpit. "We're taking off."

The soft hum of the engines roaring to life vibrated through the small shuttle.

Greyx groaned again, breaking our hot, messy kiss. He straightened in his seat, and I clicked the straps of his seatbelt in place, lest he lunge at me again before we reached the port.

The shuttle swayed, lifting off the ground, then steadily hummed ahead.

Greyx leaned back in his seat.

"Come here, Tessa." He wrapped his arm around my shoulders and pressed me to him. "Comfy?"

I nodded, snuggling into his side.

He exhaled heavily, gently rubbing my arm. "You can relax now. In a few hours we'll be home."

Home.

Chapter 22

Tessa

"Well, I'll be going now, Tessa." Lucy rolled her carry-on bag out of her room.

"The room" was basically a flower bed with an actual bed in the middle, separated from our living area by an honest-to-god live hedge.

Our apartment on Aldrai was on the seventh floor, but the building looked like nothing I'd ever seen either on Earth or Neron. The ten floors of the construction adjacent to the spaceport in Arqa, the capital city of Aldrai, were open from all sides—no doors, no windows, not even any real walls. With green grass covering the floor and live hedges instead of the walls, the building was basically a collection of hanging gardens.

Lucy and I had been here for the past twenty-four hours, or since the medical team had deemed us healthy enough to be released from their supervision.

During that time, we'd learned that our shuttle and the flight crew of three had safely made it here a few days ago. Once the *yirzi* snatched the four of us, they had abandoned the shuttle, allowing it to continue to Aldrai unharmed.

The *yirzi* had been after Greyx, who was heading the operation to expose and dismantle their facility on Zoltu. When they'd found him in the company of Lucy and me, they had taken the two of us as well, to use in their sick breeding experiments.

I hugged Lucy. "I'll miss you."

"I'll be back in a week," she assured me, smoothing down her flower-printed dress. "Just need to see all the locations where the potential future spouses for our men and women may come from."

Aldrai was called "the garden planet." However, it had not always been as luscious and green. Even now, not everywhere was suitable for living. A large part of the planet remained uninhabited. The Aldraians were still in the process of terraforming it.

The "potential spouses" could come from a city. But they could come from the countryside or even from the freshly terraformed frontier. Lucy's job was to assess the living conditions of all those territories.

"I'd better go." She grabbed on to the handle of her suitcase. "The pilot promised to stop by the sanctuary so I could say goodbye to Mittens."

The *brahlu* had been placed in the facility outside of the city. Secured and highly guarded, the sanctuary also provided the most suitable environment for a *brahlu* to thrive.

"I'm sure he's happy there," I said softly, noting her eyes brim with tears.

She nodded quickly.

"Oh, yes, he is. I'm happy for him, too. I really am." She blinked the tears away. "I just want to see him one more time. To thank him, you know, and to say goodbye." She gave me a shy smile. "In a way, he saved my sanity. Suddenly, I had someone smaller to worry about, so I stopped freaking out so much about myself. You saved my life, Tessa—" I made a gesture to protest, but she wouldn't let me. "You and Greyx, you saved my life," she said firmly. "I wouldn't be here without either of you. But Mittens saved my mind. I owe him, too."

"Say hi to him from me." I smiled. "Give him a kiss on that long nose of his."

"I will." She rolled her bag to the edge of our open floor where the small aircraft was already perched, waiting for her. "And you say hi to Greyx from me."

"I…" I wanted to say I might not see Greyx in the week she'd be gone.

He and I had been separated upon our arrival in Arqa. The moment our rescue ship landed, it was swarmed by Aldraian officials, medics, army people, and who knew who else.

The medical team had taken Lucy and me, and Greyx had been whisked away by Aldraians in army uniforms. I hadn't seen him since.

"You'll see him," Lucy said confidently. "He's so in love with you. He won't stay away for long."

She boarded the aircraft and gave me a wave as it flew away.

Was she right? Was Greyx in love with me? He'd never said that outright, but the way he often looked at me—affection and the sizzling heat of desire simmering in his golden eyes—it certainly made me feel loved.

I stood on the edge of our floor. A short hedge served as a railing. Everywhere the eye could see, the garden-buildings of various heights and shapes made up the City of Arqa. One construction smoothly molded into another, making the entire city look like a giant ocean of green waves and hills composed from layers upon layers of hanging gardens.

Beautiful, unusual, and surreal.

Another new-to-me planet. Except that this one felt…closer somehow. Must be all the greenery—it was easy on the eye.

Light breeze gently moved the garlands of flowers on the ceiling above me. I hugged myself, though the air was balmy, perfect for my outfit of shorts and a t-shirt.

Among the green hills of the buildings, life buzzed. Hundreds of light, sleek aircraft floated around, almost noiselessly. They reminded me of large birds with long wings that folded whenever they landed at the open floors.

One of the aircraft separated from the flock that moved in a continuous stream, following an invisible road in the sky. The tiny vessel veered toward my building, its red and orange paint making it look even more like an exotic bird among all the green. It pulled over to my building smoothly, then aligned with my floor.

I stepped back from the edge, keeping inside the hedge.

The large figure behind the glass of the aircraft turned. The man flashed me a bright, toothy grin. The familiar smile made my heart skip.

Greyx.

He jumped out of the pilot's seat and leaped over the hedge, not even bothering with the gate.

"You…" I breathed out as he wrapped his burly arms around me. "You came."

He hugged me tightly, and I melted against his chest. Here, inside his arms I always felt the best.

"Of course I came." He kissed my hair. It had long dried after the shower I'd taken hours ago, but I kept it unbound. My long, dark tresses were strewn over my shoulders, the ends almost reaching my waist.

With a finger under my chin, Greyx lifted my face to his for a kiss.

"I have only a few days to woo you." He smiled against my lips. "I can't afford to lose any time."

I arched an eyebrow. "To *woo* me?"

Didn't he know I was already smitten? He had conquered my heart back at the New Year's party. And then he'd made me fall for him even harder while saving my life and protecting me on Zoltu. He'd been on my mind every minute since we'd parted at the spaceport a day ago. I'd hardly slept last night. And he had been in every short, restless dream I'd had.

He held me close. "I have big plans for us this week. I'm making you dinner at my place tonight. Tomorrow, we're going dancing."

"Dancing?"

"Yes. Get ready. I'm taking you home."

Home.

I'd called home so many places in my life. Often, it'd been just a bunk bed on a yacht or a spaceship.

With Greyx's arms around me, I felt more at home than I'd ever have in my entire life. Maybe here, on Aldrai, was where I belonged all along?

GREYX MANEUVERED THE aircraft out of the city. I knew we'd left the city behind because the multi-layered "hills" of apartment buildings were gradually replaced by real, green rolling hills. Patches of flowers sprinkled the ground, creating swirls of colors in intricate shapes and various sizes.

The beauty of the landscape took my breath away. "Aldrai is gorgeous."

"This part of it is," Greyx agreed.

I watched him from the side, drinking in every detail. I'd missed him so much, my heart still ached, even as he sat right beside me.

He was dressed in a loose, cream-colored top. Its thin, soft material draped down his chest and abs, cinched at his trim waist with a wide belt of the same light-brown color as his pants. His bracers were creamy-white, matching the color of his top. Instead of the hard-soled boots he'd worn before, he had on soft-leather shoes today.

Unlike his uniform, this outfit was clearly meant for peaceful, casual events. Though Greyx didn't look completely relaxed in it.

"I feared you'd be too busy with what's happening on Zoltu to see me any time soon," I said carefully.

"I was busy." He clicked something on the control panel, and the aircraft started to descend slowly. "That's why I couldn't be with you sooner."

"Have things been sorted out there? Already?" I assumed it'd take much longer than a day to dismantle the operation on Zoltu, to re-home the animals, and to hold accountable everyone responsible. Yet here he was, with me.

He shook his head, confirming my assumptions. "The mess on Zoltu will take a long time to clean up."

"Did you find who was responsible for it?"

"All evidence leads to a major entertainment company on Aldrai. The two executives have already been arrested. There'll be more arrests for sure. The investigation is ongoing."

"And the animals?"

"All of them will be assessed and either released back in their home worlds or re-homed in sanctuaries."

"Good." A weight I hadn't realized I'd carried dropped off my chest. Knowing the arena and the entire facility would soon cease to exist made it easier to breathe.

Greyx landed the aircraft in front of a tall wall of multi-colored rocks dressed in green vines with tiny purple and yellow flowers. In the middle of it was an ornately carved gate.

"Oh, we're here?" I shifted in my seat to take a better look, but all I could see was the wall surrounded by rolling hills.

"Yes." He turned off the engines and opened the doors then grabbed my suitcase and helped me out. "Welcome to my home, Tessa."

The gate opened as we approached. A cobblestone path led to an open space surrounded by a green hedge a little taller than Greyx.

It looked like a front yard, and I half-expected to see a house next, even though I knew there'd be no building. We were already inside Greyx's home, and this was most likely a hall or a front lobby.

A carved-stone fountain was in the middle, surrounded by flower beds.

"Are you tired?" Greyx asked. "Hungry?"

I shook my head to both, too excited to see how he lived.

"Would you like to see the place first?"

"Yes," I said quickly. "Can I have a tour please?"

"All right." He set my suitcase down, not far from the entrance. "But this place is huge, I have to warn you. Let me know when you've had enough and need a break."

He led me to the left, under a tall arch peppered with multi-colored flowers, some of which ended up being not flowers at all. They fluttered up when we approached, then settled down on the hedge right behind us. With long plumes and colorful wings, they could be tiny birds or large insects.

"Do they live here? All the time?" I asked.

"They sure spend more time on my property than I do." Greyx smiled, watching me with curiosity.

I touched a petal of a large orange flower next to my shoulder. It opened under my touch, spreading into a cluster of smaller blossoms, as if showing off its beauty to me.

"Some like attention." Greyx commented. "Others not so much. But all are harmless."

"Are there no poisonous plants or insects on Aldrai?" I leaned closer to the flower, inhaling its sweet, buttery scent.

"Oh, there are plenty of both. We have a multi-level deterrent system complete with protective energy shields to ensure none of them make it inside the living areas."

"Well, that's reassuring." I felt very much relieved to hear that.

The space on the other side of the arch was as large as the one by the entrance. Instead of a waterfall, it had several shrubs with leaves of different colors and shapes. One was ombre purple, with the palest lavender on top thickening to the richest shade of eggplant on the very bottom. Another one had leaves growing in a striped pattern, from lime green to yellow and dark pine green. Others were pink or red. The path branched out, twining between and around the bright shrubs.

I noticed Greyx was now barefoot. He must've taken his shoes off while I'd admired the flying insects and flowers. I toed off my flat-sole sandals, too.

The cobblestones were pleasantly warm under my feet. Surprisingly, they also turned out to be softer than the actual stones. The material felt like firm rubber.

"This was one of the bedrooms," Greyx explained, clearing his throat. "I had the beds removed shortly after..." His voice broke off, but I knew what he was going to say.

This was his family home. Dozens of his closest family members had lived here before the tragedy took them away.

I reached for his hand, and he squeezed my fingers tightly.

Another bedroom came after that one, then another. None of them had any beds. And each was converted into yet another beautiful and unique masterpiece of living art. Flower beds replaced the beds where his loved ones used to sleep.

"This one had six beds," he said softly. "A kids' bedroom... You know what?" He turned to me after yet another bedless room. "The rest are very much the same. Let me show you the rooms where I actually spend my time when I'm here."

I was glad to leave this part of his home for now. Thinking about all the people who were no longer there filled me with sadness. Grief tightened around my heart. I understood why Greyx would avoid staying in his own home. It came with so many memories. I could only hope that with time, his pain and guilt would ease, leaving more room for fondness whenever he looked back at the times when they were still alive.

He took me across a small, curved bridge over a creek that ran along the property. We strolled under an alley of skinny trees with the trunks so tall and thin, they bent in the middle, creating an arch over the path.

Greyx made a sweeping gesture when entering the next room. "Kitchen."

The kitchen definitely looked more lived in than the bedrooms before. It was also furnished. A huge wooden table stood in the middle on a dais. When I got closer, I realized the tabletop was propped on four massive tree stumps that grew from the floor. Their roots intertwined, forming the platform that looked like an intricately carved dais.

The table appeared large enough to seat at least two dozen people, but there was only one chair, set at the head of it.

To the right was a stone countertop kitchen island with a built-in metal grill under a round cover.

"That's where I'll make your dinner tonight." Greyx gave me one of his easy smiles. "I hardly ever cook for myself. But there are a few dishes I have mastered well." He glanced at the table, scratching the base of his right horn. "And I do have a second chair somewhere."

"I'm looking forward to it." I wasn't big on cooking myself, but I could mix any cocktail known on Earth and beyond. Maybe I could recreate the one he got for me at the party back on Neron?

I touched the smooth, polished surface of the countertop on the island.

Greyx pointed at the space partially separated by a short hedge from the rest of the kitchen.

"The edge of the property is right there. I like to read in that spot after dinner when I'm home."

A pair of tall trees stood side by side, with a woven hammock stretched between their smooth trunks. The stone wall dipped on this side of the property, opening to the green landscape beyond. A dark strip of forest trimmed the horizon, and a wide ribbon of river glistened before it.

This would be my favorite place to read, too.

"Wow, I honestly don't know what's more beautiful about your home, Greyx, the inside or the outside."

He came up behind me, stepping softly, so softly, that I sensed him before I heard him. The warmth of his body pressed against my back, then his arms wound around me.

"There are a few more rooms left," he murmured just above my ear. "Do you want to see them now? Or should we have dinner first?"

It was too early for dinner, and I wasn't hungry. I leaned back against him. He kissed my neck, his warm breath fanning across my skin.

"What would you like to do, Tessa?" he asked between the kisses.

What would I like? To stay just like this, with his arms around me, his lips on me, his body so close to mine, I didn't know where one of us ended and the other began.

No, I wanted him even closer than that.

"I want to see your bedroom," I said, shocked by my own brazenness.

He hummed in approval, spinning me around to face him. "I planned to feed you first."

Lost in his bright sunny eyes, I mumbled, "I'm not hungry...not for food." I'd missed him. So much.

With his arm going under my knees and another tightly wrapping around my shoulders, he lifted me up.

His mouth descended on mine, and all sense of reality disappeared. Only Greyx remained—his lips sliding against mine, his arms holding me tight.

I clung to the horns on his shoulders, returning his kiss and craving his touch.

He laid me on my back on a cushioned surface, and I realized we'd arrived at his bed.

I opened my eyes to find a luscious canopy of light-green leaves above us. His bed stood under four trees, their trunks serving as the bedposts. A soothing sound of water trickled nearby. A melodious chirping of birds trilled all around us. So peaceful.

I fisted my hands in the soft material of Greyx's shirt. "Take it off," I whispered.

His eyes darkened, and his eyelids dropped—the look I knew so well. Heat rushed through my body in response. I arched against him, my breathing growing faster.

"I want to see you naked," I rasped.

His mouth stretched in a lopsided grin. His hand going to the clasp on his shoulder, he pushed off the bed and stood next to it.

"You want a show?" He winked, with a flash of heat in his sunny gaze.

He touched something near the bed, and soft background music filled the air.

I rose on my elbows with a hum of approval. "Nice."

He clicked open both closures on his shoulders, and his shirt slid down, bunching around his waist. I trailed my gaze down his chest, appreciating every rise of muscles and every dip between them.

Next, he unbuckled his belt and pants. Shoving his clothes down, he stepped out of them, his hard, bumpy erection bobbing high in the air.

"So?" He rested his hands on his hips, letting me gawk to my heart's content. "Do you like what you see?"

I bit my lip, taking in the wide expanse of his chest, the thick, muscled columns of his thighs, and the straining shaft of his erection.

"Love it," I confessed, heat spreading up my face and down my body. "Let me see your tail, now." I twirled my hand in the air, gesturing for him to turn around.

For once, he didn't blush when I mentioned it. His smile shifted into a wicked smirk. He spun on his heel, turning his back to me.

His umber skin darkened over the hard plates on his shoulder blades. The darker strip ran along the hard bumps of his spine and down the length of his tail. Its base was wide and flat. A few inches down from the spot where his tail connected to his body, it gradually tapered into a narrow, flexible appendage.

Greyx curled its tip, then swayed it side to side, as if to demonstrate the flexibility of the tail and his control over it.

An Aldraian tail was shorter than those of any other species I knew. It was easier to conceal.

"Why do Aldraians hide their tails?" I asked.

He shrugged, glancing at me over his shoulder. "Why do other species shamelessly display theirs? It's a cultural thing. Like wearing clothes. Would *you* run around naked?"

I smiled, shaking my head.

"Though I may insist you do around here," he added with that naughty grin on his face. "Your turn." He shifted to face me again. "Take off your clothes, Tessa. I want to see you, too."

He'd seen me naked before. But it'd been in the semi-darkness of the cave on Zoltu, in the faint glow of the stalactites, not in the bright afternoon sunlight.

"I'm waiting." He widened his stance, crossing his arms over his chest.

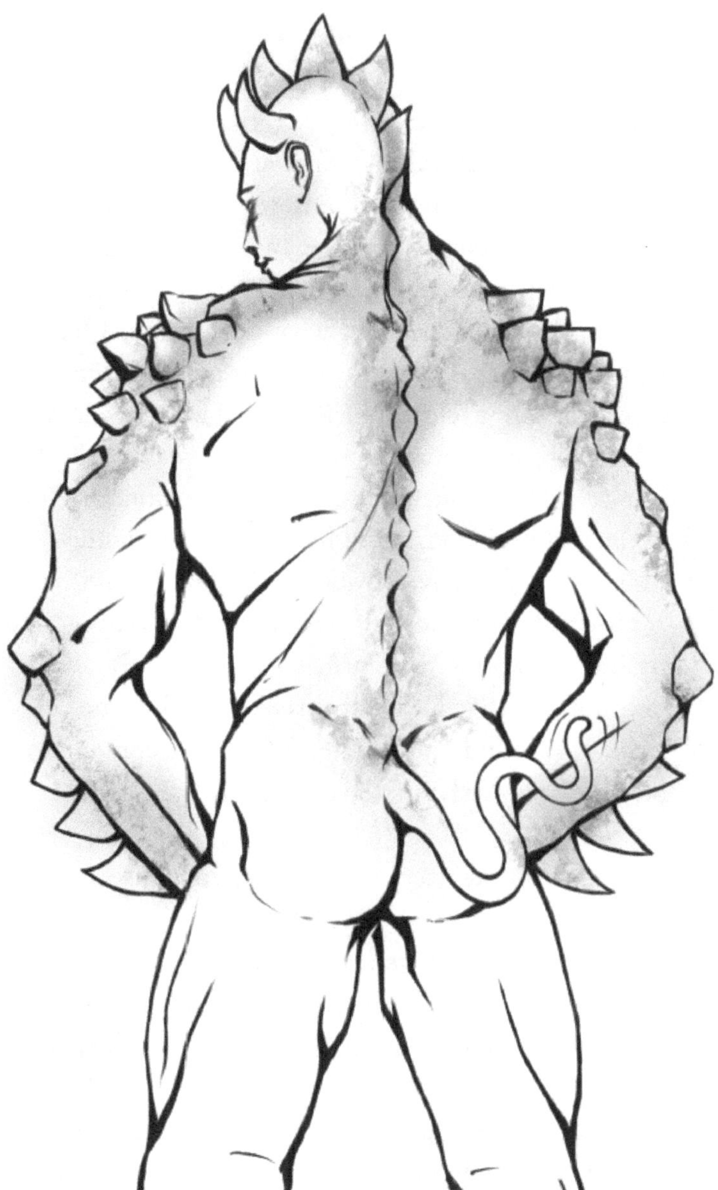

Trying to ignore his intense stare, I lifted my t-shirt over my head, revealing my white bra. After dropping the shirt on the bed, I opened the zipper on my shorts. I had to get up from the bed to take them off. Then, I stood in only my white bra and mismatched pink panties.

"More," he rasped, clearing his throat.

I awkwardly rubbed my upper arms, tentatively raising my eyes to his. I was no supermodel, but the look in his gaze, full of heat and pure adoration, gave me courage. I inhaled, unfurling my shoulders and straightening my spine.

Suddenly, it didn't matter what extra curves I had according to the Earth's standards of beauty or what I lacked compared to Aldraian women. Greyx clearly loved what he was seeing, and I didn't mind showing him more.

I reached back, unclipping my bra, then shimmied out of my underwear, and stood in front of him, completely nude.

His eyes roamed over my body with hunger and...wonder.

"How did I get so lucky?" he murmured. "What gods did I please for them to send you my way?"

How did *I* get so lucky for this man to adore me so?

His arm around my waist, he kissed me deeply and so sweetly. He walked me backward until the back of my knees hit the bed, and I sat on it.

"I want to taste every part of you," he whispered, crouching in front of me.

His kisses trailed lower. He lifted one of my heavy breasts in his hand, then sucked the tip into his mouth. With the fingers of his other hand, he played with my other nipple. I clenched and shivered at the touch.

I arched my back, pressing my breast into his mouth. His tongue flicked around my hardened nipple, his teeth scraping my skin in a most invigorating way. Hugging his neck, I pressed my cheek to the side of one of his horns. My legs fell open, making room for him to shift closer.

Letting go of my breast, he leaned sideways and opened a carved wooden door in the small hill by the bed that I'd thought was just a landscape feature, but it turned out it served as a nightstand.

He took out two wide, oval pieces from there, each with several high bumps and protrusions. They were the same milky-white color as his arm bracers and appeared to be made from the same material.

I lifted my eyebrows in questions, but before I could ask anything, he snapped the patches onto his shoulders, concealing his horns.

"Now, I can do this..." He lifted my leg then draped it over his shoulder. "Without hurting you."

My thigh rested on the soft pad over his shoulder horns.

"Talk about 'safe sex,'" I giggled.

Greyx lifted my other leg over his other shoulder, then dove between my thighs.

I hissed in pleasure when he dragged his tongue along me.

"Mmm," he hummed against my sensitive flesh. "You were so right. This is much better than dinner."

I couldn't reply, not when he twirled his tongue like that or wrapped his lips around my most sensitive spot, sucking on it like his life depended on it.

"Oh..." I moaned, feeling the pleasure rise and crest. "Greyx..."

Digging my heels into his cushioned shoulders, I lifted my hips, pressing against his wicked mouth.

An orgasm slammed at me like an avalanche of ecstasy. Every muscle in my body tensed. Each nerve stood on end. Then, the shudders of bliss rippled through me again and again as Greyx lapped at me, causing pleasure to roll wave after wave.

Languid warmth descended upon me afterward. I unwrapped my hands from around his horns and dropped my arms to my sides.

"Greyx..." I hummed, beyond sated. All other words had deserted me, only his name remained.

He kissed up my body, slowly fanning my desire back to life. It was always there, the need for him, simmering hot under my skin. With soft kisses and naughty licks and nibbles, he coaxed it to grow and burn brighter. Hotter. Stronger.

"More," I begged when his face reached mine.

"Insatiable." He chuckled.

And with him, I was. I had no idea now how I'd ever managed to go through life without him in my bed, by my side.

He circled my opening with his fingers, testing, prodding, stretching—getting me ready for his massive girth. Gripping my hips, he shifted me further up the bed, then crawled over me.

"Are you ready for more?" he growled against my ear.

Oh, was I ever.

"I want you, Greyx. Only you."

What had he done to me? No other man, human or alien, would ever be enough, would ever be this good.

He pushed inside me with a grunt, that thick, slick cock of his sliding into me, inch by inch.

"More?" He tormented me, teasing me by slipping out a little then thrusting back in.

"Oh, God, yes..."

I clawed his hard back.

A probing touch slipped between my butt cheeks. His hands were propped into the mattress on each side of my head, his cock buried inside me. It could only be one thing gently prodding at my back entrance now—his tail.

My eyes flew wide open, and he paused, a silent request for permission in his eyes.

"I—I've never done that before," I confessed, fear warring with the thrill of the unknown inside me.

He grinned. "Some other day, then." The tip of his tail rested against me without entering.

Shockingly, I felt a slight tug of disappointment. With him, I would try anything, I realized. I trusted him fully.

Some other day... echoed in my head. And I looked forward to it.

Then, all coherent thoughts deserted me as he thrust harder. The bumps along his length rubbed against the edge of my opening, tugging at my most sensitive spot above.

Pressure built low in my belly, making me ache with need.

Harder... rushed through my head, but I didn't need to say it out loud.

He pummeled into me with the desperation of a man on the brink of insanity.

Sweltering hot pleasure exploded through me, and I gripped him tighter as he roared through his release. The sound was so mighty, it must've reverberated through the hills far beyond his dwelling, letting all Aldrai know how good I made him feel.

"Tessa..." he murmured, his large body relaxing against mine. "My sweet, darling Tessa. How do you make me rage with lust like that, over and over again?"

His question didn't require an answer, but I gave him one anyway.

"Must be those *yirzi* drugs?" I teased.

He snorted a laugh into my shoulder. "The medical team found no trace of the mating drugs left in my system this morning. Whatever it is that makes me want you non-stop must be permanent. I don't see myself ever having enough of you."

Ever...

How much time did we really have to be together?

I hugged him tighter, as if someone was about to take him away from me already.

"Tessa," his voice turned serious as he shifted off me and to his side, facing me. "I sent a request to our government. I want ours to be the first human-Aldraian marriage to be approved under the new program."

"A marriage?"

This suddenly felt like what I'd imagined Christmas would be in a large, loving family—with presents that kept coming and coming.

"I've spoken to Alcus Hecear about it." He exhaled a nervous laugh. "He sent me a lot of paperwork to fill out. More forms than I've ever seen."

I rose on an elbow. "You want to marry me?"

He stared at me intensely.

"Eventually," he said carefully. "Would that be something you'd consider?"

Be his wife? Spend the rest of my life with him? Right here, in his garden home that looked exactly how I envisioned Paradise would look?

Happiness flooded me in a warm, tingling wave of excitement, hard to contain.

Greyx's expression remained pensive, though.

"Tessa, I spoke to Alcus first to make sure it was possible for me to legally make you my wife," he explained. "I don't wish to put any pressure on you. But I want you to know that I'm serious about us. You and I can have a future together if you're open to have one with me. This is not a short fling for me or just some high-adrenaline adventure. I want you. And I want you for life."

My smile grew so wide, it almost hurt. I took his face between my hands.

"You have me, Greyx. I'm already yours. I love you." I kissed his lips. "The rest is just paperwork."

His frown finally melted into a bright smile.

"Oh, I love you so much, my sweet, fearless Tessa. Come here." He took me in his arms again. "And stay here. Forever."

Home. He was the home I never had.

I murmured against his lips, "Will you let me play with your tail, now?"

He chuckled at my eagerness. "Just like the rest of me, my tail is all yours, sweetheart. Do with it whatever you want."

EPILOGUE

Tessa.

A year later.

My comm device pinged with a message.

"I'm almost there. Are you ready?" Greyx's voice said from the silver disk I'd left on the bed.

"Almost." I grunted, snapping the last buckle of my support harness in place.

Being almost eight months pregnant with quintuplets made my belly expand to an unimaginable size. The team of doctors who'd monitored my pregnancy every step of the way prescribed me the support harness made from soft, slightly stretchy material.

With Aldraian pregnancies often resulting in a dozen babies or more, apparently, the use of this device was very common. It gently cradled my humongous belly, expanding with it to give room for my growing babies inside. The wide straps and the firm but flexible back and hip support allowed women to walk and move comfortably even while carrying an entire soccer team in their bellies.

"Just need to get this dress on." I waddled to the shimmering, light-gray contraption hanging on a tree branch by the bed.

The dress was so wide that eight months ago, it would've easily worked as a parachute for me had I decided to jump out of a plane. Now, it barely closed around my middle.

"I'm here," Greyx said through the comm device.

I heard the noise of his aircraft engine turning off before he hung up. Then, the chirping of the birds by the entrance announced his arrival.

"Tessa?" He padded noiselessly along the path, barefoot. But his booming voice told me exactly where he was.

"I'm here!" I yelled, wrestling with the dress. "In the bedroom."

He appeared in the archway to our room. Wearing his white dress uniform with gleaming buckles and insignia, his horns polished to a shine, he took my breath away. I paused my hands over the buckles on my shoulders, falling in love with my husband all over again.

"You look so good," I breathed out, unable to tear my eyes off him. "And I..." I glanced down my front that had become nothing but one huge, round belly lately.

"And you look absolutely stunning, sweetheart." He brushed my lips with a gentle kiss. "But also absolutely not ready, Tessa," he scolded, tilting his head.

I huffed a frustrated breath.

"I'm trying. I really am." I got hold of the stubborn buckle on my shoulder.

"Let me." He promptly snapped the crystal-and-silver buckle in place, then closed the decorated closures on each of my sides. "Simply gorgeous, my love." He kissed my nape before spreading my long hair over my back and shoulders. "How are you feeling?" Hugging me from behind, he caressed the high swell of my belly.

"Good."

The medical team had been going out of their way to make my pregnancy as comfortable as possible. And it'd been manageable. I had no swelling or nausea. I could walk and move easily enough for someone carrying five babies.

"There is no way I can put on these shoes on my own, though." I lifted my skirt to show him my bare feet, the feet that I couldn't see over my belly.

Greyx grabbed one of the crystal-studded sandals I'd left by the bed. "These shoes?"

"Yes." Lately, I'd been wearing nothing but slip-on shoes whenever I left our place. But the fancy dress I had on for tonight required pretty footwear. The buckles on the sandals presented a challenge for someone like me, who hadn't been able to bend over for months now.

"Sit here." Greyx helped me down on the bed, then took my foot in his hand.

Warm and calloused, his palm gently supported my sole as he slid my foot inside the sandal. He quickly placed the other one on as well, then closed the tiny buckles of the straps.

"He'll be a wonderful dad," I thought for the millionth time during the past eight months. Greyx was everything a kid would need in a father. He was gentle and attentive when his help was needed. Silly and fun when he knew he could relax. Strict, protective, and firm when it was necessary.

"Thank you," I whispered when he straightened on his knees in front of me. "I love you so much, honey."

My eyes filled with tears, and I sniffled.

Damn hormones.

He gave me an understanding smile.

"No tears tonight." He kissed the tip of my nose. "I love you, too. But I'm not going to cry about it. In fact, I've been smiling like an idiot for the entire year you've been with me."

I snorted. Greyx was an optimist by nature. I couldn't imagine him ever turning into a crying, slobbering mess like me right now.

"It's the babies," I said softly. "I blame them for this."

"I know, my love." He got up and drew me closer. "They'll have to make you laugh especially hard after they're born, to make up for all the times they've made you cry already."

Of course, I knew I had no reason to cry, no reason at all. Greyx had been a wonderful husband, the one every woman dreamed of, but that I'd never even dared to hope for.

He'd already hired two sweet Aldraian women to help me look after the babies when they were born, arranged for his sister to be on standby when needed, and he was going to take a year off work entirely to stay home with me and the babies.

Just thinking about what a great man he was and how lucky I was to have met him made me tear up all over again.

Stupid, stupid hormones.

Greyx wrapped his supportive arm around my back. "Ready to go?"

I nodded, not trusting myself to speak, and blinked the tears away.

The flight to the city didn't take long. Despite it being New Year's Eve—which on Aldrai was celebrated in the winter, too—the weather remained balmy as always in this part of the planet.

Once again, I celebrated a New Year on yet another planet. Only this one was my home now. There would be no other.

Greyx pulled over and lined our aircraft up with the top floor of a large building. Hundreds of aircraft had already been parked here, clipped to the edge of the floor along one side of the building. Their colorful wings folded neatly, making them look like a flock of birds sitting on a branch.

"Let's get this party started." My husband grinned at me, helping me to get out. "We'll show them how dancing is done."

I laughed, admiring his faith in me. He still believed I could dance, even with my current size reaching that of a whale.

The Aldraian branch of the Interplanetary Liaison Committee had decided to follow the tradition started by Alcus Hecear and organized a party to celebrate the New Year.

There weren't that many human-Aldraian families yet. The handful of couples that had been paired up so far consisted of human men and Aldraian women, all matches still fairly new.

It wasn't only the Aldraians who came to the party, though. All families created through the hard work of the Committee were invited. The spacious rooftop patio was filled with Voranian men and their human spouses, the Committee employees of all races, and the members of the Aldraian Military who knew Greyx.

Linai, Greyx's sister, was already dancing with her husband. Linai was in her thirties, the same age as Greyx. She and her husband didn't have children. Aldraian pregnancies were prolific but rare, and it hadn't happened for Linai yet. That didn't stop her from delighting in *my* pregnancy. She'd been amazingly helpful and supportive. Over the past months, we'd become great friends.

Linai's husband noticed our arrival, as did many of Greyx's friends. People waved and bowed in greeting while some tried to make their way through the crowd to us.

I spotted Lucy's blonde head at one of the tables placed around a red-and-pink flower bed.

Lucy had quit working for the Committee before our spaceship went back to Earth with Bree. Instead, Lucy had accepted a position in the wildlife sanctuary on Aldrai where many of the animals rescued from Zoltu had found their new home, including Mittens. She'd been working there ever since.

Lucy had become very good friends with the Aldraian manager of the sanctuary. He was sitting at the table with her, and judging by the way he kissed her hand, they were more than just colleagues now. I wondered if theirs might be the next human-Aldraian marriage approved by the Committee.

The slow music ended, only to leap ahead with one of those crazy-rhythm dances that Aldraians loved so much, or at least my husband did.

Sure enough, Greyx's face lit up.

"Let's show these people how it's done!" He grabbed me around the place where I used to have a waist eight months ago.

"Greyx, you're not going to make me—" I started.

"Of course I am!" He winked at me. "We're dancing."

I shook my head.

"What's the problem?" He glanced down at my feet. "You're wearing just the right shoes, my love."

I could never deny him anything when he looked at me with this much excitement as he was doing right now.

"I promise you, I can't jump, not for another month at least," I warned, but followed him to the artfully shaped dance floor in the middle. "If I jump, I'd probably break a hole in the floor and fall on the heads of the people below."

He chuckled, drawing me closer.

"We won't jump, beautiful. We'll just cuddle and sway to the music. Like this." He took my right hand in his then gently placed it around the horn on his left shoulder. "I just want to have you all to myself for a few minutes before everyone else ambushes us."

He tipped the crown of his horns in the direction of the people who started gathering on the edge of the dance floor—his friends and colleagues, and the friends I'd made during my year on this planet. All those who wished to greet and chat with us.

Greyx just wanted to dance with me. And I...I would never say no to a few moments of being in his arms. Just the two of us. In the whole of the Universe.

Instead of leaping side to side to every beat as the dance demanded, Greyx swayed to every second beat with me in his arms. Instead of twirling me in the air, he pulled me in for a kiss on my lips or a caress to the side of my neck.

"I believe I love this version of the dance even more," I whispered in his ear when he drew me into him again.

"Any version works for me." He gave me one of his sunny smiles that I loved so much. "As long as you are the one I'm dancing with."

More in My Holiday Tails

Mail Order Mom

Chapter 1

Through the bent and dented blinds, I scanned the street outside my apartment for any suspicious elements. My basement window was so low, all I could see were people's feet. And all of them looked suspicious to me.

I wanted to lock myself in and stay here, relatively safe and sound, and literally underground. But my fridge was empty, as was my wallet. To put something in both, I needed to work.

I grabbed my purse and padded to the door. Pressing an ear to it, I listened for any suspicious sounds, as if the mafia thugs who stalked me would announce their presence.

All seemed quiet.

With a deep breath, I clutched the handles of my purse in my sweaty hands and opened the door. I climbed the set of crumbling concrete stairs up to the street and emerged from my underground hideout into the bright Manhattan morning.

The street was busy, like most streets in central New York. It seemed easy enough to get lost in the crowd. Only I knew that Bolshoy's people would find me. They always did.

The last time, one of them cornered me in the alley two doors down on my way from the ladies' fashion store where I worked.

They wanted the money my husband Tom stole from them. And they didn't give a damn that my dearest husband also stole everything from me—my trust, my innocence, and every single penny of my substantial inheritance. If I ever saw him again, I would punch him in the face then kick him when he fell.

Too bad he fled the country months ago, taking all my money, millions of his investors' funds, and whatever he owed to Bolshoy and his people.

Grabbing whatever he could before making a run for it, Tom had also snatched the busty secretary from his office. The two of them were out there now, probably enjoying the sun on a beach somewhere, while I was half-running to my job, scanning the street in fear for any sign of the dangerous people he was stupid enough to steal from.

It was a good thing I'd switched to wearing flats. The first day of working in retail in five-inch heels had almost killed me. Now, running was so much easier in my black, low-wedge shoes.

I reached the store, completely out of breath.

"You're late." Aileen pursed her lips. The owner and the manager of the store, she appeared to live here twenty-four-seven.

I threw a glance at the display on the cash register. "Just by two minutes."

"Five," she replied in an icy tone. "This clock is three minutes behind."

Resisting the strong urge to flip her a finger, I mumbled, "Sorry," on my way to the tiny employee-room-slash-office-slash-storage-room at the back to drop off my purse and coat. This wasn't one of the high-end fashion shops on 5th Avenue, even if Aileen liked to pretend it was just like them.

No wonder I was late. I had sat by the window for who knew how long, gathering the courage to leave my apartment. The sensation of the thug's rough grip still lingered on my throat from the last time one of them had caught me.

I kept telling them I had no money. But for some reason, Bolshoy believed I was an accomplice of Tom's and my two retail jobs were just a cover to keep a low profile. Like I would be living in a mouse-infested basement, eating frozen dinners, and working two jobs if I had access to the millions Tom had stolen.

Aileen had given me my very first job ever. I was born into money and raised in luxury homes with maids and nannies. I'd never been taught to do anything for myself. My mother wouldn't even let my sister and me make our own beds.

"There are less fortunate people in the world. We shouldn't take their jobs from them. We have to give them the opportunity to earn a living," she'd say in a dignified voice.

Mother thought herself a benevolent person by making others do things for her. She provided them with "means to earn a living" while looking down her nose at those she employed.

Customers of Aileen's often reminded me of my mother. Like her, they were snotty and self-important with no real accomplishments other than being rich. After two months of working in the store, I was still learning how to deal with them. Sometimes, I just felt like punching their well-exfoliated, made-up faces.

But I needed this job to pay the astronomical rent my landlord charged for that crawl space room I now lived in and to occasionally buy some food to eat too.

So, I smiled at the snotty shoppers and repeated like a parrot all day, "How may I help you?" and "Have a nice day."

Around noon, the bell above the door rang again, announcing the arrival of yet another customer.

I heaved a breath and plastered on a smile, then I saw my twin sister walking in.

Mara looked every bit like the customers I'd been dealing with on a daily basis. Louboutin heels. Hermes scarf tied artfully around her neck. Italian wool coat thrown over her shoulders, unbuttoned, because she'd taken a cab here, not walked like me. The handbag that people lined up for years to buy hung in the crook of her elbow.

Sliding her oversized sunglasses down her nose, she threw a glance around the store. The look in her blue eyes clearly conveyed she didn't want to be here.

Her gaze stopped on me. "Oh, there you are. I need to have a word with you."

She hadn't changed a bit. Though, just two months ago, she wasn't in a much better situation than me.

Mara's fiancé Jim would likely be at the beach with Tom and his busty secretary, right now. Jim and Tom were childhood friends, Ivy league graduates, and partners in crime—literally, as it turned out. I met them both through Mara.

Before he left, Jim had cleaned out her banking accounts just like Tom had mine. Unlike me, however, instead of taking two jobs to survive, Mara found a couple of wealthy men to pay for her expenses.

My sister and I never got along that well. And lately, she'd been treating me like a second-class citizen.

"I'm working," I snapped.

She trotted closer, expertly balancing on her sky-high heels.

"Come on, Susanna. It's important. I'll buy you lunch." She tossed another glance around the store. "It's not like there's anyone here, anyway." She tipped a chin at Aileen. "That old lady can cover for you."

Aileen squinted at her with so much disdain, another drop and she'd set my twin sister on fire.

It might be best to get Mara out of here before a fight broke out. It had been slow today. Lunchtime was close. My stomach growled, and the food truck parked on the street corner called to me. I was not in the position to turn down a free lunch.

"Fine," I said to Mara. "But only if you're paying. Aileen, can I take a break, please?"

Aileen must want Mara out of her store badly, because she didn't even argue about me taking my lunch break early.

"Thirty minutes," she sneered.

"I'll wait for you outside." Mara strolled out the door while I got my purse and coat.

After I'd joined her outside, we got gyros from the food truck, then walked to a bench nearby.

"This is not a place for a Takolsky." She curled her lip in distaste.

Takolsky was her last name. It had been mine too, before I changed it to Tom's—less glamorous—Riley.

"Which place? The store? Or the bench?" I snorted.

She sounded like our father. He always had a firm opinion about all the suitable and unsuitable places for his family to be. And no, a second-rate fashion boutique would never be considered a proper place for one of his daughters to shop, not to mention to work. Come to think of it, this chipped, worn bench wouldn't be much to his liking, either.

"You know what I mean," she brushed me off. "This is not what you should be doing with your life, Susanna."

By "this," she meant having any form of gainful employment, of course. She tossed a disgusted look back at the boutique as if it were some dirty strip joint.

"Well, gyros cost money," I argued. "So does a place to live. And since all wealthy men in Manhattan are taken..." I waved a hand in the air and took a bite of my gyro. God, was it ever good! I stifled a moan of pleasure, savoring it. Lunch time had been the highlight of my day ever since I'd first discovered this food truck.

Mara neatly unwrapped the paper from one end of her gyro too. "You didn't even try to find a wealthy man. The moment Tom left, you were applying for jobs."

"I didn't really feel like trading one asshole for another, you know."

"Well...not all men are assholes," she said hesitantly. I looked at her cynically, and she faltered. "Fine. Maybe in this city, they are. But you don't need to stay here."

I'd been thinking about leaving. A new start would be nice. Except that Bolshoy's people would find me wherever I went.

"This thing with Tom and Jim will have to end one day," I said. "Then, I'll leave. Maybe."

Mara's expression grew somber. Bolshoy had been threatening her too.

"Do you think it will ever end?"

"I hope so." I sighed.

She crumpled her napkin, her hand trembling. "They said they would cut off my head."

With a spike of compassion, I patted her arm. "They say a lot of nasty things. But sooner or later, they must realize we have no money to give them."

She sniffled and took a bite of her gyro. I ate mine, too, in silence.

"Jason believes there are some legal steps I can take," she said after a little while.

"Who's Jason?"

She perked up. "Jason Moore. He's running for senate next year. Huge prospects."

"Is he one of the guys you've been dating?"

She nodded, brushing a long strand of hair behind her ear. It was blonde, just like mine, only Mara's was much better styled, of course.

"With him, it's getting serious, though." Her eyes lit up with hope. "I think he may propose soon."

"Congratulations," I said flatly.

It was hard to muster any excitement—another man with "huge prospects." We'd been there before.

"Anyway," she sounded enthusiastic, "I have a proposition for you."

"What kind?" I asked suspiciously. Historically, all of Mara's ideas had been largely self-serving.

"Two months ago, I applied for a marriage program," she said.

"What?" I did not expect that. "Like a dating app?"

"Not really. It comes with a bit more commitment than just dating. You practically need to stay with the guy for a year before you can leave."

I blinked at her. "Is that even legal? Why on earth would you agree to something like that?"

She rolled her eyes at me. "To get off planet, of course. Away from the mafia and their threats. To save my fucking head, Susanna."

"Off planet?" It dawned on me. "Please tell me you're not talking about one of those alien wife recruitment things?"

"Why not? What's so bad about marrying some powerful alien dude and jettisoning off to another planet where no thugs would ever find you?"

"Well, if you put it that way..."

It sounded tempting, to leave not just this city or this country but the entire freaking planet. Talk about a new start!

Except that it came with yet another man attached.

"Think about it," Mara continued, her enthusiasm building with every word. "No more looking over your shoulder. No more fear. No struggle, no working two jobs just to make ends meet."

"That'd be nice..." I brought my gyro up for another bite, then stopped, staring at her. "Wait a minute. Are you talking about me?"

She chomped at her gyro with the energy of biting someone's head off. "They matched me with one—"

"But you don't like him?"

That wouldn't be surprising; my sister wasn't easy to please. Her list of requirements for a man wasn't long, but it was very specific.

She threw her hands up in the air dramatically, half-eaten gyro clutched in one.

"Susanna, you have no idea. The guy is from Aldrai!"

Aldrai was one of the four populated planets Earth had made contact with in the past few years. Neron, Tragul, and Ivodi were the other three.

"So?" I shook my head.

"Have you seen the Aldraians? They're ugly as sin! The horns, the bumps..." She shuddered. "They say they have tails too. Only those must be the most disgusting things ever, since they hide them all the time."

"Why did you apply, then?" I shrugged. "You knew what they looked like, didn't you?"

She rolled her eyes again, then tossed her unfinished food into a nearby trash can, landing a perfect hit. I couldn't help but admire her aim.

"Besides," I added. "You should be able to either accept or decline a match. If you don't like him, say you don't want him. Swipe left, or whatever they do for that."

She hung her head between her shoulders. "Yeah, well... I already accepted it. A month ago, right when they matched me."

I stopped chewing my very delicious lunch to stare at her in shock. "Why?"

Mara leaped to her feet, clearly agitated. "I was scared, okay?" She plopped back on the bench next to me again. "I wanted to get out. I didn't even read the info they sent me about him. Besides, things weren't going that well with Jason back then. I didn't care."

That was so typical for my sister, doing whatever she wished at any given moment without thinking about the consequences.

"But now you care?"

She made a face at me, as if I were the one forcing the unwanted alien on her. "Things have changed. Jason is about to propose. If I leave, I'll mess it up between us."

"The mafia may get to you before Jason makes up his mind, you know," I pointed out.

She winced, drawing the ends of her coat closer together around her.

"They've kind of cooled off a bit, don't you think? I haven't seen anyone following me lately."

I hadn't been approached by anyone for a while, either. That didn't mean we hadn't been watched. Either that, or I'd been growing insane with paranoia. Living in constant fear sucked.

"Well, at least you have a chance to leave, now," I told her.

"No!" she yelled, as if I'd slapped her. "I can't possibly marry this alien guy."

"Why not? Just because of how he looks?" I knew my sister preferred handsome men, but she could be persuaded to overlook the flaws in a man's appearance if he had some valuable assets, like yachts or private jets.

"Susanna, he's some kind of truck driver!" she said dramatically, as if revealing to me that her match was a serial killer.

"Okay. But that could've been expected, couldn't it? I would imagine people of all walks of life would apply."

She wrung her hands, shaking her head.

"It's just my luck. The first human woman who participated in the program was matched with a Voranian from the planet Neron."

"Do you find Voranians more attractive than Aldraians?"

She curled her lips in disgust. "What? No. Voranians look like goats. Ravils are cute, but their planet, Tragul, doesn't have a marriage program with us." She heaved a heavy breath. "Ivodians are pretty good-looking too. But there has only been one Ivodian ship that came here for brides, and who knows when the next one would arrive. Anyway, that first woman from Earth got married to the head guy of the entire Voranian Army. She's like a celebrity in Voran now. And what do I get? A farmer! How unfair is that?"

"You said he was a truck driver." I finished my gyro and sighed, wishing it'd lasted longer.

"Same difference," she dismissed. "It states in his application he's a captain. I thought that meant he'd be a captain of a plane or a spaceship—"

"On spaceships, they call them commanders, I think." I opened my bottle of water and took a drink.

"Well, he drives some kind of machine they use to…" she waved both hands over the pavement, "…to turn dirt or something. Apparently, that qualifies him to call himself a captain." She sounded exasperated. "He drives a tractor for a living, Susanna. How can I possibly marry him? Me, Mara Takolsky! Dad would roll over in his grave if he knew."

Dad must've rolled a few times by now, from the moment his beloved protégé Tom turned out to be a thief and scoundrel, to all our possessions being sold at auction to cover some of the debt Tom and Jim had made in my and Mara's names.

"I can't be a farmer's wife!" Mara wailed. "I can't spend the rest of my life wearing housecoats, milking alien chickens, and taking care of his bratty kids."

"He has children?"

She faced me, her eyes wide in horror. "Four of them! Imagine that." She shook her head with another shudder. "It could be worse, I suppose, since Aldraian marriages are super prolific. They say they get like a dozen babies from each pregnancy."

"Why does he only have four, then?"

"I don't know. Who cares? Just be happy it's not twelve," she groaned, rubbing her forehead.

It definitely didn't sound like the lifestyle Mara would fit into. I felt sorry for her. But even more so, I felt sorry for the poor alien guy who would have to deal with her displeasure if she ever came to his planet.

"Can you get out of this?" I asked.

She looked outright miserable when she said, "No, I signed all the papers already."

"Because you believed him being a captain meant something more exciting than driving a truck?" I wasn't impressed with her lack of responsibility. Though, it didn't surprise me, either.

She pursed her lips as her chin trembled. "At the very least, I'd hoped that captain was a rank in the army. That he lived in the city. But Aldraians don't have any real cities. Even their capital looks like a bunch of hills." She sobbed, dabbing at her eyes with her napkin. "He lives in the countryside. Imagine me out in the country? On a farm?" A real tear rolled down her cheek, soaking into her napkin. "He's expecting me to board the ship to Aldrai next week." She gazed at me imploringly. "Susanna, I just can't do it..."

Oh, I knew that look well. And its meaning.

"So, you want me to do it for you? Is that why you came here?"

She clasped her hands, pressing them to her chest. "Could you please? It'd be a win-win solution. For everyone."

I arched an eyebrow. "Would it, now?"

"Look..." She perked up, her tears drying up instantly. "What do you have to lose? A shitty job or two and an equally shitty apartment."

My sister had never been to my apartment, but she was obviously familiar with the housing situation in New York. It was no secret one couldn't afford much of a place working retail jobs, no matter how many of them one had.

"So, you think I'd do just fine as a farmer's wife and raising four kids?" I asked skeptically.

She scooted closer to me along the bench. "We both know you have more patience than me. You've been working in that clothing store for months now. Personally, I would've scratched the eyes out of that old crone at the cash register long ago. But you keep taking every pissed-off look she gives you."

"I need that job to pay my rent."

"Exactly! That's what I mean," she exclaimed cheerfully. "You adapt easily. You accept the situation, no matter how shitty it is."

"That's not a compliment," I noted, unimpressed.

She just waved her hand again. "You know what I mean. You're also much better with kids. You wanted some of your own, remember? With Tom?"

Right. I had. Until I found out he'd had a vasectomy back in college and never bothered to tell me, even after we'd both agreed I would get off the pill and start trying for a family.

I heaved a sigh. There had been so many lies in my eleven-month marriage. Now it felt like there hadn't been even a shred of truth.

"Oh, and you were always so nice to our little cousin Billy, too, when all I wanted was to rip the brat's head off," Mara continued. "Could you do it, please? For me?"

Her pleading tone brought up the memories of so many other times I'd taken her place before. Like every time she'd failed a school test I'd passed. She'd beg the teacher for a retake, then send me to take it for her. The dates she'd promise to go on but then change her mind. The group meetings in college she found too boring to attend.

We looked so much alike people could only tell us apart by the clothes we wore, and switching clothes was easy.

Sometimes, it'd been fun to pretend I was my twin, since my own social life wasn't nearly as vibrant as Mara's. Other times, she would manage to make me feel sorry for her.

Now...

"It's not just a date, Mara. I'd have to live with that man as his wife."

"But it's only for a year, according to the contract," she said quickly. "After that, you can say it's not for you and come back. A lot can happen in a year, right? They may find Tom and Jim by then and recoup what they stole. Or Bolshoy could finally get it through his thick head that we don't have his money and leave us alone. And don't worry about the wife part." She wiggled her eyebrows with added meaning in her eyes. "The alien dude doesn't want sex."

"What?" That was weird. "Did he just say it like that?"

She shrugged. "Pretty much. It states right in his application. That was one of the reasons I signed the contract in the first place. I mean, who would ever want to have sex with an Aldraian, right?"

"I don't know. I've never seen one."

"Lucky you." She made a face as if she'd bitten into something sour. "Anyway, you can fuck him if you wish for all I care, but trust me, that no-sex clause is a blessing."

I pondered everything she'd told me so far. The man's situation started to intrigue me, bringing questions. "Why does he need a wife, then? If he doesn't want sex? And what happened to the mother of his children?"

"She died. Years ago. His kids need a mother. He has two daughters...blah, blah, blah..." She took a drink from her water bottle. "Being a stepmom is so not my thing. I prefer the role of Cinderella with Prince Charming and the cool shoes."

"How about the hard work and abuse part of Cinderella's story?" I snorted, unable to picture Mara humble and industrious.

"Yeah, no," she dismissed. "I don't need any of that. I've had my struggles. I'm about to land my very own Prince Charming, who already buys me a lot of fancy shoes. I can't leave Jason for some alien farmer-ogre with a bunch of bratty kids. Can't you understand, Susanna? Please help me."

I bit my lip, mulling over her proposal.

I held no illusions; Mara's motives were purely self-serving. She didn't care if I worked myself to death at as many jobs as twenty-four hours a day would allow me. She wouldn't be here if there weren't benefits for her. But she was right. There were some advantages in her plan for me too.

I'd never worked with kids before, but it couldn't be much harder than serving the cranky, well-to-do women with superiority complexes who were Aileen's customers.

A change could be good for me, considering the circumstances.

And yes, getting away from Bolshoy and his people would be a huge bonus.

"Maybe I should consider applying myself?" I wondered out loud.

Mara gasped. "Why would you do that? When I already found one for you?"

I shook my head. "I would go on my own, Mara. As myself. But I'm not going to pretend to be you."

"Well, that can't happen, Susanna." She spread her arms, staring at me in disbelief. "The ship is leaving next week. I got the ticket for it this morning. All documents are done in my name. The papers are signed. What difference does it make whether you go as me or you? No one would know, anyway. We look so alike, our own mother couldn't tell us apart."

Maybe if our mother had spent more time with us instead of letting a bunch of nannies raise us, she would've found it easier to tell us apart. Instead, she made us wear color-coded clothes—pink for Mara, purple for me. Though, I'd always liked pink more.

"To aliens, humans all look the same already," Mara insisted. "But with us, we could alternate sleeping with him, and the guy would still think he only has one wife."

I kept shaking my head.

"Maybe, if you could bring me along—"

"Susanna!" She slapped her knees impatiently. "Are you really that dumb? Or are you just not listening to me? I don't want to bring you along. I don't want to bring anyone. I don't want to go! I want you to go instead of me."

"I'm afraid I can't help you with that, Mara."

She groaned in frustration. "But why? What do you have to lose?"

Mara was right. I had nothing left other than the seventeen dollars in my account that had to last until my next paycheck.

I'd lied for Mara before. However, I'd also been lied to, a lot. Lately, it seemed my entire life had been nothing but lies. And I was tired of it.

"I'm not pretending anymore, Mara. I'm trying to give an honest life a shot, here."

She gazed at me with so much disappointment, like she'd caught me committing a fashion crime. "Oh, you're stupider than I thought."

I was getting tired of her insults too.

"You know what? Maybe you should try to clean up your own mess, for once. Honor your commitments."

"Great." Mara scoffed. "Now, you're talking about honor. How very grand of you." She got up, hanging her overpriced and over-hyped bag on her arm. "I hope you enjoyed your gyro. Who knows where your next meal is going to come from?"

Watching her leave was a relief.

Maybe it was a mistake to turn down the opportunity to leave Earth and all my troubles behind. But I'd be going to another planet, pretending to be my sister, pretending to be interested in making a fake marriage work. I'd be living a lie. Again.

I couldn't do that to the unsuspecting alien truck driver. But more importantly, I couldn't do it to myself. I had nothing left in this life but my integrity. Giving that up would truly leave me with nothing.

"Well," I said to the pigeons that were scouring the pavement for crumbs, "maybe I should look into that marriage program myself. What do you think?"

AVAILABLE NOW

More by Marina Simcoe

My Holiday Tails
Married to Krampus
My Tiny Giant
My Birthday Getaway
New Year, New Planet
Mail Order Mom
My Pumpkin
What Makes an Alien a Dad?

Dark Anomaly Trilogy
Gravity
Power
Explosion

Standalone Novels
Experiment
Enduring (Valos Of Sonhadra)

The World of the River of Mists

<u>*Joyless Kingdom (Trilogy)*</u>
Somber Prince, Book 1
Joy Guardian, Book 2
Pleasure Trader, Book 3

<u>*Wingless Crow (Duet)*</u>
Wingless Crow – Part 1
Crownless King – Part 2

<u>*Fire in Stone (Duet)*</u>
Fire in Stone – Part 1
Hearts on Fire – Part 2

<u>*Serpent's Touch (Duet)*</u>
Serpent's Touch – Part 1
Serpent's Claim – Part 2

<u>*Madame Tan's Freakshow (Trilogy)*</u>

Paranormal Romance

<u>Demons (Complete Series)</u>
Demon Mine
The Forgotten
Grand Master
The Last Unforgiven - Cursed
The Last Unforgiven - Freed

<u>Stand Alone Novels Set in Demons World</u>
The Real Thing
To Love A Monster

<u>Midnight Coven Author Group</u>
Wicked Warlock (Cursed Coven)

About the Author

Marina Simcoe likes to write love stories with characters, who may or may not be entirely human, because she firmly believes that our contemporary world could always use a little bit of the extraordinary.

She has lots of fun exploring how her out-of-this-world characters with their own beliefs, values, and aspirations fit into our everyday life.

She lives in Canada with her very own grumpy brute, their three little kids, and a cat, who is definitely out of this world.

For the illustrations to this and other books by the author, please join her Patreon:

Please Stay in Touch

Newsletter signup is on MarinaSimcoe.com:

Facebook Readers' Group:
Marina's Reading Cave
www.instagram.com/marinasimcoeauthor
www.marinasimcoe.com
www.facebook.com/MarinaSimcoeAuthor/
www.amazon.com/author/marinasimcoe
www.bookbub.com/profile/marina-simcoe
www.goodreads.com/MarinaSimcoe